The Healer

First published by O Books, 2009
O Books is an imprint of John Hunt Publishing Ltd., The Bothy, Deershot Lodge, Park Lane, Ropley, Hants, SO24 0BE, UK
office1@o-books.net
www.o-books.net

Distribution in:

UK and Europe
Orca Book Services
orders@orcabookservices.co.uk
Tel: 01202 665432 Fax: 01202 666219
Int. code (44)

USA and Canada
NBN
custserv@nbnbooks.com
Tel: 1 800 462 6420 Fax: 1 800 338 4550

Australia and New Zealand
Brumby Books
sales@brumbybooks.com.au
Tel: 61 3 9761 5535 Fax: 61 3 9761 7095

Far East (offices in Singapore, Thailand, Hong Kong, Taiwan)
Pansing Distribution Pte Ltd
kemal@pansing.com
Tel: 65 6319 9939 Fax: 65 6462 5761

South Africa
Alternative Books
altbook@peterhyde.co.za
Tel: 021 555 4027 Fax: 021 447 1430

Design: Stuart Davies

ISBN: 978 1 84694 205 1

A CIP catalogue record for this book is available from the British Library.

Printed by Digital Book Print

The Healer

Simon G. Brown

BOOKS

Winchester, UK
Washington, USA

CONTENTS

Chapter 1	1
Chapter 2	5
Chapter 3	17
Chapter 4	21
Chapter 5	24
Chapter 6	43
Chapter 7	60
Chapter 8	69
Chapter 9	76
Chapter 10	78
Chapter 11	81
Chapter 12	98
Chapter 13	106
Chapter 14	111
Chapter 15	119
Chapter 16	127
Chapter 17	132
Chapter 18	147
Chapter 19	158
Chapter 20	164
Chapter 21	181
Chapter 22	186
Chapter 23	193
Chapter 24	205
Chapter 25	210
Chapter 26	219
Chapter 27	226
Chapter 28	233
Chapter 29	241
Chapter 30	248
Acknowledgements	251
About The Author	252

CHAPTER ONE

"Adam, I'm here. Please get through this darling, do it for me and the children. Remember what we used to say to Matthew – don't cry because it's over, smile because it happened."

I wake with a mixture of fading warmth and growing sadness. She was with me, she came to my bed, ran her hand through my hair. Her palm rested on my forehead, as though checking my temperature. I felt the warmth of her hand, her breath kissed my neck. My emotions lifted as the chill in my chest warmed with the feelings we used to share. I open my eyes, the sadness returns – she's not here.

Through my cottage window I see Borth-y-guest. I was introduced to this land of Celtic wizards and dragons, during a storm. Aaron drove us down the tree-lined lane to be greeted by waves crashing into the stones, shooting white spume into the air. Each new gust ruffled the surface of the waves, spreading the arching crests into the wind. Driving rain and spray drummed the car so loudly no-one spoke.

Aaron parked by the harbour. We sat mesmerised. The weather mirrored my emotions; I felt an affinity to the rage. Wanting to be closer, I pushed the car door against the force of the wind and walked towards the waves, letting the piercing cold rip through me, welcoming the spray and rain as it washed my body. I had an urge to tear my clothes off, shout and scream, throw myself to the sea and let my evolutionary mother consume me. I wanted to feel clean again, rid myself of the self-disgust, dissolve the past, empty my poisoned blood into the wind and water.

Aware of Matthew and Eleanor, I returned shivering and drenched. There were no words, their eyes spoke of the fear that they were witnessing their father slipping down into a breakdown. I gave them a smile, pulling myself back up the emotional hill.

"Wow, that was amazing. You couldn't pay to experience so much power and natural drama."

Aaron glared at me. "Why don't you run round the village shouting your name? May I remind you, you're in hiding."

"Do you think anyone saw me?"

Aaron smiled at the absurdity of his outburst.

"Adam can I ask you a question?"

I looked up and met his gentle eyes. I nodded.

"Do you remember a time when you once felt that everyone else was a figment of your imagination? That when we were not with you, we did not exist?"

I smiled like an eight year old.

"What if that were true, what if we are all still created out of your imagination? Ask yourself the question, why did I create these characters, why did I bring them into my life? Why did I make up the situations that have led me here? Perhaps in doing this you will let go of who everyone else is and what they have done. Give yourself the freedom to connect with your soul and find the real answers."

I knew this was Aaron's way of getting me to claim my life back, to step into my own truth and take total responsibility for what had happened.

By the time we had found the cottage and heaved our bags indoors, the storm collapsed allowing the occasional ray of sun to flit across the shiny charcoal streets.

Walking back to the harbour with a black woollen hat pulled low over my forehead, I was amazed to see that the white caps had been replaced by a gentler swell.

The small Welsh village was built around a sandy bay, the grey slate roofs contrasted with the brightly painted cottage walls. An odd assortment of dinghies, motor boats and small cabin craft bobbed on the grey water, held captive by green, slime covered chains. Laye and onto a canvas it made a picturesque setting to rebuild my life.

Matthew and Eleanor ran through puddles imitating the storm. As we walked round the rocks at the end of the harbour, I could just see Harlech castle bathed in a ray of sunlight, marking the exit to the sea .

The whistle of a steam train called out, I turned my head to see the cob drawing a line across the inner end of the estuary, underlining the mountain ranges of Snowdonia. A red narrow gauge steam engine pulled green carriages across, leaving childlike puffs of white steam floating in the foreground.

I had not expected to drop into this scene. It was the most changeable environment I had ever witnessed. I experienced mist, heavy blowing rain, sun, soft showers and gales. In the space of a day the estuary swells with Irish Sea water. Thirty-foot tides transform the landscape, draining away to a small river, exposing a desert of sand.

Even now I feel part of this changing environment. Have I become it or has it taken me? There is a wildness that pulls me back and forth so fiercely that it is impossible to stagnate. My moods change with the weather, jerking me into emotions I rarely experienced before. I throw these moods onto my canvas, not as a painter but a writer. The computer screen beckons, drawing out my experience. Writing is my therapy. I'm searching for redemption. I reach into the depths of my soul and retch them out onto this screen. It's painful but a welcomed release.

My English teacher guaranteed I would never write a book, too dyslexic to write my own name, yet here I am creating life with my words. I think of Sigeyo. Keep it simple – a clear sky, no clouds until I'm ready.

Sometimes I find it hard to trust myself. What actually happened? Maybe I did go insane at the stadium. I need a witness, someone to help tear through the delusions. Aaron will arrive soon.

Today I feel angry. My writing is poor. I resist the urge to throw things around the room. I hold onto my adult self for the sake of Matthew and Eleanor upstairs. My head pounds and then like the storm, the anger abates as I spiral into depression. A line hits my eye.

"But Daddy you could have healed her with your special hands."

The words sting their way inward and tighten around my heart. I sense tears and I swallow them down. I need to wake the children. Self pity bounds in and I relish it for a moment. My energy's draining away I must walk in the wind, blow out this damp heavy mood.

Who will read this book? Will it make it to cult status among the spiritually aware? Probably not; much of it is too base and I'm too flawed. I think people look for someone to aspire to; a guru in white, dishing out words of wisdom, leading a life of purity.

I know what I want but find myself struggling for the words that accurately describe my feelings. Right now I'm feeling clumsy and inarticulate. Oh Josephine why are you ignoring me? I need you here with your literary mind.

I push back from the table and shout up the tiny stairs.

"Eleanor! Matthew! Time for school."

CHAPTER TWO

I tried fasting just before starting this book. I needed clarity on what I wanted to write. Drastically limiting my intake of calories precipitated such a state of oversensitivity that even miniscule details provoked emotional responses. A painful reminder of the first few days after the accident. It felt as though I was sucking all my vitality from the air rather than the small amount of grains and vegetables.

I ended my fast after losing my temper with Matthew in Woolworth's. The bright screaming lights invaded my search for my soul while he demanded a plastic battery operated warrior.

This book was born standing on the top of Tryfan, Snowdonia. It was a clear day with a cold piercing wind that sliced into my being. I expanded to fill the immense vista around me and suddenly the idea for this book blew into me. I grabbed hold of phrases that flashed past. It would have been easy to write a self help book, a healing manual or cookery book, but I knew in that instance that this account will be all that and more, because this is my real life experience of living, alive instead of an abstract theory, pristine on glossy full colour pages.

My philosophy is entwined with my experience of it. Just as you cannot separate time and space, all we think we know is ultimately subjective, caught in its culture and the moment. The purity of my philosophy has certainly been contaminated by events. Isn't a dirty, used, battle scarred philosophy better than one that is clingfilm-wrapped and immaculate?

I rushed home from the mountain feeling enthused, motivated, excited and drew up an outline. But when I opened my computer I found I had no beginning. I tried to relax, to open up. I realised there is no need to write in chronological order; I can start anywhere, just flesh out whichever bones I choose.

For now I want to write about the shiatsu class. It was a time when I was drifting through life with no purpose. I had no idea where it would take me. I was a clean canvas ready to accept any form, colour and texture that life could offer me.

Having finally arrived at the point where I could move forward, I needed some wind in my sails. I needed some purchase on my rudder, to point myself towards a distant port. I thought of the advice from *Think and Grow Rich* and relaxed, with my mind as open as possible.

It happened when I had another shiatsu. Nirmala didn't say anything, the idea just crept into my head.

I listened to myself and splashed some colour on my barren background by enrolling on a shiatsu course. I took the train into London and turned up at the Primrose Shiatsu Centre. The building looked a bit tired and the inside showed early signs of flaking and peeling. The plant in the reception area was yellowing and wilting; I had an overwhelming desire to water it. I went to pay the balance of my fee. The receptionist spoke with a strong eastern European accent. There was some confusion over my name, which annoyed her. I felt like a nuisance, having apparently conspired to mess up her registration system.

As I took my trainers off, a tall slim man bounded into the room. "Hello I'm Stephen. Stephen Jacobs."

I recognised the little trick Stephen had picked up, which allowed him to say his first name twice. Stephen was dressed from head to toe in white. He had a shaven head and nicotine smoke stained teeth. It was very hard to place his age, forty perhaps. He was wiry with highly taut neck muscles giving him the appearance of a high-energy person who was struggling to stop himself from slipping over the edge.

"My commitment to you is to take you all to the point where you can go home and give a shiatsu."

He looked at each person in the room, making eye contact with each of us in turn. There were twelve of us. I sat on a futon next to a middle-aged, middle-sized, middle-class, middle-of-the-road, sort of woman.

"Please introduce yourself, tell me one interesting thing about yourself, and tell me what you want from this course. The more specific you are the easier it will be to achieve your goals. Let's start with you."

I realised from Stephen's accent that he must be Australian.

"Um, my name is Josephine. I live in Chalk Farm. And I, um, can't think of anything interesting about myself right now. I work in a bookshop at the moment. Oh yes, what do I want? Um, I don't know really."

Josephine was young, thin, pale, and limp.

"Well why did you pay the money to come? You have paid, I presume."

Josephine reddened and nodded. Stephen added that he never knew who had paid when Anouska was registering students.

"All right Josephine, imagine that it is five o'clock on the last day of the course. You are leaving to go home."

Josephine nodded. For a moment I thought she was going to stand up and leave.

"Good. Now how do you want to feel as you leave that door?"

"Um, happy I suppose."

"Excellent! Now what would make you happy? I mean, in my experience it is rarely learning shiatsu. A wonderful new loving relationship with an all-accepting, new age, caring, sharing man, friendship, something to tell your friends about, a new skill to help you feel more spiritual?"

If it was a new man she wanted, she was in for a disappointment. I was the only male on the course.

"Um, well I'm not sure. Learning something new?"

"Come on Josephine. You're walking through that door feeling happy. Are you there?"

"Yes."

"Good. Now why are you happy?"

"Because I feel closer to people."

"Thank you Josephine. No problem. That's a realistic goal. We all put a lot of energy into communicating by talking, but very little through touch. It is something I think people are not comfortable with in England."

Anouska nodded solemnly.

"By the end of this course I assure you, Josephine, you will be very good at touching people. And you know what. I think the more confident you become at communicating through touch, the better you will be at communicating on all levels."

Josephine flicked her eyes around the room in an embarrassed way as if to check if anyone had noticed her. As she did this, our eyes met and I felt a flash of recognition before she looked down. I knew we had not met before but there was something familiar. It took me back to the accident, to a flashback I had whilst dying, a moment that unblocked a distant memory I had locked away.

I was there again holding Mrs Wadkins' hand again while she lay dying in the street, feeling the life drain out of her palm as she looked into my eyes. She held my hand so tightly that I had to kneel next to her, feeling her last long breath leave her plump body.

Stephen nodded to the next student.

"Hello Stephen. My name is Wendy, I live in Hampstead, and I work as a healer. I'm interesting because I'm me! I'm very, very, very spiritual, and my goal is to be able to channel my magical healing energies more effectively."

All this was said in a loud clear voice with particular emphasis on the consonants at the end of each word. Wendy accompanied this with a confident smile. Once her speech was completed she looked around for approval. Everyone except Anouska smiled back at her.

Wendy threw a vision of her childhood into my head. I imagined her being taken to ballet classes, going to elocution lessons, throwing tantrums for attention. She irritated me because

I knew I would be taken in by her theatrics. It was all about her. She commanded a reaction. Despite being so superficial, I found her more compelling than someone wearing a suit of solemn integrity.

"I'm sure we can do that, Wendy," Stephen added flatly.

"Hi everyone, I'm Jane from Bury St Edmunds. I came up this morning with my friend Sarah. We both work in a bank. Lets see what's interesting about me. Well, I have three cats. Joey, Mouser and Miffy. And I have a great big dog called Biff."

My stomach tightened, I couldn't believe I was hearing this.

"My friend Sarah asked me to come, and I thought well, why not, it can't do any harm, can it? What would I like to achieve?"

The ability to shut up.

"Well to be honest I want to be able to give my husband, Roger, a good going over. He's the manager at a building society and honestly, Stephen, he is so stressed I don't know how he survives. He's a big bag of aches and pains. Headaches, constipation, bad back, you name it he has it. What can I do? This is my last hope."

"What else have you tried?"

"Well, nothing. Not yet. Do you really think this shitsu stuff will be of any use?"

"It's pronounced she-at-su. It's up to you."

I tried to imagine Jane giving her husband any kind of going over. Her manner was too irritating and her appearance too synthetic to even imagine her naked.

In a moment of synchronicity she cleared her throat, looked around the room and then lowered her voice.

"Just between you and me, Stephen, things have not been going well," Jane's face reddened. "You know, between the sheets. Roger seems to have lost some..." She left the sentence unfinished.

Stephen looked out of the window distractedly, his face lost some colour and his lips became thinner, Jane's revelation seemed to have triggered off other thoughts. Then he nodded at me.

I became aware of everyone's eyes staring back. I stiffened slightly and felt self-conscious. Jane's expectant smile made it worse. An irrational fear that she would hold my hand to help me through my speech was enough to launch me off. I kept my introduction as brief as possible, just outlining the benefits I had experienced with my shiatsu from Nirmala. I didn't want to go into the accident and all that followed.

As we carried on through the rest of the students I felt increasingly out of place. These were not the kind of people I would normally associate with. Where was the hard-edged, pioneering, martial arts kind of experience I had imagined?

"This is your course. Each of you has paid to be here. So make the most of every penny and get all you can out of it."

Stephen took us through an exercise routine. We stretched, jumped, rolled on the floor until even Josephine had a glow to her face.

"Right let me explain the basic principles behind shiatsu. It's based on the idea of 'ki'. This subtle electromagnetic energy flows through the universe carrying information from one entity to another. We can define this energy in terms of yin and yang. Let me give you an example. At the time of a full moon we become more yang. This means we are more active, outgoing, and generally more crazy. Now ask any insurance company and they will tell you there are more car accidents at the full moon, we also know the crime rate goes up and admissions to casualty wards increases. Some doctors are even reluctant to operate then as patients bleed more."

"Do you know, I think I have intuitively known that all along, Stephen."

Oh please, Wendy get off it. Stephen continued without even sparing her a glance.

"During the new moon, the ambient energy becomes more yin,

making it easier to meditate, be spiritual and look at our lives in more depth. So, armed with this simple piece of yin / yang information, when would be best to hold a wild party?"

"The full moon of course," replied Wendy smartly.

Stephen moved on quickly before Wendy had time to continue.

"The point of my speech is: Why be the sort of person who holds a party on a new moon, puts a lot of time and effort into it, only to find that less people turn up and then sit around talking about themselves. What if the host feels depressed, thinking he or she can't organise a decent event when all it was, was bad timing."

He had us. We were all looking at Stephen with greater interest.

"If by the end of the course you cannot give a decent shiatsu, you will at least know when to hold parties." Wendy laughed the loudest.

Stephen walked over to the blackboard and with the aid of frantic hand drawn sketches demonstrated how ki coursed through seven energy centres – chakras – and then branched out into fourteen paths called meridians. Along these meridians were numerous points, called 'tsubos', where ki could be changed more easily.

Do-In, a Japanese self-massage exercises came next. Stephen showed us how to generate a stronger flow of ki between our hands. Amazingly, I felt a magnetic sensation between my palms. There was a warmth as they came closer together and I could expand this heat field as I moved my hands apart. The strange tingling sensation I had experienced after the accident returned briefly. We then worked on tsubos on our own bodies, feeding them with ki. Towards the end I felt an emotional calmness wash through my body whilst simultaneously experiencing a buzz of physical energy, a combination I had not experienced before.

We learnt the basic shiatsu techniques over the initial days.

Jane turned out to have a very good, strong, natural touch. Stephen had banned us from wearing synthetic fabrics as they pick up static electricity interfering with our healing energy. Jane benefited twice from this ruling as it also made her look better. Lying on a futon whilst she worked on my back felt good, not as polished or as adventurous as Nirmala's treatments but she left me feeling distinctly better.

About five days into the course I worked on Josephine and whilst resting my hands behind her lungs and following her breathing, a feeling floated into my chest. I felt a heavy empty space, rather lonely and sad. I could feel myself struggling to keep pace with her breathing and then realised she was sobbing like a little girl. Somehow I managed to resist the impulse to pull away and see what the matter was. The feeling I drew in intrigued me. For a moment I tried to analyse what I felt and in the process it was lost. Returning to a kind of empty mind, just focusing on my breathing, I sensed a re-connection. The feeling returned to my lungs, bringing with it an over-riding sense of loss. The power of the emotion became too strong and I consciously tried to feed back an image of me hugging her, bathing her in warmth. I needed to breathe more deeply and I was interested to see that Josephine's breathing followed mine. The strength of the connection and a kind of emotional mixing created an ebb and flow of emotional energy between us that was enough to feel a glimpse of what it was like to be Josephine.

Stephen encouraged us to finish our treatments. I opened my mouth to tell Josephine how I sensed a kind of loneliness and loss when I heard Wendy say, "You know, I really sensed a lot a deep anger in you," to her partner. She epitomised everything I hate about new age conversations, I was horrified that I had almost slipped into the same pit.

After the class, I nonchalantly invited Josephine to have a cup of herbal tea in the village. With some careful probing I found out that her parents had died in a car accident when she was eight and she was brought up by her uncle and his family. She confided that somewhere in the process she felt she had lost the ability to receive and give love, leaving her insular and withdrawn. Josephine had been seeing a therapist for a year and she suggested trying a massage course. Shiatsu appealed to her because this sort of massage was performed fully clothed.

I resisted claiming to have felt some of this but felt re-assured in my own mind. As we parted she said softly, "I felt your warmth, even a kindness during the treatment. It's been a long time since I experienced those feelings. Do you understand Adam?"

I nodded. She turned with a shy wave. I felt a breath of emotion stir, urging me to run and hold her. Instead I stayed rooted, staring after her fading image.

I reflected on the course. My original impressions of my fellow students looked shallow, arrogant and misjudged. After what had just happened with Josephine there was absolutely nothing superficial about our training.

My mind returned to Mrs Wadkins. Now I could remember her talking to my mother, patting me on the head and giving me the occasional sweet from behind the counter. She always took a special interest in me. After she died, the subject of Anne Wadkins must have become taboo because I never heard her mentioned again.

She had been walking down the street towards me with a smile and had suddenly doubled up, holding onto a red post box for support. By the time I reached her she had collapsed. When she held out her hand, I took it. She pulled me close and I knelt next to her mauve cardigan, feeling the rough stone pavement on my bare knees. I thought she wanted to give me a message. I remained silent. There was a big commotion, help was being summoned, the distant wail of approaching sirens. I was mostly oblivious to it all, staring into her eyes, looking for a sign as she passed from this world.

"Come on lad, let go, she is gone now. Let her rest in peace."

But I couldn't, I could not let go or stop looking into her eyes. Those eyes came back to haunt me softly as I walked to the station.

On day six Stephen taught us the value of using the abdomen, or 'hara' in Japanese, for sensing our partner's ki. He called Mandy up to demonstrate his method. I noticed he tended to home in on the three most attractive women. Mandy had a naked midriff, her short pale blue tube top stretched over her eye-catching breasts.

Anouska sat in my eye line behind Stephen. Her face looked dark and menacing. I noticed her jaw tense as Stephen pulled Mandy's tracksuit bottoms down to the edge of her pubic bone. I guessed Anouska was here because of Stephen rather than to help us explore each other's energy.

One highlight was giving each other a treatment blindfolded. I partnered Jane and it fascinated me to see how much more aware I became of the quality of touching. I was able to focus more intently on the point of contact with Jane's body. Stephen pointed out that in Japan traditionally many blind people are trained to give shiatsu because without all the distraction of visual mental pollution they could develop amazing healing powers in their hands.

I noticed Stephen held onto romantic notions of what people could do with the power of their ki. He was convinced samurai were able to jump over houses, throw people down without making contact and bring people back from certain death by using their spiritual power. It made him seem rather naive in an endearing way. He obviously believed it. But then, I believed Matthew and Eleanor had brought me back from death. The difference was that I had had an experience that touched my soul. I still did not feel comfortable about it. I did not enthuse publicly or use it to justify my theories.

When Jane started to work on me, I felt a warmer, stronger connection and her presence enveloped me. I felt comforted, as though suspended in a soft invisible hammock. She obviously became disoriented and ended up working along my liver meridian, up the inside of my leg and straight across my genitals. When this happened again while massaging my other leg, she burst into a fit of giggles. Her hands bubbled with laughter. I let her amusement transport my energy, melting the more serious, uptight corners of my being. For some time afterwards I floated on her joy.

Still feeling spaced out, I was the last to leave at the end of our class. On the way out I heard an angry restrained voice that I recognised as Anouska's.

"Why you put your hands on so many girls when you love me? How come you want to when you still can't get big with me?"

I paused and heard Stephen speak slowly in a tone stressing a patient calm.

"I've explained this to you so many times. I'm just a bit too yin at the moment, my ki is too weak. It'll come back. You know I have to demonstrate and I want the student to feel my..."

As I turned to leave, my backpack caught a vase on the shelf sending it smashing to the floor. Daffodils lay among the shards of broken glass and water. Stephen sprang out of his office and tried to effect a martial arts stance whilst hauling his trousers up with one hand. Anouska stood in the doorway. Her face was puffy and flushed.

"Oh, it's you. Don't worry about the mess. I will take care of it. See you tomorrow."

I realised I had elevated Stephen to spiritual purity. This gritty domestic realism came as a fleeting disappointment. I felt stupid for being so naive.

Towards the end of the course Stephen showed us how to sense ki in another person. He chose Jane for the first time. Amazingly it was possible to feel whether my partner was thinking about the past or future just by feeling the way a hot spot of energy on the top of the head moved. Next, I tried to feel the emotions in Wendy's abdomen. It was hard to assess the accuracy of this but more importantly than trying to double-guess, I definitely could feel the energy of her ki.

CHAPTER THREE

Through Matthew and Eleanor I re-live my childhood here in Wales. I can play again and try to push back those walls to the mental freedom Aaron and I discussed all that time ago. I am able to go back and complete parts of myself that were left undeveloped. I know this is dangerous territory as I don't want to use my children to fix my own problems but there are lots of activities we can do together that fill the empty holes that were left out in my growing years.

Observing them, I am fascinated by how they make up games. What are the rules? "You're cheating! You have to count to ten first." Is childhood learning how to play in preparation for the big game ahead? Am I now playing my game? Do all the people around me also have rules, frantically playing their game of life? I suppose the prize is financial success, a big house, travel to sunny beaches. Others might play for a new skill, a beautiful lover, a feeling of superiority.

What am I playing for? How do I know when I have won? It used to be a fast motorcycle, a sexy girlfriend and an active social life. Now I don't really know. What makes me get out of bed in the morning? The awful reality could be that I am simply on autopilot, mindlessly playing an old game with prizes I am no longer interested in.

The rules have changed so much I just can't orientate myself any more. Perhaps I've seen the rules for what they are and started living outside the game. I sound like Marlon Brando in *Apocalypse Now*.

It was through my playground interactions that I formed my successful strategies. I learnt social survival. I still have those character traits and even though I now dislike some of them, deep down I am afraid to experiment with another strategy. I see the same happening with Matthew and Eleanor and want to stop them. I wish I could encourage them to leave open the opportunity for other ways to succeed but it is too frantic, they are moving too fast, it becomes instinctive.

Thinking of school I want to touch on a period of my life I still feel ashamed of. Aaron and Emily's talk on karma in the shady woods near my old home during my recovery from the accident must have affected me because I found myself assessing my history, resolving to correct the actions I felt guilty about. I now wanted my near death experience to be a defining point in my life. If I was going to make a new start in life, I didn't want feelings of shame from the old one making unexpected appearances. The thought of cleaning up my past became an obsession.

I tracked down and phoned Justin Brooks, the boy I had bullied at school. He was living with his mother in a flat near our old school. He began to stutter when he heard my voice. I persuaded him to meet me for tea in Hitchin.

When I arrived I could not recognise Justin among the café society until a man in a black duffle coat started to rise and gave me a half-hearted wave. He had put on weight, wore thick black glasses and attempted to hide a bald patch by combing long oily black hair across it.

"How fantastic to see you again Justin, it must be a good fourteen years."

Justin started to stammer so much it was painful waiting for him to spit the words out. Instinctively I reached out and put my hand on his back, and once I realised what I had done I couldn't retract it again. I could feel the stuttering vibrations of his voice through his ribs and hoped my tranquil mood would be infectious. He managed to reply and I took my hand away feeling self-conscious.

I discovered he was looking after his mother and working at an insurance company. He had no girlfriend, wife or children. When he mentioned his mother I had a flashback to an incident at school when I punched him in the face causing him to cry. He pulled out a pressed handkerchief from his pocket and at that moment I imagined his mother lovingly ironing it into a neat square and popping it into his pocket with a kiss as he left for school, unaware of the horrors she was sending him to. That thought made me feel guilty at the time and now I felt an even greater pang in my chest.

I tightened inwardly remembering how short-lived that guilt was. How quickly I recovered from my emotional stumble and reasserted myself as a grim faced rough child. I now know I could have used my influence to stop the bullying, to protect Justin, but I was too frightened of isolation. I had stumbled upon a formula that worked. Going around punching boys like Justin guaranteed me a group of friends and respect.

I did not know how to finish our time together as the small talk dried up. I certainly had not resolved anything so I blurted out how sorry I was at the way I had treated him at school. Justin looked stunned; perhaps I had transgressed some taboo – never mention school? He started stuttering badly and all I could do was give him a squeeze on the shoulder. I left saying I would give him a call and suggested he came over and meet the family. On the way home I realised I had rushed off without paying.

Justin did come round. He had a dry sarcastic sense of humour and by issuing a running commentary on our card games he made us laugh. When he wasn't talking directly to me his stammer became manageable. It was terrible to think how badly I had scarred him. In the evening I walked him out to his car. I hated the feeling that if I raised my hand to scratch my head, Justin would flinch, that he was just here so he could be my good deed for the day, that a bit of time together would somehow repair all those years when I launched the systematic destruction of his self esteem and self respect.

"I really am sorry about school. I can't find the words to express how bad I feel about the way I treated you, but I'm not just doing this so I can make myself feel better. I would like to be your friend, I want to know you better. But if you are not enjoying this, please don't do it for me. Tell me to get lost and I promise you, I'll understand."

"Same time next week?"

I smiled and slowly lifted my hand bringing it to rest gently on his shoulder.

CHAPTER FOUR

Although no interaction as dramatic as my exchange with Josephine occurred again, I was finding it easier to connect with each person I treated and I sensed I was gaining a reputation.

Stephen had asked us to bring in a friend on the next to last day so we could give a complete shiatsu under his critical gaze. I brought Justin thinking he might like to experience a shiatsu course himself.

"Please sit in a circle, place your hands in the prayer position and let's centre ourselves by chanting aah, ooo, mmm. Breathe in."

We completed one sequence and then in the silence whilst everyone breathed in, Justin let out a loud snort. His shoulders shook and he slumped up against me. Everyone looked on in silence. I felt my face flush and jabbed my elbow into his ribs. Justin tried to speak but exploded, spraying saliva across the room. He buried his head into my lap leaving me feeling exposed. Jane tried to help.

"Ha ha, the same thing happened with Roger. It's all a bit weird and wacky at first."

"Perhaps it's just a release, Stephen. You know how chanting breaks up deep stagnation." Wendy looked at Stephen for agreement.

Justin proved impossible to work with. He stiffened up at every stretch, was uncontrollably ticklish and breathed too erratically for me to find my rhythm. At the end I felt deflated. In class we were all so used to giving and receiving shiatsu it felt like a pair of dancers working in unison. Throw in Justin and it degenerated into a wrestling match.

On the last day we each gave Stephen a shiatsu so that he could feel our technique for himself. I caught him loosening his trousers and pulling them low when Wendy massaged his hara. I looked over to Anoushka, our eyes flashed into each other's before she stood up and left the room. I took my turn last.

"Promise me one thing, Adam."

"Yes?"

"You will use that energy in your hands. You have a special strength there. I cannot remember feeling such a powerful touch." He sprang up and shook himself like a dog. "Fantastic! I feel goooooooood!"

Wendy was standing nearby and turned to Stephen.

"I think Adam should see Sigeyo," she turned to me. "Sigeyo is this amazing Japanese healer I do some work for in return for treatments. You really should meet."

I felt quite emotional when the course ended. We had grown to be a temporary family and I had become fond of the others. I looked forward to their daily news, to working together, exchanging their energy with mine. That night I felt emotionally flat as I lay in bed. The thought of meeting Sigeyo kept a flame alight in my heart. I didn't want my new direction in life to peter out so soon, I needed to keep the wind in my sails.

I noticed a steady improvement in the movement of my arms. With the exception of a few difficult shoulder stretches, I felt virtually back to normal.

After the course I still felt incomplete about my encounter with Josephine. A few days later I arranged to meet up at her flat in Chalk Farm to practice our shiatsu. Her lack of enthusiasm was slightly disturbing, but I persevered.

We met in Primrose Hill village for tea and then she took me back to her studio flat. She seemed a bit stiff and self-conscious when we entered her domain. The room was bare save for essentials. There were no DVDs, no CDs, no pictures, art or any of the items on show that give you clues to the character of the person inhabiting a space, just several piles of books in the corner.

I suggested that Josephine give me a shiatsu first. She began tentatively and initially it all felt weak and slow but then as she progressed I felt a greater warmth and energy in her hands. When it was my turn, I again felt a strong connection but not the same intensity of sadness. Josephine did not talk much but I found that the little she said had a profound quality. Perhaps it was just a case of placing a greater worth on her words for their rarity value.

"Adam, apart from the shiatsu in the class, I have had reiki and reflexology from professional practitioners, but none change my energy like you. Just imagine what you could do with more experience."

I hope I did not fool myself into thinking Josephine smiled more and was a little more open as I left. I would like to think she had found some of that closeness she craved at the beginning of our course.

CHAPTER FIVE

The weather is grey, cold and wet and as I walk down Porthmadoc's high street. I find myself enticed by the smell of coffee. Moments later I am drinking a strong espresso and filling my mouth with the creamiest cake on display. This is my first coffee for over a year. Soon after my heartbeat races and I feel slightly dizzy.

One question enters my caffeine driven head. How do I want you to feel when you have finished reading this book? I would like to alter your perception of yourself and the world you live in. Not a philosophy prescribed by me but to give you the freedom to explore your own unique take on your universe. I hope to arouse your curiosity, to inspire you to go beyond your normal boundaries in search of new ways to perceive the relationship you have with your world.

Fourteen hours later I am lying in my wooden cottage bed with my head splitting with ideas. My skin is clammy and I cannot sleep.

My mind races ahead. I am looking at the stars through my bedroom window. I am thinking no two people can ever see exactly the same view at the same time. It is physically impossible. Even if our eyes are separated by a few inches, our views will differ. I open one eye and then the other to see my perspective of the room change subtly. I suppose the same happens with my ears and less obviously with my other senses. The thought that I am totally alone sends a chill through my chest. No one else will ever share precisely the same experience.

Ideas are pouring through my cells far too quickly. I reach for the bedside light and find a note pad to try and hold onto a few strands of my argument.

Reality is what most people in a community agree on. If we all agree on a certain religious belief and follow it, it becomes our reality. Similarly if we all agree to use simple maths it is real to us.

I use many concepts, and still do, but ever since Sigeyo explained her ideas on conceptual thinking I am clearer in my own mind they are not reality. Take a concept as simple as addition. Two plus two equals four. But when you add two drops of water to another two drops of water you end up with one. Even if you try to do it by weight the drops will be evaporating, collecting dust and the weighing machine itself will be expanding or contracting, so it is only possible to say you have measured the weight of the four drops of water plus or minus a certain percentage. The concept does not match reality. Even one as beautiful as simple maths is an approximation that only works in certain situations. The more complex the concept, the more layers and variables distort the connection with reality. I no longer believe any concept accurately describes reality. Concepts are our clumsy attempts to explain the world we live in, reality is our unique personal experience of life.

For me observations are different. We observe things like the weather, nature or human behaviour and these are true for us, it is only when we try extrapolating our observations out into a general theory of life that we undermine ourselves. The human mind is lazy and because of this we find it easier to take an event that happens a few times and then expect the same results in every situation than to try constantly to deal with the unknown.

Reality is personal. Because we are subjective beings our whole world becomes coloured by the way we want to see it. We all have control over how we choose to perceive our reality and this ultimately affects every aspect of our lives.

I once perceived my universe in a way that made me angry, wanting to blame others, especially those parents who fed their children junk food. Perceptions are habitual. I still fight to replace those that isolate me with a set that is more accepting and less judgemental.

I am determined not to slip back into the general banality of common belief. I cherish what I have developed. Is there a like-minded woman out there? Right now I crave for such a person to be lying next to me, to feel her warmth envelop me.

If I am lucky, I probably have forty or fifty years left. The big question emerges. What do I need to do between now and then to feel content, complete and satisfied when I reach the end? And how should I perceive the world to achieve it?

The sun's coming up and I haven't slept. Thinking about Sigeyo has inspired me to write about my first meeting with her.

Wendy arranged for me to have tea with Sigeyo. I was not sure if that was her first name or her surname. She lived in Camden Square, not far from Primrose Hill and the healing centre. I was surprised by the solitary doorbell to see that she occupied the whole house. Wendy opened the door and gushed forth with a big smile, and an even bigger hug and kiss. She asked me to remove my shoes and led me through to the living room. It took a while for my irises to open enough to see properly. Heavy drapes hung around the windows blocking out most of the light. On every available surface I could see piles of books, newspapers and rolled up scrolls of paper. These were tied up with red ribbon. I could just pick up a mild smell of musky spice. It was a large room divided by concertina doors, with windows at both ends. Each half had an impressive floral ceiling rose and intricate cornicing framing the white ceiling. Thick maroon patterned rugs appeared to have been thrown over the wooden floor at random. Wendy ushered me to sit on a low cream sofa. Just as I was about to make contact Sigeyo walked in. I mis-timed the re-bound and fell back into the chair for a second time as I tried to stand up.

Sigeyo was dressed in dark loose trousers, a white sweat shirt and a maroon Liberty print kimono style jacket. She bowed and I followed. Wendy made the introductions and also did most of the talking for both of us. I could see Sigeyo found her amusing in an affectionate way. I assumed she liked the contrast between Wendy and women from her own culture. She referred to her as her noisy angel, apparently oblivious to the impression of conceitedness she presented to others. Wendy introduced me as being the star of the course. She continued telling me some of Sigeyo's history. She studied in Japan with a man called George Ohsawa. It took me a few seconds to register that name and connect it with the book Aaron lent me.

"Zen Macrobiotics," I blurted out.

"Ah, so you know macrobiotics?"

"Yes, my wife cooks me a macrobiotic diet."

Sigeyo looked me up and down again and waved to the chair. We sat down and Wendy poured genmaicha, green and roasted brown rice tea.

Taking over her story, Sigeyo told me how she had spent several years working with George Ohsawa and had then been sent to London to spread his teachings. Other students had been sent to New York, Paris and California. Sigeyo was shy, keeping a low profile compared to her colleagues, preferring to work directly with clients and taking on the occasional student. She had written three books, one on macrobiotics, another on shiatsu and a final book on Japanese nine ki astrology and feng shui. Wendy pulled them off the bookshelf opposite. Sigeyo fell silent in mid-sentence.

Wendy explained how she looked after Sigeyo's appointments. She worked from home. Looking at Sigeyo's face, I imagined she was in her seventies. Her hair was immaculately groomed, tied back and authoritatively grey. Two small almond shaped, dark eyes looked through me. Overall she created an impression of wisdom and kindness. Every movement was made with ultimate dignity and grace. She conjured up a feeling of efficiency. Sigeyo appeared comfortable with silence, letting Wendy fill in the long gaps.

Then with no warning or introduction Sigeyo asked me to turn to the window, pulled back the curtain and peered into my face. Sensing my discomfort, Wendy explained she was reading my face and needed more natural light.

"Excuse me Mr Saunders but you have a very interesting face. I see you seek variety and adventure . Sorry to say, but I do not think one woman is enough for you."

I drew a surprised if not uncomfortable smile and Wendy giggled. Sigeyo leaned forward and looked straight into my eyes. "I think you are coming to a big decision. I think you have wandered along a familiar path without much thought so far, but now you are out in the open with no directions. Be careful of your emotions. Depression can be dangerous for you. You need to learn to keep your energy here."

Sigeyo thumped her abdomen with such force it made me jump.

"When I was young I used to be very jealous inside and wasted my energy. Aikido taught me how to focus my ki and direct it." Sigeyo turned to Wendy. "So what do you think Mr Saunders' nine star ki is?"

"Oh, I think he has a lot of thunder. Maybe mixed with a softer energy… earth? What's your date of birth Adam?"

It felt strange being discussed and analysed like a rat in an experiment, although I have to admit, unlike the animal I enjoyed being the centre of attention.

"The first of July 1970."

Sigeyo smiled. "You are right on one count. But the softness you see is from water. Sorry Mr Saunders, you must think us rude, from your date of birth you have thunder as your deepest ki. It feels similar to the sunrise in spring. The energy of the night and winter, we call water, controls your emotions and on the surface you have the ki of the lake, the sunset in autumn."

After a short silence.

"You are a very sensitive man with lots of interesting ideas. I think you have the ability to do much," Sigeyo snapped her hand into a tight fist. "If you can catch the tide, you may rise high. If you do, please make the most of it, as unfortunately you have," she paused. "I hope you don't mind me saying this, a self destructive side."

Sigeyo asked me to hold my hands out in front of me with my palms facing each other, approximately a foot apart. She then placed one of her hands between mine. With her eyes shut Sigeyo appeared to doze off, leaving her hand in place for an uncomfortably long time. I struggled to focus on my breathing and trying to generate an energy field between my palms.

"Mmm, yes, your ki is quite strong but so dispersed and unfocused, like your emotions."

All this was said as though she had found an interesting shell on the beach. Sigeyo seemed completely detached and I suspected she would be amazed if I took offence to any of this. Again I felt like an animal, this time a horse being examined before a sale. However, my discomfort was overwhelmed by my interest in this woman. I had the growing feeling that she could be a significant part of my life.

My first impression was that Sigeyo was a genuine master of her art. Perhaps it was because she was Japanese, perhaps because of her age, or maybe it was her dry, minimalist, matter of fact style of communication. Sigeyo obviously did not feel the need to sell her beliefs in the way Stephen did.

She must have indicated to Wendy that the session was over because Wendy stood up and thanked me for coming all this way to meet Sigeyo. We all proceeded to the front door and I turned to say goodbye.

"May I say I like your house Mr Saunders?"

I stood in the open doorway confused.

"I have one small suggestion to make. Your kitchen is at the back of your home to the east?"

It was at the back but I could not remember which compass direction it faced.

"Does it receive the morning sun?"

"Yes, yes it does." I was relieved I could respond but still dazed by this turn in our conversation.

"Please put a bowl of fresh water on the table so the rising sun hits it each morning. I think your entrance is in the centre facing south-west. Why don't you try putting a bowl of sea salt next to your front door. And excuse me Mr. Saunders, one last suggestion, I suggest you turn your bed so your crown chakra faces south-east."

Wendy ushered me down the steps, "I'll explain later," she said.

Sigeyo stood at her door, bowed and remained there watching me walk away. Each time I turned she raised her hand into a slow wave. I was relieved to turn the corner, out of sight. My mind was racing and my emotions too turbulent to think clearly.

I phoned Josephine and arranged to meet her at her home. It was almost twenty minutes walk but I was still disorientated when I arrived.

Josephine's pale face flushed slightly and her eyes danced around my face as I told her of my meeting Sigeyo. She appeared openly enthusiastic.

"Will you go and see her again?"

"I'll have to talk to Wendy."

It was only when she had finished giving me a shiatsu that I felt calm again, even then I gave her a rather distracted and poor massage in return.

On my train journey home I phoned Wendy and she explained how Sigeyo could see the layout of my home through its imprint of ki on my face.

"Over the years the atmosphere of your home has created a pattern in your outer ki energy field that Sigeyo could read. I think she likes you."

"What did she say?"

"Just that she felt comfortable with you. Do you want to meet her again?"

"I would love to."

At home I described the meeting and Sigeyo's comments about our house. In the retelling it sounded incredulous to me and I could see Christine trying to hide her scepticism. Matthew found a compass and sure enough the front door did face south-west and the kitchen was in the east. I looked at Christine and raised my eyebrows.

"Perhaps there's more to this woman than you imagined. How could she know that?"

I reiterated Wendy's explanation. It felt as though we were indulging in some kind of dark magic ritual as we turned our bed so the tops of our heads faced south-east. It meant having our bed in the middle of the room and I expected Christine to protest, but she was surprisingly open to the idea. Christine even found some sea salt and an attractive bowl for the water and helped me place them as Sigeyo instructed.

A few days later Wendy called to arrange for me to meet Sigeyo at a Japanese restaurant, Miyama, in Clarges Street, Mayfair. Sigeyo requested that I bring my wife. We set off early to make the most of our journey into London. I found all of Sigeyo's books at Watkins book shop off the Charing Cross Road. I was slightly nervous of meeting her again. She was unpredictable and during that first meeting she had shown the ability to completely stun me. My biggest anxiety was fed by the thought that she might repeat her theories of 'one woman not being enough' in front of Christine, given my recent failing.

We wasted time browsing for CDs in HMV by Piccadilly Circus, another passion from my youth that I could not shake off, and then walked towards Green Park.

Aaron had suggested we experience the circle of thirteen trees on the east side of Green Park. They were arranged with an opening to the east-north-east that must have let in the morning sun. Standing in the centre of the circle holding Christine's hand, I felt a sense of purpose and destiny.

We arrived at the restaurant early. I imagined we would be

sitting on the floor with Japanese lanterns and the ubiquitous aquarium near the entrance. Instead the atmosphere was very clean, quite Zen in a way, with cream walls, simple elegant furniture and interesting three-dimensional linear artwork on the walls. The only hint of the orient was the low wooden lattice screens between the tables and girls dressed in traditional Japanese kimonos.

Christine and I drank a lager each whilst we waited. There was a slight flurry of activity and a black suited manager ushered Sigeyo and Wendy to our table. We stood up and all bowed to each other and then shook hands.

Sigeyo ordered for everyone in Japanese. Wendy was different around Sigeyo, much more respectful and certainly less prepared to push herself forward.

The food began to arrive. Sigeyo had choreographed the whole event so that different dishes arrived with their dipping sauces in a set sequence along with different types of sake. I regretted ordering the lagers before she arrived.

Neither Christine or I had used chopsticks before. Wendy tried to bend my fingers around the wood to make the correct scissor action. I was having severe difficulty lining the ends of my sticks with the consequence that instead of gripping the food I tended to flip it over, once or twice sending a spray of black shoyu across the white table cloth. Under Sigeyo's guidance Christine was learning quicker.

"Think of chopsticks as extensions to your fingers. We use wood instead of metal as it is softer, more gentle for eating."

Two eel sushi arrived for me and a dish called nabe for Christine. Sigeyo explained her choice. "Christine, this should help you relax. Spread your energy out from the centre to the surface a little."

It looked like a noodle soup with tempura vegetables, oysters and white fish in it. Green leaves and mushrooms gave it some colour. "I think maybe you work too much. You need to relax and let other people do some of it."

I was beginning to feel uncomfortable.

"This eel will give you strength, Adam. Help you wriggle and fight for what you want. Ah, here comes gobo kimpira. Please eat often, you need the burdock if you want to take on more."

Dishes came and went but two stuck in my mind. Natto oroshi was made from raw fermented soya beans and grated radish. Sigeyo considered natto to be some kind of wonder food, imploring us to eat it. Wendy declined, she had tried it before and failed to acquire the taste. I enjoyed the flavour but the texture was a shock. The whole mixture could only be described as slime with soft pellets in it. It was later to become one of my favourite dishes. Maguro yamakake consisted of chunks of raw tuna mixed into another slime that Sigeyo explained was a mountain root vegetable possessing great strength. When grated it transforms, I observed, into something with a similar consistency to sperm. It was this association that put me off the most, although the taste was interesting and likeable. Sigeyo hinted that this dish could improve a man's sexual vitality. Christine squeezed my hand and murmured her approval. A little disingenuous, I thought.

Once we had run through some polite small talk and felt the warm glow of the sake, Sigeyo turned to Christine, "May I ask your date of birth?"

"Certainly, I was born on Valentine's day, the fourteenth of February 1971."

"Oh interesting, very interesting you are all soil ki. The perfect mother I think. Very practical, very methodical. You should listen to your wife, Adam, I think she may be right more often than you think."

Sigeyo laughed and we all joined in. She persisted with her theme.

"You two so different. Let me say like this, a kind of opposites attract relationship, exciting certainly, but hard to understand each other. Not bad if you can accept the differences, although sometimes, I think, Christine you are the mother and Adam is the little boy."

We all laughed again, although I was slightly uncomfortable at the accuracy of her reading. Christine asked her how she knew all this.

"I have a very simple system I use over and over again. It is based on the five elements, eight trigrams and what you might call the magic square."

I was familiar with the five elements from the shiatsu course. "When you know a subject inside out and have used it for more than fifty years, an intuition develops that allows me to read into the charts more than is there." Sigeyo raised her hands in an expression of wonder at how this happens.

"Adam, what was your mother's date of birth?"

"Twentieth of November 1947."

Sigeyo's face lit up.

"And your previous girlfriend's?"

"Um, let me see I think Jackie was the thirty-first of May 1973 and Sandy was the fifteenth of August 1969."

Sigeyo nodded whilst appearing to count on her fingers. I heard her mutter something softly in Japanese to herself.

"Very interesting," came again. "You are looking for your mother. All your lovers have the same emotional ki as she did. I wondered why you have such a strong attraction to such different energy. You must remember Christine is your wife!" Sigeyo smiled.

I looked up to see Christine staring back into my eyes. She raised an eyebrow. After a brief silence Sigeyo continued in a more serious tone.

"I think you must have lost emotional energy from your mother that you are still looking for. Maybe the connection was severed too quickly, perhaps there was something you wanted from her but never got. Sons and mothers, daughters and fathers, I see it often. But I think it is a little difficult for a wife to be her husband's mother or for husband to become wife's father. Unreal expectations and easy to be disappointed, don't you think?"

I nodded uneasily, I was clearly the object of her musings. I felt slightly deflated, a heavy feeling passed down through my chest.

Without warning, Sigeyo suddenly announced, "If you want me to help you, Adam, you will have to stop eating ice cream. I am not interested in your difficult moods."

Everyone looked at me. True, ice cream was one of my favourite foods growing up and yes, even now I do occasionally have one with the children. Just as I felt the indignation rise up inside me I realised that she was also offering to help me.

"Don't worry, if it helps his moods I will make sure he never sees another ice cream," said Christine. "What else would help my darling?"

Sigeyo appeared not to hear and rose folding her napkin.

"All I can do is show you the path; after that it is up to you."

Back in bed, I lay awake for a while next to Christine's warm, rhythmic body. What did Sigeyo mean regarding my mother? I rewound the film. When I became rebellious in my teens, I was no longer mum's loving little boy. Although I initiated the fracture, I lost the warmth, closeness and affection in the process. Did a gene become active that pushed me into becoming independent; forcing me to move from the woman I had loved so much for my first twelve years? Had I consciously transferred my source of those comforts from my mother to Sandy, Jackie and now Christine? Deep down I felt a flutter as I recognised it to be true. I turned and slid next to her naked skin. I loved the feel of her.

I called Wendy the next day to thank her for making the introductions.

"What did she mean by helping me?"

"Sigeyo works very differently from us. You may never hear from her again or she could ask you to come down tomorrow. I have been working with her for nearly a year and I never know what she wants me to do next. All I can suggest is to keep your diary open and be ready to come down at a moment's notice."

Two weeks and no contact, then Wendy called, inviting me for tea with Sigeyo. It only gave me just over an hour to drive all the way into London.

Wendy looked as pleased as ever to see me. I imagined Sigeyo fed off her unbridled enthusiasm for life. Where it used to irritate me, I now found myself drawn into her constant euphoria.

During the tea and small talk routine, I took my cue from Wendy and sat calmly listening, only responding when appropriate. After the tea was cleared away I sensed the mood change.

"Excuse me but I'm going to speak frankly, Adam. I see you as a blunt stone. I might be able to help you become more focused, but a little guidance is all I will give you, the rest is up to you. I will only embark on this journey if you accept the seeds, plant them, nourish them and share the fruits generously."

I nodded solemnly.

"I am aware of my mortality and now I am ready to pass into you some of my experience in the hope that a part of me will stay alive through your work."

I tried to memorise every word as I knew I would need to work out what she meant more carefully on my own.

"So let's begin here. Kneel on the floor, Adam."

I did as she bid.

"Not bad, not bad."

Sigeyo walked round and adjusted my toes slightly so that one big toe rested over the other. She then stepped back and looked at me with her head to one side.

"Sorry, but I think you are not breathing well. Please allow me to line up your chakras."

My lower back was straightened a little, ribs tilted and the back of my head was pulled up.

"Now let your breath come in lower, deep into your abdomen. Only finally should you feel your upper chest expand."

I was surprised at how much more air I could take in with my new posture and technique.

"Very good, please adopt this position when you eat. I hope you can try and chew fifty times each mouthful. When you eat, please consider the food, the nature and people who brought it to your plate. To eat well Adam, you need to develop endless appreciation. Once you have placed the food in your mouth, rest your chopsticks and lay your hands palms up in your lap like this. Be humble."

I phoned Wendy for more explanation on the way home.

"Sigeyo considers food to have a living energy, life force or ki, feeding your soul. I think the appreciation is so important so you can love and respect the energy that your food brings into your body. Once inside your body the food becomes part of you. Being humble also means being slightly empty emotionally so you can take in more ki. What do you think?"

"That sounds a good explanation. I find her a little confusing at times, it is good of you to help like this."

Back at home I put my instructions into practice. I felt apprehensive that Christine and the children would laugh at the sight of me sitting on the floor, straining to keep my stance and making a mess with my chopsticks. Somehow they managed to maintain a supportive attitude. Matthew and Eleanor were enthusiastic to try eating with chopsticks and enjoyed spearing their vegetables.

That night I woke to feel the mattress trembling and Christine in fits of laughter. When I asked what it was she just gripped me, shaking as a new wave of hysterics ran through her.

It was very difficult to keep the food in my mouth for more than twenty chews. It required considerable concentration to push each mouthful to the front of my mouth and stop it sliding away. Needless to say, I was not very social during the meals. In fact part of me would have preferred to eat alone but I knew this was the one time the family was together.

When Justin came round, he took advantage of the situation, waiting until I had put the food into my mouth before embarking on topics he knew I had strong opinions on.

"I think George W. is a lot more intelligent than we think. He may not be the most eloquent orator but perhaps it is just his camouflage. I think he really does have a master plan that is slowly taking shape, leading the world into a better age."

I wanted to spit the food out, preferably into Justin's face and respond. My chewing sped up dramatically but somehow Justin managed to move on just as I reached fifty.

"Christine, did you see The Simpsons last night?"

He knew this would arouse Matthew's interest and by the time I was ready, no one else wanted to go back to my intended monologue on the evils of leaving someone as stupid as Bush in charge of the world's most powerful nation. I could see Justin eyeing me as I inched the next mouthful to my lips. I tried to trick him but he was too canny and again I was trapped with a full mouth as he expounded his crass views on the benefits of identity cards. Hardly the humble, tranquil, ki absorbing scene Sigeyo had envisaged.

Sigeyo suggested I keep a food diary to show her on my next visit. Ten days later Christine and I were invited to Sigeyo's house for dinner. She and Wendy prepared a meal of miso soup, brown rice, barley and aduki beans, a vegetable stew, steamed greens and a pressed salad. Each dish had a garnish to decorate and flavour the main ingredients.

Before we started, Sigeyo and Wendy placed their hands in a prayer position, I followed trying to think of all the people who had brought this food to the table. Sigeyo warmly invited us to eat. I felt rather self-conscious as I tried to sit in my correct posture and reach fifty chews.

"You have improved Adam. I think soon you will begin to feel the difference. When you learn how to focus the way ki comes in, through your food and breath, you can start to work on focusing the ki you project."

We were amazed at how the dishes, essentially the same as the ones we cooked from our macrobiotic recipe books, tasted so different.

"I let it come out from within naturally. Anyone cooking from a formula will never make food with vitality."

My wife looked at Sigeyo confused.

"Practice, practice and play with the concepts until they become part of you, but forget them when you touch the food. Once a basic understanding of yin and yang is inside you, it will find its own way out."

To complete the meal Wendy brought out four small bowls of stewed hunza apricots.

"Ah, here is little yang, big yin."

This was sweetest, unsweetened fruit I had ever tasted.

Christine cleared her throat. "Sigeyo could you please explain yin and yang to me, I have heard so much but still do not really know what it means."

"We only sense change. If you lived somewhere with a constant temperature you would not know that hot and cold existed, yes? We only see objects because they have different colours, or shading. If you were in a room where surface was the same colour you would not see any forms. Silence is simply no variation in sound. It is the same with all our senses."

We nodded. "So we live in a universe that is in a state of flux, always changing. You are changing, I am changing, the world around you is changing, that is how we experience life. It has a rhythm. Whenever one entity alters it causes the rest of our universe to change. You pull a string here and the world adjusts. Yin and yang is an attempt to make some sense of the way we react to the changing universe we live in. So sorry, I think am I confusing you."

"No, please continue, your explanation is very interesting."

"Practically you can observe how you react to different changes, for example weather conditions, foods or environment. Yin and yang is a tool to understand the connections better and so we can discuss them a little more easily." Sigeyo smiled. "But in the end they are just a pair of adjectives."

"How do you apply it to your life or to healing?"

"Basically if I feel too yang, let's say stiff or tense, I eat more yin foods and do some long slow stretches. When I am too yin, lethargic and cold, I make an effort to cook more yang foods and do some more vigorous exercise. I try to think very simply. Keep a basic idea, play with it and if I am comfortable with it use it in the same way repeatedly until the concept becomes irrelevant. Then I am working from my intuition and I have mastered the subject. I think in terms of how I feel and look at the rhythms around me. Full moon, new moon, sunny, cloudy, spring, summer, autumn and winter, night and day, hot, cold. Then I observe what I eat and how I respond. Not difficult or complicated, no magical secrets, just time, but who has the patience?"

I resisted the temptation to raise my hand. Sigeyo continued explaining how foods that help us feel more energetic and focused are more yang and those that make it easier to relax are more yin.

I thought this was a good time to give Sigeyo the food diary she had suggested I keep, but she appeared surprised and confused, giving it a rather cursory flick through, making no comment as she handed it back to me.

"Have you thought about the energy of food?" She picked up a carrot. "This contains the energy of the land it grew in, growing season, speed it grows, direction it grows, its own moment in its evolutionary cycle and even its place in the evolutionary cycle of our universe."

"Wow, who would have thought." Christine looked amazed.

"When we eat this food we take in all that energy with it. If you want to be more at home in your local surroundings eat vegetables that grow there. If you want to feel the rhythm of the seasons, eat fruits and vegetables in season. To calm down try foods that grow slowly; even better, cook them slowly. Move energy up your body using green vegetables, growing up above the ground. Strengthen the lower parts of your body with root vegetables. For a more youthful energy eat seeds, whole grains, nuts, beans all at the beginning of their life cycle. I think good for greater curiosity and a more open, flexible mind. For greater wisdom please try foods closer to the end of their life cycle, like vegetables, meat or fish. If they are wild they have the experience of how to compete. To access more primitive feelings of survival and reproduction eat ancient foods closer to the beginning of the whole evolutionary cycle, sea vegetables, fermented foods, oysters, mussels or clams. Where do they grow? Fruits are often higher in the air giving you an energy that makes it easier to connect to the world of souls." Sigeyo looked up. "Wild leafy green vegetables are exposed to the dark and light, hot and cold air, the wind, making them helpful for becoming adaptable, don't you think? Vegetables growing in the ground have a very stable environment, not much change in temperature, but have to work hard to push past stones. Yes, it is important we consider all these carefully Adam."

As usual I was blown away by Sigeyo's insights. She must have noticed as her next comment was more cautionary.

"Remember these are just ideas, opinions, please do not lose your common sense and only eat any food that is in season or that grows locally. Only an imbecile would take someone else's idea and follow it literally. You need to learn for yourself when and how much to follow. Try it, experiment but keep your sense of non-credo. Please, never let yourself become enslaved to a concept."

After some more small talk Sigeyo pulled her chair forwards so that she formed a circle with us.

"I want you to consider this. If we are made up of energy, of ki, how do you mix your ki with your husband or wife?"

I was not sure whether she was thinking out loud, preparing to voice the answer or wanted us to try.

"By being close," Christine offered.

"True but when you are close your ki mixes but only passively. How do you stir it up?"

"Sex?" Wendy piped up.

"Yes, Wendy, when you have sex your ki becomes active and you charge your chakras up so your ki flows from one to another. Afterwards you each have more of your lover's ki coursing through your veins."

We waited for Sigeyo to continue.

"So if your ki mixes most strongly during sex, the way you have sex will also have a lasting effect on your relationship. I think, because the way your energies interact during the passion creates a pattern, a flow between you that continues, affecting the way you behave with each other. You could say it defines your relationship on a deeper level. Think, how you have sex and how this influences you. May I suggest you two try doing the opposite of what you do normally see what happens to the way you relate to each other."

I turned to Christine playfully. "Something to keep us busy!"

I sensed Christine was slightly uncomfortable. Her acquiescence was barely audible.

CHAPTER SIX

Aaron is staying this weekend. He has been reading through my work, with the result that I will have to take out the clichés and be a bit more imaginative with my choice of words. Reading the previous chapter he shook his head.

"Verbose, verbose, verbose. You're not being paid by the word. Can't you be more concise?"

Sometimes writing feels like sculpting, moulding words into shape, re-working, trying to massage the slippery sentences into more elegant forms. I cannot always mix the water and clay correctly, my style alternates from being too dry, stuck looking for the correct expression and sliding into a loose, watery outpouring that embarrasses me in later readings. It feels weird writing about Aaron whilst he is here but it does make it easier to describe some of his traits. I feel like a painter observing my subject.

I am going to write about the time just after the accident, the turning point that led to my learning shiatsu.

After my accident and whilst I was still in hospital Aaron turned up. He swaggered up to my bed, wavy golden hair flowing over his shoulders. I had seen Aaron with a shaved head, a Mohican, various hair dyes, but this suited him best – the Mediterranean hippy. His skin was tanned, his clothes were frayed and he had a Jimmy Hendrix style purple felt hat on his head. Not finding excitement in our current popular culture he had gone back in time, whilst I followed musically.

It was Aaron I most looked forward to seeing. I was closer to him than anyone during my teens and even though our time together was punctuated by his travels to spiritually elevated places, the bond remained. He was back from India.

Aaron smiled as he approached me and by the time he sat next to me he couldn't stop laughing. His good humour was infectious and I could feel myself laughing through the bruises for the first time.

"My best friend's turning into a psychopath! First you try to kill your wife and then yourself. I'm surprised you didn't take the children with you. What's with the death wish?" All this was said with a huge grin whilst his eyes danced around my body.

Christine had obviously seen him first.

"OK, I overreacted to Christine not having my coffee ready, but you can relate to that."

"Christine said you experienced an amazing resurrection. I thought you might be ready for these, Jesus," Aaron placed a pile of books on the table next to my bed. "You know, maybe this is some kind of turning point for you. This could be the start of a new life as a motorcycle stunt man."

I tried to kick him as he giggled.

"Let's face it, you were going nowhere with that motorcycle repair crap, your relationship's a mess, and you may as well not have children for all the time you spend with them. But look who's talking, what do I have to compare to that? As Janis Joplin said – freedom's just another word for nothing left to lose."

I could never feel upset with Aaron, somehow he dived into the most tender areas of my life in a way that made it all appear trivial and comical. With a dash of self-deprivation thrown in, it felt we were really in it together. However his words stirred the deeper, darker waters of my mind and over the next few days I began to examine my life.

When Christine later flicked through the books Aaron had left she pointed out that he had thoughtfully written a little note inside each for me.

Inside *Zen Macrobiotics* she read out 'a new perspective on life rooted in the most powerful diet you can experience. This is all about living the biggest life you can.' Emily would second that statement.

Inside *Stalking the Wild Pendulum* he wrote 'Cosmic man. Some incredibly mind expanding stuff. You should seriously try to open up to more possibilities!'

'This one is more your scene – science meets eastern philosophy. Perhaps you should start here' summed up the *Dancing Woo Li Masters*.

Inside the cover of John Irving's book *A Prayer for Owen Meany* he simply scrawled 'The ultimate book on destiny.' Finally for *Think and Get Rich* he wrote 'a crass title but if you can crawl below the surface there is a mind blowing thought in here'.

After a few days rest at home Aaron cycled round to see me.

"Why do we have emotions, or at least dark negative ones? What is the point?"

Aaron raised an eyebrow. "Do I detect a depressed soul?"

I persisted. "Surely evolution should have weeded out all the depressed, miserable people. Our genes should be free from it by now. I can understand how anger, jealousy, impatience, boredom or loneliness can be helpful, but why depression? What possible service to the human individual or race is someone feeling too morose to function?"

"Good point, I'm just beginning to ask myself the same question."

I smiled back. "Seriously Aaron, who would want to be with a depressive or have children with one? Surely they would be pushed out of society, not have children and their breed would die out. Perhaps the clever depressive gene does not strike until after you have had children and already passed it on. Are those post natal blues the first sign it has become active?"

"For Christ's sake, I'm not wasting my afternoon with one of your dull monologues. Just accept it. You're feeling down. No big deal, embrace it and move on. The more you analyse it, the longer you'll stay there".

My body was distorted, thin and misshapen. My plasters were off, revealing severely atrophied pasty arms. My left was permanently bent at the elbow and my right shoulder too stiff and weak to lift my arm. I had put on weight in all the wrong places. My stomach hung forward resembling a pregnant beer pouch and large creases cut through the fat across my back. Pink blotches from too much time in bed coloured my pallid skin. My physical state reflected my mental attitude.

I pulled out a photograph album and found pictures of a twenty-year-old Adam. In my swimming trunks I looked athletic, broad shouldered, supported by a flat stomach. The edges of my muscles were defined and toned.

After a while Christine came in to see what I was doing and I confessed.

"I cannot face the workshop, just a lot of hard work to pay the landlord, rates and taxes. I'm thirty-two and I have no career to fall back on. It used to be worthwhile because I loved the bikes and hanging out with their owners, but the thought of race tuning a Ducati doesn't do it anymore. At least the insurance money will buy us some time."

Christine's lips tightened and her face turned a shade paler.

"You do what you think is best and I'll support you."

However the way she closed the door left me feeling stripped of any backing.

I began to look at myself in a way I can only describe as utterly self-destructive. I would wake at night hating myself. I picked through all those dark, heavy times that made me someone I no longer loved.

I recalled the times I joined in the bullying at school, the way I maintained minimum contact with my parents in their last years, the times I was unkind to Christine and her parents. I was selfish, cruel and manipulative.

Strange is that feeling when your self-esteem departs. The bravado, arrogance and ego slip away leaving a vacuum inside, a big painful empty space that was once filled with pride, confidence and self-belief. I had no future, no direction – a sailing boat that had become becalmed. It didn't matter which way I turned, the rudder there was no purchase, no movement, no bearing.

"Christine, I promise you my depression has nothing to do with you or the children, in fact quite the opposite, you three are the sole reason for me to try to find a way out of this darkness."

Since the accident I was having dreams of sitting in a chair in a field feeling different sensations wash over me. I was not entirely sure it was me. I was inside the body of a man but I could not tell if it was mine. The feelings I experienced were not familiar. Sometimes I was very sad, missing someone close to me, other times I felt anger, then a desire for revenge, a savage rage in which I wanted to kill and confront evil. Most of all I felt a numbing tiredness.

A few days later Aaron came round again and against my wishes he insisted on discussing my future. He threw his kaftan on the floor and sat on my bed. I could see some dried mud on his brown leather boots, and for some bizarre reason this held my attention as he talked.

"You have got to start rolling again A. If you stagnate you may as well be dead."

I tried to explain the emptiness and sleepless nights; waking feeling so heavy I could hardly breathe.

"All that means is you need something new. Don't be so unimaginative. Here's your chance to be creative with the rest of your life, be cool for a change, stop being boring Mr Normal. Come on, get up, we're going for a walk."

"But it's raining."

I had hidden myself away for so long that it was quite a shock to be out in the elements. It felt good even though cold raindrops were running down my spine. The wind blew away some of the negativity. I even found myself mildly interested in Aaron's idea that the planet is surrounded by a mass consciousness. Ideas are energy and therefore cannot be destroyed. They drift out of our heads, circulating around the globe.

"All you have to do is relax, keep moving and be open to letting new possibilities into your life. If you are open enough you'll find all kinds of interesting challenges come along. The solutions are out there waiting for you."

Aaron waved his hands around as though he was conducting his own thoughts. He had a bracelet of green beads on one wrist and a wooden ring on his middle finger. They caught my eye as they spiralled across a background of earth and faded leaves. Then he swung round, grabbed my jacket collar, shaking me slightly as he looked into my eyes.

"Get interested in life Adam. Look at the world, feel it, engage in it, develop your natural curiosity. Look at Matthew and Eleanor, the way they question everything. Come on Ads, why do we have five fingers? Think about it why two eyes, two nostrils, two ears, two tonsils but one mouth? Why do you feel the way you do? Why did you storm off and nearly kill yourself?"

When we returned I actually enjoyed kicking a football around in the mud with Matthew. Aaron stayed for tea and then left to see a girl he had met the previous night.

On leaving he spat a few words of advice to Christine over his shoulder, "Don't let him stagnate, clean sheets, fresh clothes, showers, throw him out doors as much as you can. Keep him fresh. He's rotting emotionally."

To me he simply said, "Read those books," and gave me a piercing stare.

I could tell I was beginning to drag Christine down. I don't know what I expected of her but whatever it was she did not have it. I think I really wanted her to feel my pain, to understand. I dismissed all her practical suggestions. We danced an emotional tango where I tried to trap her into behaviour that would allow me to carry on lying in bed feeling depressed. Sometimes when I sensed she was about to give up, I would feed her a glimpse that her efforts were finally working and suck her back into being matron.

When I came out of hospital she started wearing provocative clothing but now she was back to her baggy tracksuit bottoms and oversized sweatshirts. It suited me as the one thing that would have made it difficult for me to remain entombed in my dark mood would have been abundant sex.

Despite wearying of me, my wife religiously followed Aaron's advice and true, it was having an effect. I looked forward to my crisp clean sheets, my freshly ironed clothes, smelling of the sun and wind. I felt an immediate change throwing off my old rags, having a shower and putting on clean clothes. I now had three different circuits for my walks and I was reading Aaron's books. I had taken over walking Matthew and Eleanor to and from school. I was moving again, I could feel the twitch of the rudder, the slight tilt as the sails of my emotional boat filled.

My sister Emily came to stay from Canada. Emily and Aaron had once had a brief relationship that only seemed to last long enough for Emily to be infused with Aaron's enthusiasm for macrobiotics. Where Aaron tended to flirt with the macrobiotic movement from the outskirts, reading books and learning through experience, Emily plunged into cooking classes and courses. To me she became a zealot, a macrobiotic warrior whose only role in life appeared to be to convert me. Later the full-on macro persona softened to more motherly, earthy tones and my diet ceased to be an issue. Inevitably with Emily's arrival a new diet started to appear on the table. It was suspiciously similar to the macrobiotic regime in George Ohsawa's book. No more meat, dairy food or sugar. I ate lots of whole grains, mostly brown rice mixed with barley, rye or whole wheat, along with vegetables, seeds and beans. I had fish twice a week.

My protests were thrown back.

"Until you get your energy back and start behaving as though you really are alive, my dear brother, this is what you eat."

My heart sank as I witnessed Christine enthusiastically joining in and chopping vegetables. I was still too fragile to make a stand and to be honest, the food became appetising. Next I said goodbye to coffee and found myself brewing up herbal teas.

Alcohol was out of the question as it would exaggerate all the depressive emotional energy running through me.

Emily explained the macrobiotic theory that sugar leads to depressive blood sugar lows, once my natural insulin kicks in. Meat and dairy food make my blood stickier reducing my ability to take in oxygen, starving my mind of positive energy. Acid forming foods harm my bones and joints, so a huge amount of alkaline forming vegetables were piled onto my plate.

I sensed she revelled in my predicament, that she was milking the opportunity to finally impose the foods I had been so dismissive of. This should have been enough of a reason to snap back into my assertive, healthy self but instead I just sighed.

Aaron found me a shiatsu practitioner. It was not quite the sensual experience I had looked forward to. I imagined I would meet a wholesome girl dressed in a white tunic mixing up oils, that there would be an undercurrent of sexual tension as I undressed. Instead I found a middle aged Indian woman with cropped hair, wearing a tai chi outfit. I kept my clothes on and experienced an hour of being stretched, pressed, squeezed, pounded and manipulated in ways I had not imagined possible.

Every now and again Nirmala would stop and lay her hands on me, asking me to breathe slowly and deeply. "Forget the past, don't worry about the future just focus on the now," was her mantra.

She lived her own philosophy, showing no interest in what had happened to me, dismissing my attempts to tell her my story. I soon began to appreciate the silent routine, no need to suffer meaningless conversation. I did notice a lasting difference after each treatment. Not only did the range of movements in my arms increase but I also felt emotionally uplifted.

Following Nirmala's philosophy of living in the present was hard to do. Does it exist anyway? Surely we only have the past and future. The present is simply the transformation from one to another. You could divide time into the smallest segments possible and you would always have the past and future in there. Our senses would be too slow to ever get close to the turning point. I imagined that with a huge effort we move slightly closer. I now know that the more concepts I believe in, the harder it is to edge my nose up to the line. That whole process of matching whatever reality throws up and comparing it with what goes on in my head slows it all down too much. To feel really close to the turning point I would have to lose all of my beliefs. How many of them served me anymore? Very few, if any.

Still, I understood Nirmala's point. I was wasting too much of my mental energy trying to analyse my history and worrying about the future. Nirmala encouraged me to focus on every breath, to simply consciously initiate every in and out breath and feel my body respond. I struggled to do this each time I felt my heavy heart sinking.

It was easiest to be in the moment when I was being competitive or in danger. This was the sensation I used to experience when riding my bike.

I loved to ride fast enough to demand every brain cell of concentration, scrutinising the winding road for any sign of debris, puddles or shiny surfaces that might precipitate a slide. Following the white lines framed by the blur of the trees and hedge. Accelerating to oblivion and back, swooping through the corners like a bird.

My most vulnerable times were when I was bored.

"Initiate each in and out breath. Once started let the rest of your breath take its natural course. Then focus on feeling the sensation of breathing, Adam."

Walking barefoot in slow motion sometimes did it. For a few minutes I could be totally absorbed in feeling my weight gradually shift from one foot to the other as the sole of my foot made contact, rolled and broke again.

My main aim was to try to stop my mind spinning with irrelevant ideas and focus on what was really happening or at least what I wanted to make happen in my life. The quality of everything, however small, was all that mattered.

I finished all the books. I felt high chasing around all the possibilities of time, destiny and connectedness with Aaron. He sat with his legs crossed listening to my monologue on the turning point between the future and past. When I paused he moved the discussion on to tell me how he thought we are all connected by an invisible energy called chi.

"This is our sixth sense and gives us incredible powers."

We talked, relaxed, laughed and for the first time since the accident I felt mentally free as we drank our lemon and ginger tea.

It was during our teens that Aaron defined himself as a colourful visual experience. Cultivating the look, being associated with the right sounds, finding new philosophies to try on. He explored Zen Buddhism, he practised Tai Chi, embraced macrobiotics and developed a cool, spiritual superiority. I was curious as to what made him take that particular turn, being on the cusp of a change myself. I asked him one cold morning as he joined me on a walk, clad in heavy coats and wrapped in scarves.

"Fathers are meant to be role models but mine became an anti-role model. I looked around and all I could see were beaten down hamsters in treadmills, running for another glittering plastic household object. It was all so overtly obvious and predictable, you know how an insurance salesman leads you through a set of questions that always ends in you needing a savings plan?"

I nodded.

Aaron shook his head.

"Seeing them come back from another Saturday afternoon shopping expedition with the glow of their latest retail fix still smeared across their faces made me sick. I was a lamb being herded to slaughter. My escape was to search for alternatives so I could be the master of my own destiny. No disrespect Adam, but I just don't see the need to have all my decisions skewered because I have a horrendous mortgage and debts hanging over my neck."

"Marriage and kids change all that."

"Do you see me with a wife or children? The further I distance myself from all that, the easier it is to see it for what it is. An army of miserable people marching towards the end of their lives, trying to excuse the insanity of it all by grabbing hold of a few possessions along the way and indulging in mindless entertainment."

"You make it sound so depressing."

"Not at all. If I make any investment, it's in myself. All I have is me, the rest comes and goes, I'm moving forward. Maybe one day I'll find somewhere to rest if the desire is strong enough."

The issue of me having a family and Aaron being the free man was a theme we visited often. I remember a snippet of conversation from around this time. Christine had become less intimate and I was feeling sexually frustrated. Emily was making a pot of miso soup in the background.

"Thinking back, all my relationships were most vulnerable during periods when we weren't having sex. Sometimes I feel I could do anything for Christine when she's brought me to the edge of ecstasy."

"Maybe that's why I always bale out after the honeymoon period. As soon as the arguments start and the sex dries up, I'm off to explore new pastures."

"Not all of us have that luxury. Don't you ever want to work through all the challenges and grow yourself?"

"What and miss out on all the euphoria? No. I don't know how you guys manage it, but good luck to you. To be honest when I look around at all the couples we know, I haven't seen much growth, just two people bringing each other down and regressing into childhood tantrums and silly mind games."

"Perhaps you're right."

Aaron laughed.

"Have you two finished?" We looked up at Emily. I groaned. I could see where this was going.

"How can you two be so dependant on someone else for your happiness? I wish you could hear yourselves, you both sound like a couple of poodles waiting for a few crumbs of cake so you can wag you little tails for a few minutes. So tell me Adam, if you never had sex again would your life end?"

"No, but..."

"Aaron, think back. Is it at all possible that you might actually feel closer to someone if you have variety of experiences with her? Can you not accept that two people taking on a huge challenge together might find out more about themselves and each other and as a result live a bigger life? What is the point of putting all this energy into living your amazing philosophy and then being so one dimensional and shallow in relationships?"

Aaron laughed and threw his hands into the air.

"Let me have a few simple pleasures even if they are superficial. Please?"

Emily smiled and turned to me.

"I think it all started with your relationships with mum. The patterns you developed in her arms are being transferred onto Christine. I think many of my relationships are based on finding people who remind me of dad and then using them to try and repair my past."

"Oh, and who did I remind you of?"

"No one Aaron. That's why it didn't last. Anyway I wanted more than a few romps and nights out in a bar."

My next thought-provoking verbal exchange with Emily came as we walked through the soft shady woods close to my home. Matthew and Eleanor ran on ahead, in and out of shards of sunlight that beamed through the branches, running away and back again, screaming, laughing, kicking last year's leaves and throwing sticks. Even though Matthew was a couple of years older than his sister the chemistry was harmonious, reminiscent of Emily and myself. The ground was covered in a sea of bluebells, a truly magical day.

Today's topic was reincarnation. Emily was convinced that, "Every action tips the balance of the rest of your life, leaving imprints and shaping your destiny."

I was relieved to find she did not trot out the idea that I might be reborn a rat for the mistakes I'd made in life. Taken to its ultimate conclusion, Emily's version meant that, "If you take the right actions you will build up enough good karma to attract positive energy into your life."

Emily implied that the universe had the power to hand out rewards for good behaviour.

"It sounds more upscale New York than Rwanda, Emily. Interesting that the 'universe' decided to focus its rewards so tightly on selected parts of the globe. It might work in the land of opportunity but not in a desert. I can imagine even the right kind of smile might win you friends, a good job and a relationship in a city of plenty but would the ravishes of nature respect your past deeds? Can a volcano single out good from evil? And how does karma decide what is good or bad? The interpretation of the moral code changes so much depending on time and culture."

Emily gave me a despairing look. "Don't give me that. You're taking it out of context. Wherever you are, you can always improve. And who is to say that a drop of water in the baking desert is not worth more than a million dollars in shiny New York. You're looking at it with materialistic eyes. We're not in an Ab Fab episode."

I suspected Emily thought my accident was some kind of lesson dealt out for bad deeds. And true there were parts I wished I could rewrite.

"No, it's not a punishment, but more about trying to see the accident happening for a reason. Working through why it happened and finding a way to turn it into something positive will give you a new force in life. That accident changed your destiny. To me that's exciting."

"I'm not good at change. I used to dream of adventures and

excitement but right now I just want to curl up and return to my old life."

"Going back and putting right some of those things you're not happy about will change your karma and might enable you to move forward more freely," she offered, brightly.

I was not sure this was karma but the idea of cleaning up my past appealed. Perhaps I would no longer be haunted by old deeds.

Emily expounded her belief that, "After we die we spiral out carrying an energy that sums up our experiences in life into infinity and then return to take this forward into our next life."

"How does the population increase if we are the same energy coming back over and over again? And if our life force floats out into infinity and back again, we would have to pass through a phase where time does not exist. Infinity implies no defined space, which must mean that time breaks down. If this is the case, we could come back at any time, including the past. We might have already lived future lives as well as past lives. Anyway, who is to say that our energy does not mix with other energies during its journey out to infinity and back."

I was impressed by my ability to match Emily in these free-thinking ramblings and even add in my own original thoughts.

"Look, Adam, I did some things I regretted. I resolved them, I felt better and I'm moving forward more freely."

"You mean with mum and dad?"

"I was terrible to them, you know, with the Buddhism and dropping out of school. Don't you remember all the arguments about my macrobiotic diet? How we stopped talking and I left home. I felt they had done me the harm. They didn't understand me, all they were interested in was exam results and fitting me into the shape of their ideal daughter. If only I'd worn pink floral summer dresses, taken up horse riding and gone out with mum for tea with the awful Perrines."

We laughed. I remembered hearing mum complaining to me

about Emily and dad asking me for advice on what they should do. I wasn't any help, by then I was lost in beer, gigs and sex. Somehow a son forming a drinking habit and running wild was acceptable or at least tolerated, whereas a daughter experimenting with another take on life and a weird but essentially healthy Japanese diet was not. It never made sense at the time. I don't think Emily falling in love with Aaron reassured my parents either.

"I mean who's to say that my life was any poorer than that of a frumpy middle class cow setting out her stall to ensnare a rich city bull? If I was happy, surely that should be enough to make them happy. Anyway it got worse, I used to shout at them about their meat and eggs and they labelled me as being brainwashed."

I remembered Emily's vegan declaration. I remember witnessing the leather shoes, belts and bags dramatically being thrown out with the rubbish. I recalled her animal-free shelf in the fridge. Most of all, I could still access the "ugh!" and sour face whenever any of us ate meat in her presence.

"You were pretty extreme and aggressive then, kind of the opposite to this peaceful, accepting, loving person you claimed Zen macrobiotics was all about."

"Yes, I know, but it was during a Zen meditation course that I finally got out of my head and saw that my war with my parents had become all consuming. I invested so much in being right but there was no right or wrong, it was just my choice to be vegan. It was all in my head, it was just my assumptions, my expectations, my judgements. Why should mum or dad have the same views? I had confused opinions with fact. So I ran round, made the biggest, most humble apology I could and told them how much I loved them. Mum became tearful and couldn't stop hugging me, dad stroked my head like he used to when I was little. After that they became more accepting of me and that tornado that spun around my head lifted."

Aaron walked along the path to meet us. We lay on the long

grass in a small clearing. Emily summarised our karma conversation and soon we were laughing at how many people claimed to be a reincarnation of exotic historical figures. I love the way that however passionately Aaron believed in an idea, he was quick to see the paradoxes and giggle.

Watching Matthew and Eleanor climb a tree, I brought up the topic of my coming back from the dead.

"You know they somehow pulled me out of that golden tunnel. I still don't know how it happened and sometimes I find it hard to just see them as children. And yet despite that power they seem blissfully unaware."

There was a long pause before Aaron spoke slowly.

"Remember when you were that age, anything could happen. Look at them. Maybe they are still not yet fully materialised, perhaps they still see energy."

Emily's eyes sparkled.

"Remember how Matthew used to draw people with a halo around their heads, like an aura."

"Yes, Eleanor still does."

Emily touched my arm.

"Have you noticed how babies often look just above your head?"

I thought back to my death and being a child again. I remembered seeing that light haze around my mother's head.

"Yes, I think you're right."

Now it was Aaron's turn. "Children have no limits, life has not hammered them into socially acceptable beings yet. I believe they must have picked up some of your soul as you were dying and reacted to it naturally. Adults would block it out. If it is not within our perception of reality, it does not exist. We live in very small worlds, Adam, limited to the scraps we believe in. The walls of mental rigidity close in as we grow up and suddenly all we are left with are neatly tied parcels of thought. Zen monks spent their lives breaking down those walls to see it all and experience freedom."

I became a spectator as Emily carried on. "Yes I suppose the more we believe in the concepts the harder it is to except reality when faced with observations that don't fit.

"If a pink elephant flew through the woods, would we block it out? Our adult brains probably wouldn't register it. Meanwhile, Matthew and Eleanor would be jumping around pointing."

CHAPTER SEVEN

Whilst steaming vegetables for our supper I have a flashback. As we walked with my father on a cold winter's day across frosty leaves, he explained how we only use ten percent of our brain-power.

Ever since, I have wondered what the rest was for. I tried to focus every part of my mind on a cup, willing myself to move it with my brain waves. Much later I tried levitating myself and more recently I attended a séance. It was only with Sigeyo's guidance that I started using some of my extra capacity. I still cannot conceive what it would be like to turn my mind on to full power. The idea that within me lie hidden secrets that even I am not aware of intrigues me.

I finally felt I had found a new direction in life. I was on a roll, riding the crest again. With Sigeyo I felt a whole new world was opening for me. Just as I previously had some use, purpose and social value with the motorbikes, I now had it with healing. Aaron, Christine and Josephine lapped up my latest encounters and were happy to recommend me to friends. I was soon giving two or three healing sessions a week.

One issue was whether I should charge a fee for my work. I remembered Sigeyo's instruction to remain humble and as I had not qualified in any aspect of my healing, I felt more comfortable giving my energy for free. When I discussed it with Sigeyo she appeared to deliberately misunderstand me.

"It would be very easy to abuse your position and try to enslave people to your ideas on healing. You must ensure anyone you work with remains in control. Your job is merely to educate people into healing themselves. You should empower rather than enslave anyone to your ideology."

"Yes, but do you think I should charge a fee for my work yet?"

Sigeyo's voice became terse.

"I sit at home and wait. I keep myself clean, I am a receptive, empty vessel ready to accept. When someone calls, I ask what they want from me and what they want to offer. Then I can decide if it will work for me. I have never advertised or promoted myself. I don't want money that is tainted with resentment. I give freely and I prefer to work with people who give freely too."

I assumed this meant different prices for different people. So far she had not charged me. I felt uncomfortable, perhaps I should have made an offer.

"Sigeyo, I am aware and grateful that you have not asked me for anything in return for your training and wisdom. I would be happy to give freely."

Sigeyo looked at me quizzically. I felt there was a potential for misunderstanding.

"I mean I would be happy to pay you."

A frown creased Sigeyo's forehead and she stared straight into my eyes. "My wish is to give you my experience, your reply is to use it. I thought we discussed this."

One person who did not take my re-invention seriously was Justin. Perhaps he could not believe that this aggressive, mildly violent, nasty bully had somehow transformed into a kind, benevolent healer. Justin's way of dealing with it was to ridicule my conversion. He enjoyed mispronouncing the words in my new healing vocabulary and he laughed about the food – especially my attempts to eat it. Christine would often join in and I liked it. It was funny and I could see it was amusing to witness a grown man clumsily putting on a different set of clothing, assuming airs and graces, and pretentiously taking on a new language; ki, yin, yang, chi, the five elements, a trigram or a meridian dominated my new dictionary.

I couldn't complain because I had always smiled inwardly at Aaron's spiritual, new age persona. Later, I wondered whether Justin was trying to maintain a part of our traditional roles because it ratified his past. Did he resist my conversion because it risked crumbling up the rock that he had built his emotional life on? I dismissed my inner psychobabble, but who knows.

It was a sunny afternoon when Christine and I lay on the sofa after lunch, enjoying the time alone together. Here was the opportunity to try Sigeyo's ideas for a change in our mating habits. I resisted the urge to make our closeness more sexual. I let Christine take the initiative, becoming more passive as we reversed our normal pattern. Our lovemaking was slower, with pauses to talk, more caressing. I came first and then gave her my full attention as she reached her orgasm. I enjoyed the change. Would this adjustment to our most primal energies reach out and fine-tune the more evolved feelings in our hearts and minds? Would it ultimately have any effect on our relationship?

When the day ended and I fell asleep, I had another of those memorable dreams. This time I finally fell asleep in my deck chair only to wake, my heart pounding, to the sound of the bell. Men were shouting as I scrambled to my feet. No more wistful thoughts, just running across the morning dew. I woke up to find myself halfway across the room in a sweat. I must ask Sigeyo what she thinks.

I was gratified to reflect on how much I had learnt during my next visit to Josephine. I noticed how cold she was inside. This was different from her cold hands, the need to cup hot drinks with her artistic fingers or to squat down and cuddle up to a radiator. I could see and feel a chill inside the bones of her long spine. Without thinking, I suggested she had miso soup with grated ginger and root vegetables everyday, I explained how to make a nabe and suggested she try eating more hot cooked foods for a while.

I wanted to energise her kidney energy. I prepared hot ginger water, dipped a hand towel in the steaming liquid. She lay on her front and I helped pull up her sweater and vest. Josephine undid her bra strap and I pulled her jeans down a little. I was aware that she was ill at ease. During the preparation she became stiff and tense. I was not sure if she thought I was going to make an advance, if so there was no need to distress herself, her thin pale bony back did not act as a visual aphrodisiac. I wrung out the hot gingery cloth and laid it over her bony spine as instructed in Sigeyo's book. After frequently refreshing the compress, her back had a red glow. Josephine got dressed and I was sure I could see a difference in her face.

I was alone during my next visit to Sigeyo. Wendy had made a light lunch before she left for her drama class and without her presence we ate in silence. Afterwards Sigeyo made some tea and to my shock insisted I smoked a cigarette with her. She handed me a Davidoff. She must have registered the look of surprise on my face. "Two people eat the same food, drink the same tea and smoke together, they begin to vibrate at a similar frequency. We are tuning into each other. I think you will understand me better."

I thought of American Indians passing a pipe around.

"I think it may be easier to sit as I do. Breathe with me for a while."

This was said as though it had only just occurred to her, a sort of surprising discovery. As with many of her statements I felt she was not really sure herself, just thinking aloud. We knelt facing each other on the wooden floor.

This was followed by a long silence during which we smoked our cigarettes. I watched and followed her breathing. Sigeyo then appeared to doze off. She knelt motionless with her chin resting on her chest and her eyes closed. I followed, fearful that I might mess up the transfer she alluded to if I moved. I could feel a growing pain in my ankles. It was spreading up to my knees. I began to shuffle, trying to shift my weight by leaning forward onto my knees. Whilst Sigeyo looked serene and dignified I was hunched over in agony searching for way to alleviate the pain, praying for Sigeyo to get up. Finally Sigeyo started talking. "Adam, let's sit in the chairs. I think you will be more comfortable."

I rose stiffly and found that the blood flow to my legs had been restricted so much that they could not support me. I fell forwards, just managing to cling onto a chair. I struggled to drag myself up and gingerly shook each foot in an effort to force the blood back. As I walked forward, my legs buckled and I was back sprawling on the floor again. I lay on my side writhing around, pounding my legs until the strength returned.

Sigeyo watched the whole performance with an amused, quizzical expression. To my amazement Sigeyo inhaled slowly and with a powerful out breath jumped straight up onto her feet from her knees, and spoke.

"Consider oneness. There is an essence that runs through all we know. We might call it ki but this is only part of it. I want you to meditate on the universe. Go out at night and connect with the stars. Wake early and feel the dew rise off the grass with your bare feet. Feel the sun rising and setting. Experience the full and new moon. Next time we meet you will know the rhythms of life, night and day, the seasons, the phases of the moon."

Sigeyo fell quiet again and then continued softly.

"Adam, when you look at the stars look for ways you can see basic patterns repeating, the spiral in a sea shell, your ear and the cosmos. Consider how the form of our solar system is reflected in atoms. You will start to see and recognise the same flow over and over again."

I think the chestnut tree outside the window distracted Sigeyo and we returned to silence.

"Every now and then I like to look at what I am doing and strip it down to its bare essentials so that I can clear out anything that is unnecessary. When I do this I work on the assumption that the only thing that is real is how I feel – my thoughts and my emotions. This is my reality. Your reality is your thoughts and your feelings."

Then she appeared to falter.

"Can our realities merge? Did my mother's reality somehow

programme mine?"

Sigeyo looked confused and left the question floating above her head. She paused before taking in a long breath, looking up at the ceiling as though accessing something deep inside her mind.

"We can watch the sun rise and set, look at the moon, feel the rain, listen to the thunder. However, no one else can experience the world exactly as I do."

I nodded. This was not new to me but somehow hearing it from Sigeyo gave it greater drama, it was as though time stopped and the atmosphere of the room dropped to the ground. There was an incredible weight and gravitas to her sentences. She started again, speaking very slowly.

"Human nature drives us to try and explain the universe we live in. As such we develop concepts to make sense of it. I think it is essential to remember these are simply different people's ideas and not reality itself. We can measure light as a wave or particles moving in almost straight lines. Quantum physics is based on probabilities not certainties. Personally, I do not believe the concepts I use accurately reflect reality. Yin and yang, five elements, trigrams are all different people's attempts to explain the way ki moves."

I had thought of Sigeyo as a wise grandmother who had intimate knowledge of the eastern approach to healing but now her intellect slightly disoriented me. I struggled to find my balance.

"So why bother with the concepts at all?"

There was no answer so after a few minutes I repeated my question a little more firmly.

"Concepts help me learn about other people's thoughts and understanding of a subject, they help me discuss issues in more depth, they contribute to a body of knowledge, intellectual cohesion and structure."

Sigeyo turned to look me in the eye.

"Most importantly, the concepts I use alter my perception of the world I live in. My studies with George Ohsawa radically altered my perception of the way humans interact with their food and I have been able to confirm much of this through my own personal reality. Healing solely on the basis of the feeling of ki at the time would mean decisions are made based on a snapshot of experience. Ki is always changing. Simply being in someone's energy field means I have altered their ki and I would be affecting my reading of what is happening there. For this reason, I need some kind of objective structured view to give my work greater consistency."

I stared back blankly trying to understand what she was saying whilst struggling to keep up with every word she uttered.

"It does not matter that the concepts are not real, it allows me greater flexibility, more room to think and a greater appreciation of my observational reality. I believe too great an attachment to concepts means people can no longer connect deeply with the world around them. Concepts create a filter that matches what really happens and how this compares to the concepts we hold dear. If observational reality throws up something that does not match our concepts there is the risk that we favour our pet theory and ignore reality. When this happens a person can edge into a world of delusions and lose any connection with his soul."

I wanted to formulate a question but in doing so realised I still had not thought through Sigeyo's ideas.

"Before you go, try this exercise with me. Kneel facing me."

I sighed at the thought of another gruelling leg numbing session. We knelt facing each other and Sigeyo held my wrists firmly.

"Now try and push me backwards or to one side."

I pushed hard in various directions.

"Try harder Adam, there is no need to constrain yourself on my behalf."

Again, I tried but however I directed my force she was able to shift her weight over my arms and change the direction of my thrust, leaving me struggling to stay upright.

"Please let me try." We changed so that I was now gripping her wrists.

Before I could blink, Sigeyo had pushed me off balance and swung me round onto my back. I did not feel any force, just being gently led.

"Now you know what to expect, let's try again."

This time Sigeyo let me hold her wrists for a longer time before flipping me onto my back.

"This is a lesson in using the rhythm of life. If you can catch the wind or the tide, natural forces will take you, if you fight against them you will struggle. What rhythms did I, an old woman, use to overcome you, a larger, younger man?"

My mind stumbled. All I could think of was heartbeat but surely Sigeyo could not mean this? She smiled.

"True but you over-estimate my abilities. I watch your breath. When you want to move against me I breathe out and deflect your ki, when I want to push you I wait until you start to breathe in and with my out breath I overpower you."

It was so simple. I resolved to try it on Aaron.

"Good, do you have any questions before you leave?"

"Yes what are all those rolls of paper?"

"Oh these are my clients' charts and notes. Please excuse the mess."

She undid one and rolled it out to reveal a beautiful page of Japanese characters surrounding what I now recognised as the magic square from her nine ki book.

"I roll them up to contain their energy and fasten the paper with a red, yang coloured ribbon but as you can see, it's not very practical for filing."

On the way to Josephine's flat I thought of the rolls of paper. How interesting that Sigeyo should think that flat paper could lose its energy and therefore presumably the energy of her relationship with her clients. In a way it made sense. I was fascinated by the way she thinks, her attention to detail. I gave Josephine the usual de-briefing when I arrived. It was therapeutic for me, a form of mental release but more importantly allowed me to go over each session with Sigeyo in a way that helped me retain the information. This only worked because Josephine was genuinely interested, she didn't interrupt or ask questions, she just absorbed it all. Josephine suggested I make a list of all the tasks Sigeyo expected from me.

I felt very relaxed and comfortable around Josephine. It was now second nature to give each other a shiatsu. She had been trying my advice and had even made a miso soup for me. She said she felt stronger for it and it showed in her touch. It was only when I gave her another ginger compress along her spine that she tightened up again. I remembered how she had chosen shiatsu over other forms of massage as she could remain dressed.

CHAPTER EIGHT

The combination of the macrobiotic foods and silent lengthy chewing made me feel light headed. As the weeks slipped by I became highly perceptive and clear minded. My moods were becoming more consistent. I had not had a major black depression for some time now. Although at times it took tremendous will power not to join in with the children's snacks and occasional ice cream, my body's attachment to those foods was weakening. It helped to think of food as energy. I had a completely new perspective on food and a new set of values when choosing what to eat.

During this time I identified two different types of cravings. There was the physical craving when my blood sugar ran low, and the habitual emotional craving formed by attachments I had formed with certain foods. I associated ice cream with a childhood treat for being good or more recently when having fun with Matthew and Eleanor. Any time there was a conscious or subconscious need to relive those emotions an ice cream would act as a conduit.

The challenge was to build a new positive emotional relationship with healthy foods. Roasted nuts and raisins became my staple uplifting snack. I put my feet up and listened to my favourite music of the hour and read a heartening book; Josephine had urged me to read *Pride and Prejudice* for this purpose. As the warmth of contentment spread through my body I chewed my 'bird food', as Justin referred to seeds and nuts. I tried to apply the same principle to my healthy meals, making the whole experience as happy as possible.

Sigeyo claimed that as time went by my body would actually tell me what I needed in the form of a physical craving. She pointed out that this only worked if I consumed a wide range of foods so that I could subconsciously form biological relationships with a variety of certain tastes, textures and smells along with the ki and nutrients they give me. Are the powers of the human body that great?

In this heightened state my attention was focused more closely on what was happening immediately around me. I was pleasantly surprised that thoughts of my finances no longer brought feelings of anxiety. Sigeyo's opinion was that alcohol, coffee and sugar drove me to a state of chemical instability, where insecurity and anxiety naturally followed. At one time I would have treated a statement like this with derision but now that I had the experience, I nodded.

I began to experience the rhythms of nature as Sigeyo instructed. I made notes in my diary for the timing of the new and full moon, I woke to see the sunrise and walked to the brow of a hill to watch the sunset. I was amazed at how aware I became of myself as I was standing in the field behind our house at midnight. I felt each breath with every heartbeat. This contrasted with the sight of the stars. All my problems seemed irrelevant compared to the size of the universe.

Christine and I continued to reverse roles during sex. It was definitely having an effect on our entire relationship. I felt more accepting, more open to her ideas. She took the initiative more, coming up and tickling me unexpectedly, fondling my bottom when I talked to a shop assistant, jumping on top of me as I relaxed on the sofa.

One disappointment was that Aaron became slightly distant from me and subtly critical of Sigeyo. "All the best changes I have made are through my own experience and challenges. Without Sigeyo you'd be stranded. If I fail I know I have the resources to go out and do it again – to change and evolve. You are more like someone who has just won the lottery and if you lost the money you know you would never get it back again."

I explained that Sigeyo was a helping hand up the ladder.

"Strong oaks don't grow in the shade of others. You are

becoming lazy and dependent," he challenged. "I expected more from you. Don't you think that all you are doing is transferring from learning how to fix bikes to learning how to fix people? As Ken Wilber says, you're just in a process of translation, not real transformation. Where are the challenges and resources to keep evolving yourself?"

Despite agreeing to differ I saw less of Aaron. I felt uncomfortable relating Sigeyo's teachings in front of him, which was sad.

During my next encounter with 'my guruess' as Justin referred to her, I learnt how to see an aura. The trick was to have a white background and focus my eyes halfway between the subject, Wendy, and the wall.

I could see the haze around Wendy's head when I relaxed. Sigeyo encouraged me to confirm what I saw by feeling the ki around Wendy's head with my hands. I could just see a tinge of colour in the haze, however, it was hard to make much sense of it. I trusted it would become clearer with practice.

I walked to Josephine's to practise my new skill. An element of self doubt crept in as I wondered whether I was imagining it, a sort of self projected image formed by an optical illusion produced by poor focus. Whatever it was, the result was different from looking at Wendy. Josephine's aura appeared more intense and active, a deeper hue of yellow and much more uneven. A yellowy dark purple haze extended higher above the right side of her head. I was surprised. I assumed Wendy had the busy active mental ki. I guess it is all in how much you verbalise. Josephine was still a creature of few words. Her facial expressions were very understated and her body language was almost non-existent. I was intrigued that there might be so much more inside Josephine that was a mystery to me.

My latest homework was face reading. Sigeyo wanted me to find a busy location, somewhere to sit and observe different facial features. The mission was to spend an hour looking at lips, then move on to an hour of noses. The objective was to observe the differences. Full or thin lips, wide or narrow mouth, pale, red or purple lips, creases around the mouth.

Josephine suggested Camden Lock market and it occurred to me that it would be fun to take Christine and the children. The market is situated in a large Victorian warehouse area filling the space between the canal, the railway arches and the road. There was a vast multicultural explosion of food, furniture, clothing, art, junk and music. It was a cool place to hang out and be a part of the sea of souls that had opted out of the synthetic shopping mall experience and were looking for a unique purchase.

I sat on a wooden bench observing whilst the others explored the endless stalls. I had picked my site for its close proximity to a Turkish lady selling pitta bread, humous and falafels. As the morning evolved and I moved on to eyes I realised we are all face readers. It is the one part of each other that we see the most. I must have hundreds of characters and their matching faces stored up in my brain. Each time I meet someone I can probably make some kind of association between certain features on his or her face and personalities from my past, making a rough reading of my own.

My family and Josephine kept popping back at intervals to dump off purchases at my feet. Christine surprised me with an authentic Second World War pilot's jacket.

That night I tried out Sigeyo's instructions for feeling ki. Christine undressed and lay on her front. I then ran my hands up and down her spine, close to her skin, noting the areas that had warmer ki and places that felt deficient. I firmly ran the backs of my thumbnails over her skin along either side of her vertebrae. I watched two red lines slowly form beside her spine. I was reassured to see that where I had felt an excess of life force the red blush filled more quickly creating a broad line, leaving the areas where I could sense less energy with a pale thin line.

Sigeyo's next challenge was for me to go on a one week fast of brown rice and vegetables. The first day was surprisingly easy.

During day two the cravings began to kick in. Days three and four proved to be the ultimate test of will power. All I could do was chew and use this as a way to absorb the maximum out of the food. My record was one hundred and fifty three chews for one mouthful of brown rice, rye and barley. Having survived the worst my body seemed to go limp and give up. By the sixth day the deprivation was replaced by a mildly hallucinogenic calm.

Apart from the lethargy, I felt serene, colours jumped out and surfaces looked grainier. Towards the end I found my world had become softer, shimmering and slightly translucent. The edges of physical material forms almost melted into a fuzzy haze – subtly similar to the auras I had seen.

Sigeyo had advised me to come out of the fast slowly, bringing in soups and fruits. In fact, by the seventh day I was tempted to carry on. I had reached a weird dreamy state of independence from food. It all came to an abrupt end when I saw Justin in a café in Hitchin and found myself ordering an éclair, followed up by passion cake. As the ice cream and a monster-sized hot chocolate arrived I saw Christine and Aaron come in to the cafe. My initial attempt to hide under the table was thwarted when Justin called out to them. Christine stared open mouthed at the remains of my binge. I still had cream and chocolate around my mouth, pieces of cake lay in my lap. Justin added fictitious chocolate fudge brownies and scones to my indulgence.

On the way home I felt dizzy and sick. I wanted to throw up but could not bring myself to force it out.

My spiritual elevation was followed by two days of nursing a sore stomach and headaches. It annoyed me to think Sigeyo would see it all in my face and perhaps find it amusing.

My next lecture with Sigeyo took the theme of humans essentially being emotional beings. Sigeyo related how we were just made up of universal ki that had become concentrated and as a result more intense and active. In this form the ki took on the hue of what we call emotions – and that is all we are – emotional energy, mixed into water, contained in a bag of skin.

Sigeyo showed me how to read the ki flow through the face. She drew a face map connecting the various features with ki from different parts of the body. Lip with intestines, nose with the heart, cheeks with the lungs. She helped me look at the details on my skin in the mirror to read my own internal ki.

"Ki on the inside drifts out leaving its mark on the surface."

As I explained to Josephine, physically she saw liquids, tissue and bones but what interested Sigeyo most was the way each of us uniquely manifested the emotional ki of the cosmos.

"It is as though we are outlets for our environments emotions. Sigeyo thinks our emotions simply reflect whatever is happening around us. Food, people, environment all combined to create different outpourings within us, like a mountain spring. All our bodies do is to influence the way universal emotions come out, gushingly, constrained, violently, nervously."

Josephine appeared to absorb the words but gave no obvious clues as to her reaction. I knew she was taking it all in seeing her eyes flitting around my face with heightened alertness and interest. So I continued.

"Everything we do is done emotionally. We add numbers emotionally, we see emotionally, even the way we exercise is just emotions transposed into movement, and this energy, this ki is universal – it's not ours. Despite what we think, they are not even *our* emotions. We're just a conduit for the emotional ki coursing through us and sometimes it comes out as happy, sometimes sad.

"The point I'm trying to make is that your diet, the place where you live, your lover, could have just as much influence on the way you feel as your past or childhood."

The implications were exciting but I had to admit to being sceptical. What about Sigeyo's nine ki astrology, our upbringing, genetic make up? The whole point must be that there was no separation. No separation from our emotions.

"In Sigeyo's opinion, emotional isolation equals death.

Emotions and physical forms are one."

When I completed my discourse Josephine tilted her head to one side, looked into my eyes and smiled. One great contrast I had not yet understood was how someone who tended to be so shy, evasive and withdrawn, appeared comfortable maintaining eye contact for long times. It was sometimes unnerving but mostly I found it quite intimate, as though she knew me deeply.

"I don't know Adam, my whole life has been built on what happened as a child. I have been to three therapists in the last four years and the connections all make sense. You can't write it all off as my diet."

"Well I don't have the benefit of knowing what happened to you, but…"

"I thought you felt it in the shiatsu class, Adam, that was closer than anyone else has been."

"True, and I'm not saying she is right, but if there is any truth in what she is saying it means you can change. Different foods, a new home, someone else close can possibly change the way we feel."

There was a long pause – I had run out of steam and Josephine just stared at me.

"Adam, I will admit that since you came into my life my emotions have changed, I do feel different."

This was not quite what I meant or expected. I was thinking more of a Christine, Matthew or Eleanor type relationship, not a couple of shiatsu students swapping sessions and exchanging ideas.

Josephine reached out and touched my hand. My first instinct was to retract it but managed to relax and leave it under hers.

"You're a very special person, Adam. If you can have this effect on me there must be so many others you could help."

I left with a glow. After seeing Josephine, I experienced a surge of self-belief and confidence.

CHAPTER NINE

I finally felt comfortable chanting at home. I still dreaded the effect it might have on the children and tended to voice my mantras when they were at school.

With Sigeyo's help I could now direct the sonic vibrational energy into different parts of my body. Essentially the lower the pitch the lower down in my body I felt the vibration. I could now chant from my sacrum right up to the crown of my head, starting with a low growl and ending in a high pitched hum.

Aaron came round with his new, very young looking girlfriend, Jade. We went out for a long walk and I was surprised when he asked me what my latest session with Sigeyo had revealed.

"Sigeyo thinks we all live in a world of self created delusions and one of the challenges we all have is to strip down those delusions and see ourselves and the world for what they really are."

I was conscious that I was quoting my guru rather than expressing my own thoughts, so I tried to continue with my own observations.

"It's more about how your emotional energy colours your perception of the world, how you build your own version of reality – one that suits your belief systems. But unfortunately the further we walk down that road, the further we wander from reality, the more we get lost in our delusions."

"Exactly, if I was overly materialistic, my delusion would be that wealth makes me somehow superior."

"Or does the idea that being spiritual elevates you to a superior level, create another delusion?" Christine said pointedly.

We both scowled at her, knowing she was right.

When we returned, Elizabeth Archer came round for her healing session. Liz was my first definite healing success. She had come with asthma and eczema. Now her skin was clear and she no longer required any medication for her breathing. A combination of macrobiotic food, skin scrubs on the unaffected areas, and my hands, had worked. Where I saw a dark blue haze I could now see light yellow, where I used to feel coldness in her chest I now sensed warmth radiating out.

Liz recommended her sister to see me for her back ache and a friend who suffered from migraines became a regular. My clientele was picking up and someone came round every day.

I kept it all very bohemian, no appointments, clinic room or even fees. Some people left some cash on the hall table or pressed money into Christine's hand. I refused to take money directly or set any fees, people gave what they wanted to. Clients just turned up during school hours and if it was good for me I spent an hour or so with them, if not they came back later. One Friday a small queue of four people developed. It was like my motorcycle workshop – I was back in demand. It felt good. I loved that sense of being useful, having something to offer.

CHAPTER TEN

Weeks passed without hearing from Sigeyo. Finally I made the call. Sigeyo sounded surprised. We ran through the pleasantries and then there was a long pause. In the end I had to break it.

"I was wondering if you wanted to see me again soon?"

Another pause.

"Maybe it is time to continue on your own. I am tired and slowing you down. I think you should be free to go where you want and live your own journey."

I could not believe she was telling me this. There was no kind of completion to her teachings, we were only starting. I knew there was so much more. Had she lost faith in me as a student?

"Sigeyo, why? Have I done something wrong?"

"Not something wrong. Of course you do something – it is not for me to judge whether right or wrong. We have come to a fork in the road and I am taking another route by myself."

I realised by the tone of her voice there was no way back. I had been born and this womb was closed to me.

"Well, I can't tell you how grateful I am, you have given me so much..."

"No thanks please, I did what I wanted and I hope you did too. I must go now, I am not sure if we will see each other again, bye. Oh wait, excuse me, I nearly forgot, so sorry. Those dreams, I think when you came close to death some energy crossed over. Someone else's ki became muddled into yours. Do you think he could be a wartime pilot?" the line disconnected and I slowly replaced the receiver.

I was stunned. I felt stranded. Suddenly all my confidence drained away. What did she mean by – I had done something. I thought back and could not find any action that could be construed as a reason to end our relationship.

A pilot? That did make sense. I remembered the flames when I was dying. It did all start then. I wonder what happened.

I called Aaron and we arranged to meet. "I warned you not to depend on a guru. Anyway, that's not the point. I don't want to rub it in, not for too long anyway. Now do you see my point? You're lost, like a chick who has fallen from the nest." He sighed. "I suppose I'll have to come and look after you again."

"Back off! I didn't come here for a lecture."

"Well where do you go from here?"

I shrugged.

"What would you honestly like to do with the rest of your life?"

I just started to say that I wanted to work in a shiatsu clinic when Aaron talked over me.

"Come on Adam here's your big chance. Why don't you see it as breaking free rather than losing a mentor. You already have the skills you need, the whole point is you can help people heal themselves. What you need is exposure, to put yourself in a position where you can meet lots of people." He thought. "How long does it really take to help someone heal themself? Forget all the small talk, how long does it actually take you to see or feel someone's energy and help it change with your hands."

Aaron had an intense look on his face, staring straight into my eyes.

"About ten or fifteen minutes. I don't understand, what's your point?"

"You need to become a mass healer, give more people the chance to benefit from your gifts. Wait – I've got it! Shopping centres. We'll go to different shopping centres so you can heal the masses."

"Why? What's the point?"

"Adam, here is your big chance, take what you have and offer it to the world."

It was very close to the contract I made with Sigeyo.

After a long talk with Emily I felt more secure and found some of my confidence again. Perhaps it was all for the best, but if only my relationship with Sigeyo had ended differently. I wanted her blessing, some kind of pat on the back and recognition that I had succeeded.

"Adam, it has got to come from inside. Other people, certificates and bits of paper mean nothing."

I knew Emily was right.

CHAPTER ELEVEN

My original focus is changing. I am now hoping you will be like the character out of Sex with Lucia. Come and track me down to my Welsh cottage and walk straight into my life. I'm beginning to crave the passion and lust I lost. Despite this I have become too selective. No one measures up. Christine spoilt me. I have not met the woman worth compromising for. It sounds conceited and arrogant but it would take an amazing forceful, provocative creature to light that fire inside me.

Even though I realised what the dreams were, it did not stop them occurring. Last night I was in my plane homing in on the enemy. Our geometric patterns descended into chaos and I was lost between emotions of hate and fear. Hunter became hunted in the ebb and flow of battle.

I woke briefly with my heart racing. Rolling towards Christine, my accelerated rhythms calmed to her sleepy cycles and I started falling, floating, drifting into other dreams. That moment when you are actually aware of passing into sleep is similar to dying. Sometimes I check myself when I know I'm losing consciousness, a primal fear? Every time we go to sleep it is rehearsal for death. Is that why some babies and children fight sleep so?

I felt ridiculous driving to the Luton Arndale shopping centre with Aaron. This had all the makings of an embarrassing disaster. All we had was a fold up chair. Walking through the artificial fluorescent indoor streets no one looked the type who would want to dabble in healing. The shiatsu class and my clients were primarily made up of well-educated females who had some interest in the spiritual side of life. Here among the cheap electrical goods, video games and trainers, the bargain hunters looked decidedly uninterested in opening their souls to me. I wouldn't if I was one of them.

Aaron was not deterred. He revelled in the challenge. This was a complete contrast to the clean, zen minimalist trendy clinic I had imagined. Where were the plants, natural light, rural views?

My heart sank as Aaron unfolded the chair and started shouting to anyone who wanted to be healed. People stopped to look at him, bemused by his offering, but they kept their distance whilst I reddened and looked sheepishly at their feet. It was only when Aaron finished by saying it was completely free that an elderly woman shuffled over. Six members of her family were with her but they hung back.

As she walked over I could see blackness on the side of her veil. Aisha sat down and told me she had a tumour in her head. Vision in her left eye was impaired and she was in pain. I lay my hands on her and felt the dead, numbness under her skull. Minutes edged by but I could not feel any change. Aisha's family gathered around; I could feel someone's breath on my neck as they strained to see what I was doing. I began to sweat. The ten minutes passed without me sensing any change at all.

Desperate to make some kind of progress I started to massage her neck. Working up her vertebrae I experienced a strange sensation as I reached her cranium. My left hand was still resting on the side of Aisha's head when I felt the faintest spark of ki between my healing hand and her head. I continued to feel around the ridge of bone at the base of her skull. It only required a gentle touch to stimulate her energy. Too much and the feeling disappeared. Each time I found the correct pressure and location the spark felt a little stronger. Now I was totally absorbed, lost in the experience, so when Aisha cried out I jumped back, my heart racing.

"My eye, my eye, it feels better. Oh my God, this is a miracle! Thank you, thank you sir – in the name of Allah thank you." After a little more healing I stepped back. It took Aisha a while to realise I had moved away.

"Look Zaid, I can see more clearly, the pain is less."

"Please sir, take this." Her husband pressed some notes into my hand.

"Can I see you again?"

Aaron assured her I would be there next week.

The big lesson I learnt here was that I always need a reference to measure myself by, a feedback system. It does not matter whether I am comparing leg lengths, shoulder flexes or feeling the ki change in another part of the body, without that functional feed back it all risks becoming delusional. Having that ability to feel the changes as they happen meant I was able to accidentally find a new solution.

If Aaron's street performer warm up speech wasn't enough to draw people in, this certainly did. The crowd swelled and had surged forward to see the source of the hysteria. Aaron landed me another victim, this time a man with a headache. A clammy cold forehead countered by a hot neck. This proved easier, I simply focused on letting the heat from his neck move to his forehead, whilst Aaron massaged his large intestine four tsubos on his hands. Another satisfied customer. This one took Aaron at his word regarding the free treatment.

As is often the case, a small queue developed and then a longer queue quickly formed, trailing back towards the car park entrance as people did not want to be left out. A couple of security staff leant against the wall but to my surprise, they were content to watch.

After Aaron had set me up with an attractive teenage girl, he shot off to find better reception for his phone. Zoe was breathing a little better when Aaron ran back waving his hands.

"They're coming mate, they're coming."

I raised my eyebrows – was this the police? Should we fold up the chair and run?

"The BBC, you're news, man."

I slowly worked through the queue and surprised myself that I was not experiencing any bad results. I would have expected a few people to react well, most to feel mildly better, and a few to think it was a complete waste of time. Perhaps no one made negative remarks because it was free.

The television crew turned up and Aaron acted as my spokesperson whilst I carried on uninterrupted. A variety of people were filmed from different angles whilst I lay my hands on them. At times the camera lens almost touched my nose. I was struggling not to lose my rhythm. They interviewed three or four people and then the security personnel came over and we were asked to leave.

I was relieved, I was exhausted, I just wanted to go home. I saw Aaron writing out phone numbers on bits of paper for anyone who asked. Please don't let it be mine. Once home I pulled myself onto our bed and slept. Christine came and woke me for the evening news. We all watched expectantly. It was only at the end on the local news, Look East, that they ran the piece. The camera panned along the queue with an intro, a quick sound bite from Aaron, someone being positive about my ability to help her back and close ups of my hands and then onto the local weather. The whole clip lasted less than fifteen seconds, but there I was.

Aaron hugged me "I knew you could do it, you're the man now."

Christine gave me a hug whilst the children jumped excitedly.

"So how did you manage to get the BBC to film me?"

"I just phoned up the news desk said there was this sensational Jesus character in the shopping centre healing the masses for free. I think they like the idea of hundreds of people queuing to see you."

I could understand why Sigeyo did not want to walk with me.

The following day Aaron answered a call from a promotions company representing a shopping centre in Reading asking if I was interested in doing some healing there. They understood it was free to customers and their clients were willing to pay five hundred pounds a day. They were desperate to draw people to their building rather than a new rival centre. At least we wouldn't be kicked out this time.

The pre publicity ensured that I would be healing a human conveyor belt from 10am to 6pm. More positively, I was building up an incredible amount of experience very quickly. I became an expert in headaches, stiff necks and tense shoulders.

With Aaron acting as my agent, I travelled to various shopping centres during the week. I refused to work weekends, preserving these two days to spend with my family. I could now see the point of Aaron's strategy. Go to where the people are rather than expect them to come to a new age clinic.

Inevitably we were invited back to the Arndale shopping centre where I met Aisha again. Apparently her tumour had shrunk slightly taking pressure off her optical nerve. I continued to work with her each time I was nearby and helped her onto a macrobiotic style diet. Aisha's story later broke in a national newspaper. It was all backed up with medical records and reports. She put it all down to my healing and diet. Aaron's phone chimed continuously. I appeared on a daytime chat show, was interviewed by one of the tabloids and featured in a leading woman's magazine.

It was soon after this that Aaron received the call. His usual composure left him as he spoke to his all time guitar hero. Keef had a degenerative liver disease and wanted healing.

I thought I would be immune to the glamour of a rich and famous man but it did affect me. We were collected in a 1960's Bentley and driven to his mansion. The house itself was awe-inspiring. Huge double vaulted entrance hall, chandeliers, sweeping dark wood stairs, marble floors. Keef revelled in showing us around, being as hospitable as possible, "Do you want to swim?" "Gin and tonic?" and "Here, have some of my latest CDs".

Once he had exhausted his generosity Keef lay down so I could begin my healing. Keef had too much energy. His ki was compacted and bursting through his overworked liver. I tried to find ways to disperse some of his excess energy. After fifteen minutes his rate of breathing increased and Keef began to let out long moans. What had started as wriggling became writhing and Keef began to shout. He let out a long wail, cursed his wife, Suzy, and someone called Pete. I tried to maintain contact and smooth the release. I half expected him to leap up in his rage and become violent – it was hard to keep my concentration.

After what must have been several minutes his anger turned to tears. Keef sobbed as he complained of the way he treated Suzy. Finally his breathing found its natural rhythm and he became subdued.

I gently covered his body with a blanket and left the room. Aaron was lying by the pool with a pair of headphones on listening to 'some amazingly cool riffs', drinking a beer. He raised his eyebrows and I raised mine. I sunk into a bean bag. I might have fallen asleep because when Keef waltzed into the room I had the feeling time had elapsed.

"You wizard, you amazing wizard man. I don't know if that did my liver any good but it sure sorted me. Suzy I feel so light. I could take off. I've been cleansed. Same time next week?"

I gave him some food ideas, made sketches of stretches he should do and encouraged him to live in the style of a Zen monk.

"You're talking to the wrong man here, why don't you email everything to Suzy, she'll make it happen."

"But you need to take responsibility, it's your life, your liver."

I could see I had lost Keef, so Aaron and I exchanged hugs with him and left.

On the way home I reflected on my last few weeks. Now I really did have a new direction in life. I was close to being self sufficient and running with the healer baton. It is interesting how when you are up and on the move people become attracted to you. Now I was making progress with my life everyone wanted to be my friend. It obviously wasn't for money because despite being in demand I only received money from the shopping centres and the occasional donation. We could pay the bills but not much more.

It had been two years ago that I had had my accident and on that second anniversary I made a list of what I had achieved:

New healing career.

Open, constructive, loving relationship with Christine.

Become a real dad.

Gone back and tried to sort out some of my past.

Found and lost a mentor.

I can see and feel ki.

I can choose foods for their life force and the way they change my energy.

Met a new friend – Josephine.

Closer to Emily again.

I'm now less judgemental and open to finding people's good qualities.

Healed myself – back to full strength and mobility.

I reflected on how Sigeyo simplified her ideas. Rather than complicate, mystify or build up layers of concepts in a more masculine manner, she stripped everything down to its bare essence and left room for intuition. George Ohsawa had described viewing the world through magic spectacles using yin and yang, yet Sigeyo had even reduced this to basic life force. It was even clearer to look at a vegetable and see whether it grows up or down or choose a food that is at the beginning or end of its life cycle. This was easier for me to communicate because it was not rooted in any culture as yin and yang is.

Wendy arranged a shiatsu class re-union at the school in Primrose Hill one Friday evening. We all chipped in for wine and snacks. Surprisingly everyone made it. It was good to see Stephen again. The person I most wanted to see was Wendy.

"What happened to Sigeyo? Why did she cut me off?"

"My guess is as good as yours. She is very private about some things."

Of course everyone had heard of my shopping centre adventures. I might have been mistaken but I formed the impression that Josephine basked in my glory more than I. In fact I felt slightly self-conscious with my shiatsu friends and particularly Stephen. Deep down I knew they could give wonderful massages and yet somehow I had become the centre of attention. Thanks to Wendy I was guided by Sigeyo, and thanks to Aaron I had my moment of fame.

The sad truth is that you can be amazingly accomplished and never make your mark whilst people with inferior talents work society, talk the talk and eek out a good living for themselves. History is littered with writers, artists and musicians who were never fully appreciated in their own lifetimes. It would be reassuring to think they came back in another life as someone who benefited retrospectively. Perhaps an art dealer or publisher making money out of their own works from a previous life. I knew better than that.

I was surprised and glad to see Stephen slip his hand into Anoushka's. She turned to give him a kiss.

I wanted to relive the feelings we shared on the course, a group of people spending the day together giving each other massages. Now they had put me on a pedestal, I became slightly untouchable. For the first time I had a feeling of isolation and I felt sad. Everyone was very friendly and gave me hugs but it wasn't the same any more. I didn't feel I was one of them. Perhaps that was just the point. It was the way I felt, their reaction to me could have all been my assumption. I withdrew slightly as it occurred to me that I was the one putting myself on a pedestal.

I walked Josephine home. As we crossed the railway bridge she slipped her hand into mine. It was done in a kind of childlike way, just as Eleanor would have done, a sort of unconscious act, gently swinging back and forth. I felt like her father for a moment.

All she wanted to hear were my stories of television interviews and Keef. I don't think she had heard of him but the idea that I had a famous client clearly impressed her. I was beginning to feel that even my relationship with Josephine was being consumed by my success. The more she talked, the more frustrated I became. Unfortunately when I confronted her all my words sounded sharp and piercing.

"Is this all you're interested in? Have I suddenly become a one-dimensional character? I thought we were real friends who felt close and couldn't give a damn about who Keef is or what I do at shopping centres. What is happening Josephine? Surely you're not taken in by this healer hysteria. I'm the same Adam I was when we first met."

Tears started to roll down Josephine's cheeks and she had pulled her hand away to find a tissue. She looked crushed and almost frightened. I sighed and put my arms around her, pulling her head against my shoulder.

"Look, I'm sorry, I feel weird around everyone. I don't know how to fit in right now. It's not your fault. Come on, let's get you home."

Josephine didn't talk all the way back to her flat, just held my hand tight. I tried to make jolly small talk about the children, a television comedy I'd seen last night. I knew she enjoyed discussing literature, but it was like trying to extract water from a stone.

When we stepped up to her front door there was an awkward silence as I thought of a way to leave with a more positive ending to the day. It was Josephine who had the words.

"Adam, don't you know how much you mean to me? You're the only person I really care about. I don't think you realise how boring my life is working in a bookshop every day. I'm sorry I wanted a little taste of your exciting world. I won't bother you any more. We can talk of the weather, friends and television like all the other boring people. What a shame that you have such an interesting life but want to shut me out."

I was tired of talking and I also knew she was right, so I simply held her head and pressed my lips to her forehead.

"I'm sorry, you're right, good night."

I left and on the way home I wondered what Josephine meant by me meaning so much to her. I hoped she was not falling in love with me. Should I be a little more distant? Although if I was the first person she had felt close to, it would be terrible to abandon her.

As usual and as Sigeyo had once predicted, Christine had the sensible solution.

"Adam, she is so much younger than you and even though she may have a crush on you, I doubt she would want it to turn into a physical relationship. I had a massive crush on my history teacher at school and then again with a university tutor. I would have been shocked if either had tried to turn it into something sexual. I just wanted to feel special, to have a sort of substitute dad whilst I made the transition from child to woman. You had Sigeyo for a while, perhaps that's all she is looking for. Some kind of mentor to help her along until the right person comes into her life. Maybe it is a kind of practice run for being close to a man, knowing that she is safe with you. She is, isn't she?"

"What do you mean?"

"You wouldn't have sex with her, would you? Can I trust you?"

"In this case, I can assure you that there is no physical attraction."

I felt a bit more comfortable taking on a fatherly role. I called Josephine and arranged for her to come to one of the shopping centres, hoping she would see how mundane it was.

We drove to Brent Cross together and Josephine took on the role of being my assistant, talking to people in the queue and giving further explanation of my advice to the people who left me. One memorable moment was giving a healing to a little boy, Sam, who had a blood disease.

"Mum believes in me and thinks I will go on forever. But if I do go to heaven I will meet Jesus."

When I put my hands on someone I believe they will heal themselves with every cell in my body. Once I make that connection and feel their life force, my energy rears up and gives me an amazing feeling of stillness. In that moment I am convinced I can feel them changing, just as I could feel Sam's blood bubble with greater vitality. It is only afterwards, with my hands in my pockets, that the doubts return. It is all so intangible and dreamy. When I took my hands away I so wanted it to have worked for Sam. I offered his mother the opportunity to come to my home for some more treatments. I hoped she would follow my food recommendations.

Working with Sam precipitated a more serious effort to help Matthew and Eleanor onto a healthier diet. So far they had eaten the parts of my macrobiotic diet they liked and left the rest. The grains were popular, a little soup if it was pureed was accepted, however, so far Matthew only liked carrots and broccoli and even then they were pushed to one side if slightly overcooked.

I explained the difference between saturated and unsaturated fats, how too many saturated fats eventually clogged up the body. I drew a graph of imaginary blood sugar levels going up and down erratically after eating their sweets. I taught them how whole living foods were nutritionally complete and how processed foods decayed through oxidation. We cut an apple in half to see how quickly it turned brown. We put a variety of whole grains and beans on a damp cloth in a cupboard so they could watch them sprout.

Christine started a vegetable garden with Matthew and Eleanor and got them involved in some of the preparation of the meals. I knew from my experience that some of the macrobiotic foods were an acquired taste so we introduced a rule where they had to try a little of everything at each meal. I did my best to persuade them that if they did not like the taste of something one day they might the next. True enough, they both hated stewed pumpkin but liked it pureed in a soup. Combinations and cooking styles were just as important as the ingredients in determining whether they were eaten.

With the aid of dips, humus, tahini, cider vinegar and ume vinegar, even Matthew slowly edged up to liking twenty different vegetables. Generally we let them eat whatever they liked when we went out or they went to a party but the macrobiotic style food at home became sacrosanct. I observed that my children preferred clear boundaries and mealtime routines even if it was not their first choice but I also wanted to leave them the freedom to develop their own intuition and experience with food when outside the home.

We stopped having processed sugary snacks at home and watched our children adapt to nuts, seeds and fresh fruit. Fresh juices replace the now extinct canned soft drinks.

My new life consisted of Keef and my regular patients. The shopping centre phenomenon had petered out. Christine made Wednesdays my open surgery day.

After three months Keef was given a clean bill of health by his consultant and Aaron, Christine and I were invited round for a celebration. In keeping with his new diet Suzy had organised a buffet of vegetables, couscous salad, smoked tofu, dips, fresh juices and fruits.

Keef had invited friends from the music business, media and band. We sat rather self-consciously in the corner, until to my shock Keef stood up and proposed a toast to the man who had healed him. I felt my face flush as eyes turned to me. Keef insisted on us being photographed together. I was suddenly included in his circle. A journalist did an impromptu interview. People who had shunned us smiled and nodded. Someone asked if I could help his wife. I was engaged in conversations, jokes were made about Keef and his liver.

We were taken home by Keef's driver, basking in the afterglow of our first rock and roll party, despite the drugs and alcohol being replaced by health foods and juices.

Two days later the photo from the party was pasted across one of the tabloids with the headline 'Keef cured by shopping centre healer'. There were quotes from Keef, his friends, his doctor and a little piece on me.

Now everyone wanted part of me. I was back on daytime chat shows, radio and filled numerous features for magazines.

The media coverage ensured I was inundated with requests to heal. Everybody who had any kind of serious illness thought I would be their salvation. Gone were the days when I was honing my skills and people just gave it a try because it was free. Now it was serious.

This was not true of course. I knew that the results of what I did were random and a lot probably depended on the person's attitude and whether he or she took any of my advice seriously. Perhaps it was all a placebo and some people believed in me so much that it precipitated some kind of spontaneous self-healing. The whole process was self perpetuating as the more people I gave my healing to the more people came out and claimed it had worked. There was a kind of media frenzy in which people kept popping up claiming they had been saved.

Now it was all cancer, heart disease and other life threatening illnesses. Non stop experience in sensing the tumours, cancerous cells and decaying flesh. I dreamt of weak auras, the empty numb feeling in my hands and the smells. The whole random method was unsatisfactory as in Keef or Aisha's case I saw them many times and the turn around only happened over a period of months. Here, I never knew how often I would see someone – it was all left to chance.

I reflected on the way so much of what I had learned had become synergised into one ability to sense ki. Seeing auras, feeling ki, face reading, observing someone's posture, listening to his or her voice, touching, it all became one and producing an instant feel of how he or she could change. It felt so much more accurate than using one system or plodding through it all manually.

A combination of everyone's need to hear my story and for me to put my hands on people's bodies meant I no longer had any other life. I felt I was falling down an ever tightening spiral and as the helter skelter G-force increased, I spun faster, pulled away from my family.

Eventually after another sleepless night I couldn't face leaving my duvet. I froze, blinded by the intensity and volume of interest in me. Give me a deep dark cave, sheepskin rugs and enough wood to make a fire. I craved obscurity. In fact I spent most of the day in bed with Christine. Sex, cuddles, sleep, love, more sex – my nerve endings began to calm and I could almost consider life beyond the covers.

I realised one problem was that by giving it all for free demand infinitely outstripped supply. On a typical day I could only see a quarter of the people who wanted my help. I knew I could start charging and put up my prices to a level where I would just see a small volume of people, simultaneously making my fortune. Tempting, but somehow I would feel a fraud. What would I do about people who did not recover? On a more philosophical tack, if I was simply focusing some kind of universal healing energy, could I honestly say it was mine to demand money for? What about the agreement I had with Sigeyo? By accident I had reached what I considered a middle ground where some people would make an unprompted donation.

Aaron came round the next day to see what the matter was. He had similar feelings.

"Yes, this isn't working, I don't even have a sex life any more. Instead of being pioneering and wild we've become a healing factory. There's a guy from America that you gave some healing to who wants to meet you. Thinks you should be looking at big events rather than one person at a time."

I met Steve the next day in a London hotel. Aaron made the introductions. To my embarrassment I could not remember him. Just shows the depth of my current interactions with people. Steve was a head shorter than me but compensated by being twice as wide. He gripped my hand with his stubby fingers and wet palm. When Steve opened his mouth the words flowed out effortlessly, a slow drawl I found soothing.

"Look, Adam, I can see you're on a treadmill, overwhelmed and running on empty. There's no point in trying to help others if you are washed out yourself. Your mistake is that you are trying to work with everyone individually. Tell me this, what is more important, your advice or your hands."

It was a good question and one I couldn't answer. From Sigeyo's perspective it would be the advice as this helped people tap into the healing powers around them and become self-sufficient.

"I'm not sure but I suspect some people respond to my hands better and others follow my advice and recover using that."

"OK, so lets say it's fifty-fifty. If you gave talks to groups of people it is possible that you could help half the people right there by giving them help to heal themselves."

I nodded cautiously; I could see where this was leading.

"Second, is it possible to teach people how to heal each other?"

"Yes, there are techniques I could pass on that would help."

"Adam, imagine standing in front of thousands of people giving your message, think books, DVDs, websites whatever it takes to communicate your message. I know you don't want to charge people but we could make it all non-profit. What do you think?"

At least it was an alternative to the crazy state of my current life. Looking at Steve whilst he talked, I tried to focus on what it was that he came to me for. There was a slight purple hue to the tip of his nose and a darkness across his chest. Heart attack? Steve's energy flowed up easily, a mix of inspiration and practicality. I tried to guess his nine ki energies. A lot of springtime, sunrise ki but is it more thunder or wind.

"What's your date of birth Steve?"

Steve looked perplexed.

"He wants to work out your nine ki chart. Just humour him – it's easier in the long run."

"Oh, well I was born on March twenty five, 1961."

"Let's see three, um, five in February, yes you're a three four four. All tree energies! Thunder, wind and wind. I thought so. You must be an up, positive sort of person. Excellent at making things happen."

"Thanks, I guess I am."

Aaron tried to steer the conversation back to its original direction.

"Big seminars, books, DVDs…"

"Interesting. I like the big talks best. If we did it on a Woodstock basis at least some could be free."

"That would be a start."

I suspected Steve was brushing that to one side. I looked at Aaron.

"It has to be better than what we're doing now A."

Aaron nodded.

"OK, let's give it a try."

We shook hands.

"Let me know when's good for you and I'll book tickets and organise everything. We'll be based in Philadelphia."

I hadn't realised he meant America. Although right now it sounded appealing. I would have to see what Christine thought, of course.

I made a detour and saw Josephine on the way home. She gave me a restorative shiatsu and I told her Steve's proposal. As always she was enthusiastic and supportive.

"You must travel Adam, make it accessible to everyone, write a book."

Christine agreed with the logic of the proposal but was less keen on staying alone. I suggested she come too, but we both knew dragging Matthew and Eleanor out of school into a hotel lifestyle was not an option.

Even Aaron bailed on the idea. He was off to Thailand with Mia for a month of beach huts, diving and Thai massage. So when the time came for my adventure, I left from Heathrow on my own.

Before agreeing, I asked Steve to be clearer on how Christine and I would live through this adventure. With Steve there was no hard bargaining involved as he had read my concerns and offered more than I expected.

"I'll take care of your needs in America and all the monies that come in from donations, and I can assure you there will be plenty, I will send on to your wife. If there is not enough coming through I will make it up out of my own pocket or if you're unhappy we can send you home."

CHAPTER TWELVE

I think I might be ready to write more about Christine. It is difficult, I want to preserve my most cherished memories but if this is going to work in terms of my writing I am going to have to be honest and put it all in.

Our relationship was at an all time low before my accident. One incident I have not been able to wash out of my head would sum it up.

I woke alone, slowly trying to kick off the heavy fug left by the residues of last night's wine, the bedding next to me still warm with the imprint of my wife's dreams. I could hear Matthew and Eleanor playing in the garden – laughter, screams, shoes kicking the gravel.

I wandered downstairs, unshaven and unwashed in my jeans and white T-shirt. I wanted to be on my own, hating the children see me hungover. I still wanted to be their hero.

"I am leaving to finish the Yamaha, it's due Monday."

Christine spun round as though I had re-opened a festering wound with my jagged selfishness. I watched her violet skirt sway back and forth.

"Adam, you promised to stay with us. I thought we were going for a picnic. Please don't let Matthew and Eleanor down again." And then more pleadingly. "You deserve a rest."

The words were reasonable but the delivery carried a bitter poison that had seeped below the sweetness. My mind chose to settle on her turning her back on me last night whilst I lay looking at the ceiling, imagining all the couples enjoying wild drunken orgies and me separated from Christine by those few inches that had turned into a void that evening. I felt a wave of angry self-indulgence.

"No, it can't wait. I'll be back soon."

I wanted to avoid a confrontation, I was not feeling strong

enough to resume our little war, but Christine was already primed, startling me with her blitzkrieg tactics.

"What is your problem, Adam? No, really what is it? I would so love to know what goes on in that twisted stubborn head of yours."

She left short gaps for answers but when none was offered from my blank, consciously unresponsive face, she moved on. "Why is it so hard to spend any time with us? Is it me? The children? Are we that boring? You're never home any more. What is the point in having children if you aren't prepared to be with them? Don't you think they deserve a father?"

I kept my emotions entombed, my face remained static as I suppressed the urge to tell her that it was her endless nagging that was driving me away. Too many humiliations from the past kept my mouth closed, Christine always came out of these skirmishes victorious. Those childhood feelings of not being heard or understood resurfaced abruptly. Rather than try to see my perspective, it always twisted back to her version of me being selfish. She was even turning the children against me with her criticisms and negativity, slowly chipping away at my self-esteem.

I had dropped into my emotional hell. I craved praise and respect but languished in a blazing nightmare where my faults were blown out of proportion and continually revisited.

She started prodding me. Firm jabs to the chest. "If you hate us all so much, just piss off and I'll find a decent man. Someone who has the guts to be a real..."

Backing into the table I could feel my defensive line of sullen disinterest begin to crumble and I knew she could sense this and was rallying for the final attack. She now spat out a long list of crimes I 'always' committed, tasks I 'never' completed. These two words peppered her critical reviews of my performance as a husband. She synchronised a machine gun jab with every word aimed at the shell that protected my pride. Inevitably it cracked.

I let fly, pushing past her I grabbed a vase from the sink and smashed it on the floor, I kicked out at a stool sending it skidding across the terracotta tiles and to my dismay, it smashed into Matthew's red fire engine. My next target was one of our kitchen chairs. I aimed a ferocious sidekick at the back hoping to see the wood spindles splinter dramatically. Instead my socked foot wedged itself between. With one foot painfully elevated I lost my balance and resorted to thrashing out at the chair with my free foot from the cold stone floor.

Breaking free, I leapt to my feet, fists clenched. When I looked around for my next target the knot in my abdomen tightened as I saw Matthew and Eleanor watching from the back door. They were open mouthed and their huge eyes flitted between mummy and daddy.

The next time I saw Christine, I was in hospital.

I floated off into a dream, lying on a deck chair in a warm breeze under a clear sky. I was so tired, infected with a mixture of fear, apprehension and excitement. I wanted to sleep but waiting for the bell prevented me from letting go.

When I opened my eyes Christine's face entered my mind. She looked pale and gaunt; her skin translucent with purple pools below her eyes. Her dark hair hung down across the sides of her cheeks, merging into her black top, making her face appear tall and thin. She looked at me pleadingly.

"Why, Adam?" was all she could say. I focused on her lips noting how thin and drained they looked.

Christine leaned forward and held my better hand to her breast. I saw her skin become blotchy and her eyes start watering.

"Thank God you're still alive. Please, let's never argue again, you're so special to us. The children were so upset. Somehow they knew before the police called. I thought I heard Matthew shouting to you. They were both distraught. I couldn't calm them."

My skin became clammy, a chill crept up my back, making me shiver as I remembered my children calling to me in my other world.

I forced myself back and dredged up the essence of my experience for Christine. She gripped my hand and tears rolled down her cheeks as I described the children crying out. My voice became thinner as I felt warm salty drops running across my face. She put her arm around me and lay across my chest. Her heartbeat, her breasts, her warmth, I wanted her to stay forever.

My memory of the tunnel and Matthew and Eleanor calling, floated by on a river of dreams. Finding out that she heard the children too generated more questions than I had answers for now but it was therapeutic having someone to talk to who was part of that extraordinary incident.

Familiarity, the gentle scent of oranges and home. Christine set me up in bed, our bed this time, and insisted on giving me a wash. Weeks of pent up sexual energy quickly became apparent. She obviously had similar feelings and began to make encouraging movements with her hands. Her cool, soft, wet tongue explored my mouth as her hands gently stimulated me into a frenzy. I groaned as I felt myself slip past the point of no return. I had flooded but not run dry and soon Christine was sitting astride me.

It had been so long since I had seen her naked. Her breasts looked full and swayed erotically with every movement. Her body was curved and womanly in the way mothers can be so seductive. I wished I could grab the flesh on her hips, run my fingers around her nipples, slide my hands up the inside of her thighs but all I could do was lie there with my arms passively at my sides.

"Welcome home, Adam Saunders."

Christine smiled, letting her long hair fall across her face, as she slipped me inside. The ebb and flow of her movement, the sensation of Christine's bottom rising and falling across my thighs kept me on the edge – she felt so soft against my hard bones. We both came on a rising flame of passion. There was an extraordinary similarity between this feeling of surrender, of slipping over the edge, and the feeling of accepting death. For a moment I emotionally relived my journey into the ether, then she washed through me and I felt strangely clean inside, a purity I cannot remember experiencing before.

"I have never felt so close to anyone as I feel to you just now, Christine."

Somehow our bodies merged into one, she came into my being. To my shock I started crying. She squeezed her cheek tight against mine.

"Rest, my angel."

Christine laid her hand on my forehead and I felt myself drift away. I floated back to that deck chair, looking at a small creased, glossy, black and white picture of my girl, wavy mousy hair, a raincoat buttoned up to her neck, half smile, slightly wooden – Christ, I've forgotten her name, I cannot remember my fiancés name, I began to panic, what is it?

"Adam, Adam, what's the matter, you must have been dreaming."

I saw the concern in Christine's eyes. They felt wrong, the wrong eyes staring. Then they vanished, like the shake of a head. I slipped back.

It was during my recovery from the accident but before embarking on the shiatsu course that I tore our relationship apart. I'm not sure whether there was some unconscious motive but I cannot bring myself to write about it now. I will skip ahead to the consequences.

Christine turned away and cried into the night. I did not want to make excuses, so I lay in silence. When I later made a tentative approach to put my arm around her she pushed me away forcefully. When I woke I was on my own. Christine had slept in the spare room.

For the next few days I sensed our relationship was coming to an end. Christine packed for herself and the children but then appeared to change her mind. I bought flowers, tried to be extra helpful, wrote her poems, left cards of apology and gave her the space she wanted from me. The big ugly showdown I dreaded never materialised, perhaps I had wounded her too deeply.

I phoned Emily hoping she would offer to come round and help us through this. Instead she screamed at me down the phone. Later she called back and slowly I came to the realisation that I had abused our relationship. Before the accident I had sabotaged so many of Christine's attempts to build the life she wanted and since, I have simply used her as a cesspit for all my rotten emotions and failings. She has always been there for me and now I have tried to kill her off. It was a weird and new situation where my chief enabler had lost interest. Thanks Emily.

"Look, Christine, please let's make this a turning point, let's salvage something out of the pain I caused you and use it to make our relationship stronger. I promise you I will be different. Losing you like this has made me realise how much you mean to me and how close I am to you. Please give me one chance to show you what I can do."

It took time but slowly the threads that connected us started re-growing. Having tea together, family walks, talking in a way that implied our relationship would last. Christine found me bearable again. I didn't feel the time was right to ask her why. The thought of being apart from Christine, selling our family home and just seeing Matthew and Eleanor at alternate weekends filled me with dread. A few days later she spoke about it.

"When I married you it was for life. I have built my whole future around you, Matthew and Eleanor. There is nothing else. However much I wanted to end our relationship I could not create another future in my mind. Do you understand?"

I nodded.

"That was a mistake Adam. I think I was addicted to this idea of middle class family life, being a wife. Well I'm going to try and wean myself off that."

I could feel myself tense up again. Where was this leading?

"Like a recovering alcoholic, I'm just going to take it one day at a time. If we have a good time together and I don't project any values into our relationship that will be a good day. But in the end I will be free to walk out of your life if it's not working for me."

I felt shocked. Not only by the implications it had on our relationship but by Christine. It seemed so out of character. Where has this Zen Marriage attitude come from? The words were being delivered by Christine but I imagined from a script that had been written by Aaron. My first reaction was to feel betrayed, as though Aaron was plotting against me.

Over the next few days I realised we were building a different, better relationship without silly games or taking positions. It was one where we were freer to be ourselves but equally free to kiss each other good-bye if it was not working. Slowly the patterns that had defined the way we behaved together broke down and left room for interactions that felt more real. I knew I could not offload onto Christine any more. It was time for me to start giving, be her caring husband instead of a needy son.

My recovery from the accident felt complete. I began to wake up with energy, I had enthusiasm and a desire. For the first time in my life I focused my attention on my home, organising sunny picnics under leafy trees, games in meadows next to gently flowing rivers, outings to museums and grand old country houses, nostalgic trips to steam railways, wild and adventurous camping expeditions, and walks in the shady woods near our home.

Christine and I began to talk more, touch more and be together more. Finally she came back to our marital bed. With Christine's Zen approach to our relationship I did have more freedom but my old crutches had buckled from under me. If Christine did not feel like putting up with my moods she just did something else. We rarely criticised each other and we tried to catch ourselves before making assumptions or judgements. Eventually I had a real family life and I loved it. We cuddled on the sofa, I read to the children until they slept. Christine and I spent more time together and our sex life bloomed.

My period of success here was an extraordinary occurrence. Up to that point I had failed miserably as a lover, partner or husband. Looking back, I had no training or role model for these parts. My parents were mum and dad, not passionate romantics. As far as I can remember all they showed me was how two people can function very well together to create a harmonious home and bring up well-behaved children. The rest took place behind closed doors or after our bedtime. Consequently I made up my own formulas for what I thought would produce a successful relationship.

I have witnessed all my friends having accidents in their relationships but I do not sense any kind of collective learning. We did not discuss the problems, or look for solutions. Instead we supported each other in building walls, digging in and surrounding ourselves with razor wire ready for the next attack.

I still don't know how I fell into that period of bliss and therefore I do not know if I could find it again. Somehow I strayed out of my defences, lost my way and stumbled into a pool of love.

Floating on a high of altruism I had no idea of how to sustain it and relied on Christine to show me the way. It was on this high that my life of healing started with the shiatsu course.

CHAPTER THIRTEEN

Are there any accidents? Is it all part of our destiny or a reflection of our condition? Are we trapped by our karma? Did I drift off into a lifestyle that could only be corrected by putting myself through a near death experience? Looking back there were so many ways in which I could have prevented my accident. In fact, if I had wanted to experience such an event, what would have been the odds that it would all fall into place with such perfect synchronicity?

I approached the old railway tunnel at speed. A dark brick arched hollow with perfect acoustics for turning my exhaust note into a howling heavy guitar sound. The usual procedure was to open the throttle until halfway and then close it turning the howl into a jarring rasp.

As I leant forward to keep the front wheel down and lunged into the tunnel, I saw my symphony was not going to happen. A green and yellow tractor pulling a stack of straw was lumbering up to the tunnel. The tractor was slower than I thought and I was almost out of the tunnel as the shadow slid across its engine.

A white shape, glinting in the sun, moved out from behind the trailer. The deep thud was louder than I expected. My rhythm stopped. Just me floating, tumbling, watching the sun move slowly though the sky, freezing or jumping ahead. Little black holes punctuated my journey. A pain in the side of my head, my shoulder burning, my left hand ice cold. Spinning again. Winded by a heavy impact to my back, and then still.

I could feel a lightness pervade my being as I began to levitate and spread out. There was an incredible sensation of unwinding as I felt my soul slither and unravel. I was pain free and empty.

I could see the farmer kneeling next to my body. A woman was running over from a silver saloon, shouting into her mobile. My right forearm was bent at a strange angle. A white van had a crumpled 'V' struck into its bonnet and an older man sat on the verge holding a handkerchief to his bloody forehead.

My bike had partially buried itself into a ploughed field. Fragments of the bright yellow paint and chrome winked at me. Most of the distorted machine was camouflaged with mud and parts of the hedge it had torn through.

I start again, falling back through the tunnel, old bricks were replaced with golden leaves. Flashes of silver light, warmth, dense, confined space. I feel a need to push forward, am I swimming? Then bright light, gasping, sucking in air. Cold followed by the reassuring rhythm of a heartbeat. Lying on bare skin. A nipple for comfort.

I could vaguely make out round shapes, they came in pairs. Light and dark moving patterns held my attention. I saw colours and shapes around faces, I saw eyes and smiles. Huge temperature changes, such cold, being wrapped, seeking warmth.

I float onwards. The grandfather clock ticked slowly, filling the room with a reassuring sonic rhythm. My back warmed by the glow of burning embers in the grate. Wind and rain battered the window. I feel secure, connected to my mother by the sound of her voice, chatting to Margaret in the kitchen.

Big strong hands held the wings of a Spitfire for me as I tried to slide the round red and blue transfers into place. This was the man I wanted to please. How I craved his praise and respect. Why did I choose the hardest nut to crack when my mother could provide it in abundance?

Winning fights at school. Gaining the reputation as the toughest boy in my class. I came top in daydreaming but last in anything academic.

Sailing with Dad, the rush of nervous excitement as I was allowed to take the rudder. Laughing with my sister, Emily, as we made up imaginary stories.

Sitting in The White Horse with Alfred and Derek, before jumping onto our bikes and off to Sophie's party. Wrestling Sandy to the ground playfully, hands creeping down over each other's underwear.

Wearing my green overalls with greasy hands in a small red brick workshop, feeling the cold metal of a large oily spanner.

The village church where I married Christine. Her eyes sparkling, framed by her radiant face.

Floating funerals. Feeling my father's unspoken pain at my mother's funeral. Lifting his coffin onto my shoulders a few years later. Overwhelmed by insecurity.

Being there at the birth of Matthew. Later sitting in The Rose and Crown drinking heavily, feeling left out. Clinging on to my teenage lifestyle. Craving happiness past. My life slips on by.

Watching Matthew and Eleanor follow an ant trail in the garden. Being drawn into the field of innocence around them, I was beginning to feel lighter; my essence thinned. An incredible sensation of love pulsed as I drifted away.

Matthew looked up as if to say goodbye but tears were streaming down his freckled cheeks. I touched his fear. "Don't go, Daddy, please don't leave us. Daddy, I love you Daddy, pick me up."

Eleanor began weeping next to him. Her sobs drowned out his words. I could see her wringing her little hands together. I sensed heaviness enter me, sadness stained my soul. The spell was broken, emotion spread like blood soaking into a tissue. I began to panic, fighting my way back to my broken body and broken family.

I was swimming against the tide, fighting to escape the slippery gas and find something solid to hold onto.

The black holes came back. Each new moment of consciousness brought new sensations. A dead numbness enveloped my arm, an unbelievable pain exploded into my head. There was a rhythmic pressure on my chest. Cold air blowing into my lungs. I had a taste of salt in my mouth. Through one eye I watched the ambulance man talking to me. My other eye was filled with blood. I did not respond.

I fainted as they moved me onto a stretcher. A flash of lightening entered my mind as I felt myself falling, the increasing sound of an engine revving out of control, flames and smoke around my legs, struggling to find and operate the lever. I had waited so long and now it was here, I was consumed with naked fear, fighting to escape.

The numbness faded as we arrived in a white fluorescent casualty ward. I was consumed with screaming pain. No other thought could survive. My clothes were being cut off and someone in a white coat pulled my eyelid up. Finally a drip was inserted in my arm and the anaesthetic crept into my blood stream.

"Adam, count to ten for me please."

I think I reached three before it kicked in and the pain dissolved into a surreal dream. Images splintered, colours collided. My father came into the room and it was one of those fantasies where I could actually feel him touch my arm, smell him, know he was there right next to me. Nothing was said but I thought he wanted me to be a better father, take responsibility and live a life he could be proud of. Did he really want that? Or was it me projecting my own thoughts into him. Had I always done that? A sort of self imposed stern critical father figure, all my own creation.

The next time I was fully conscious I tried to rationalise the last twenty-four hours. I reasoned that I must have had a near death experience and that I had travelled back through my life again as I fell through the golden tunnel. I had read about a man drowning, the floating away and reliving his life. Somehow the children had caught me.

I had heard of clairvoyants and psychics but never given them any time. Did our children possess some kind of supernatural powers? Could they have brought their dying father back to life? In my world, if you could not see, feel, hear, smell or taste it, it was a figment of the imagination. My scientific background was rooted in things I could quantify with instruments, objects I could make or take apart. If I could not measure it, it did not exist. I wanted to find some logical explanation, to rationalise it so I could put it in a compartment and let go.

But Christine knew, so there was no chance of going into denial.

"Please keep it a mutual secret so we can explore it together without having to fend off outside curiosity," I begged her. I shuddered at the thought of trotting out my amazing story at every social occasion.

All my thoughts were interrupted by the scream of "Daddy!" as two colourful fizzing life forms homed in on me. I managed to catch them painfully with my plaster and hold them close. My reasons for coming back were now pressed against me, wriggling like eels, bubbling with words.

Christine tilted her head to one side and gave me a sympathetic, loving smile. A few days ago I would have resented the sickly 'see how good these quality moments are' kind of look but this time it felt genuine. Perhaps it always was and I just felt guilty and reacted badly, or maybe the truth is I didn't know how to join in.

CHAPTER FOURTEEN

AMERICA

Steve met me at Philadelphia's airport and took me to a small apartment he had rented for me. I showered and put on fresh cloths to rid myself of seven hours of cosmic radiation and recycled bacteria on a 747.

Sleep came quick that night. Steve arrived early in the morning and suggested we go out for breakfast. His behaviour was edgy for while, then he came out with it. He had a heart problem and wanted to know if he could continue with his treatment. Of course I was generous with my response, hoping that this was not the main reason I was here. He must have sensed my concerns and spoke earnestly of bringing together a committee of people to make it all happen. Our next stop was to meet them at his home. We picked up Mike and Marlene on the way.

Mike must have been in his late fifties, thin, wiry, emitting a nervous energy. He wore a brown cowboy hat with a feather in it. Under the rim his round metal framed glasses magnified his eyes slightly, drawing in my attention. His eyes constantly flicked around, never making contact with mine. He spoke quickly in short bursts, mainly about his health food shop.

Marlene looked slightly younger than me. She appeared full of life and projected herself so well that her personality filled the car. Physically she was full and rounded. Her red top contrasted strongly with her black skin. She had complemented this by braiding red beads in her hair. I could easily imagine Marelene filling a huge space merely with her persona. Words mattered. She articulated her sentences in a way that was easy to understand. I was finding it difficult to assimilate more than the occasional word from Mike's rapid-fire mouth.

When we first arrived, Steve introduced me to Pauline. She looked attractive and feminine but somehow hardened by life. Her sinewy body gave the appearance of a tough fighter – take me on if you dare. She looked me straight in the eye as she gripped my hand shaking her long brown hair to one side.

"I'm so happy to meet you Adam, really. I'm in sync. It's so right that you just do it all for free and so right that you try to give people the power to do it for themselves. You wouldn't believe how corrupted up some of the healing scene is here. Money and manipulation."

She was interrupted by the arrival of Stoosh, who lived up to his reputation with long frizzy hair, John Lennon style glasses and a tie-dyed multicoloured T-shirt. He walked past my outstretched hand and gave me a hug.

"It's so cool you're here man. Wow, feel the power."

Suddenly, everyone became organised, deciding Steve should be the chairperson. He leant forward onto his beefy knees. Steve expressed his desire to put some of his wealth back and devote more time to worthwhile projects. Speaking slowly and making eye contact with each person, he kept my attention.

Mike spoke next, I could make out 'supporting organic farming'. I think he said he wanted to reverse the decline in American's health followed by 'homemade miso', then it all scrambled again. I nodded earnestly.

Pauline's style was very different. She tensed up, I could see lines bulge in her neck as she pulled her jaw back, took a deep breath in, open her large brown eyes wide and lifted her hands.

"I just think it's time we did it for real. Let's stop pretending to be concerned, committed, engaged and take action for a change."

Stoosh looked up at the ceiling showing his disinterest.

"You can try and look bored Stoosh, but what have you done in all these years? What have any of us done? My point is that if we are doing this let's get off our butts and make it happen."

Pauline slammed her fist into her hand.

There was a slight pause whilst I presumed everyone reconsidered their positions.

"Well, let Stoosh have his say."

"Well, unlike," he waved dismissively at Pauline, "I believe we each have our own responsibility to this universe and I don't believe in this moralistic crap, telling other people what to do. Yeah, let's give them more choices, yeah, let's spread the horizons, but please don't go out and shove this man's stuff down everyone's throats."

"I didn't mean that. Sometimes you just have to take action and work it out as it happens."

Marlene spoke over Pauline putting an end to her duel with Stoosh. "Right, well I am here because I'm excited by Adam's work and I'm going to give him the support he needs to get his message out. There is a huge listening out there, your time is right, Adam."

Steve unfolded his muscular arms and nodded to me. I was suddenly very conscious that I had no big speech and lacked any passion to express myself.

"Well, I think you all know what I do and I just want the chance to reach more people."

No one spoke, I think waiting for me to continue but I had said all I wanted and sat out the silence. For an awful moment Pauline tried to start a round of applause but stopped abruptly, leaving Mike making a couple of claps. Steve broke the hush, insisting I was not overstretched. One day a week healing with Pauline at her clinic, another day at Mike's shop and then a talk in three weeks time. Marlene would take care of PR, and Stoosh offered to find a venue. I was beginning to enjoy joining a team, decisions were made quickly.

I started my day with Pauline healing AIDs patients and drug addicts. I felt a chaotic buzz along the spine of some addicts, as though their nervous system had lost the ability to contain the ki normally running along its core. I sensed that some of the connections had partially broken, leaving a lack of synchronicity between different parts of the emotional body.

Pauline demonstrated little tolerance for excuses. "Do you want to recover? What is the point of coming here to see this man for a diet that might heal you if you say you can't do anything he suggests? Come on Joe, do what he says and stop finding reasons to die!"

Then with another man who claimed he did not have time. "Jeff, you're lying to yourself. That's not reality. You're finding an excuse not to get better, which is fine if that's what you want to do. If not, make recovery your top priority. Be honest with yourself, the reality is you are dying of AIDs every day you are getting weaker. Why do you think that will change if you make no changes yourself?"

I was surprised by the explosiveness of her delivery and slightly nervous when talking to the rest of my patients.

One girl, Cheryl claimed she needed drugs to live through rejection from her parents. After my healing Pauline spoke more compassionately. "Cheryl, is it really true your parents did not love you."

Cheryl nodded.

"Is there no possibility your parents might have loved but still turned their back on you? Not even the slightest chance they might have had their own hang ups, pain, challenges."

Cheryl shrugged.

"You don't know for sure. It is an assumption you created in your head."

"But they didn't cuddle me or buy me things or take me on holiday with them. How do you think I felt when my friends had all this and me nothing?"

"You had an expectation that cuddles, presents and holidays equals love, right. You saw your friend having that and thought that's how everyone should be."

"Hmm."

"You made it up. You can believe they did not love you if that makes you happy but if not what's the point in thinking like that? Especially if you say it is the reason you poison yourself with drugs?"

Cheryl looked up.

"Check out Zen Buddhism Cheryl, you don't have to feel like this. It's all in your head. Stay in reality, find that love of yourself and you won't need drugs."

Pauline took me out for a Japanese diner that evening. When we ordered I discovered Pauline ate a vegan version of macrobiotics. I started to order some sushi but then asked Pauline to order for me instead.

"You should try cleaning out from animal food for a while, Adam. I haven't eaten any for nearly two years. I feel more pure, more myself. I have not been contaminated by consuming the emotions of death. Doesn't it make you want to turn to violence when you see how people treat factory farmed animals."

"I thought being the sweet vegan you are you would prefer to organise a peaceful meditation outside the gates of the farm."

She had an interesting characteristic where she would be highly confrontational and opinionated and then retract it quickly if I had a different view. The intensity of her expression made the engagement stimulating. She obviously had far greater experience and knowledge of healing and spirituality than I. She lost me a few times talking about shamanism, Zen Buddhism and tantric yoga. Watching her I sensed she had incredible internal frustrations – with what I didn't know – but it distorted the natural flow of her emotional energy. One clue came out later.

"Somehow I have to except I will soon be too old to have children even if I could find a man to father the child."

She was thirty-six and single.

Pauline changed subjects faster than I could re-orientate, leaving me with the feeling I was playing catch up. Sometimes I gave up on the words and just looked at her as she tilted her head letting her brown hair fall across her cheekbone, her eyes narrowing and opening wide as she made another point.

Then it suddenly it was my turn. I talked on auto pilot.

"The healing scene in the UK is vibrant. There are more alternative health practitioners than doctors. You can hardly open up a conversation without yoga, tai chi or meditation coming up. I bet more people go to these kind of activities than any of the main religions."

"That's hardly surprising. Talking as a woman, who in their right mind would want to be a part of a religion that treats you like dirt? No, I mean it Adam, why would I get involved in any organisation that will never let me become a leader just because I'm a woman, that tells me what to wear or that orders me not to use contraceptives or that feels it has the right to dictate whether I can have an abortion or not. If any of this was said by a woman perhaps I could take it on some level, but for a man to stand there giving orders on subjects he has no experience of just because he's male is the ultimate in arrogance. Why would anyone be surprised if all the women just left and took up a form of spirituality that was inclusive and accepting? It's no wonder so many yoga classes are full of females, don't you think?"

The taut lines in Pauline's neck were back, the crease between her eyebrows, the intense stare. Sitting opposite her I felt like the representative of the Catholic, Jewish and Muslim faiths rolled into one.

Pauline stared me out waiting for my answer. I was still stunned by the speed at which she could change her expression. I wanted to tease her and tell her not to worry about these big complicated issues and to go back to smiling and looking pretty but I did not know her well enough.

The couple next to us were having beef fried at their table. Pauline raised her voice.

"Did you know that meat eating contributes more to green

house gasses than everyone's travel put together. Just think of how much land would be freed up for trees if we did not have to grow all that food to feed billions of animals just so some people can have some beef."

The woman looked down at her napkin and the waiter glared at Pauline. I slid down my chair a little and looked away trying to focus on the long haired waitress on the other side of the restaurant.

"It's not as though it's even healthy. Adam look at me! Why? Why ruin the planet to rear animals in barbaric conditions, put them through a ghastly slaughter experience just so we can raise cholesterol, have heart attacks or get colon cancer. What kind of idiot would want to be a part of it all?"

"Excuse me lady. We can all have our views but can't you keep your voice down. We came here to eat not to hear you mouth off." Pauline smiled back and mouthed "I love you too." Being around Pauline was dangerous but exciting. What next?

The healing at Mike's whole food store, the Organic Basket, was easy in comparison to Pauline's clinic. Basically the regular shoppers gave it a try to see it they felt any different. I enjoyed the way his customers were so quick to praise and recommend me. One even picked up her cell phone whilst my hands were on her temples.

"Jeanne get this I'm with this guy Mr Saunders and he just has the most incredible hands. Oh my goodness I've just felt this weird buzz in my head. You've got to get your butt over here honey! He's come all the way from London...no it's completely free. I can still feel his hands even though he's taken them away. Wow, what a trip!"

I imagined Pauline's comments on mixing my healing energy with microwaves. An hour later her friend did turn up with two others.

Marylyn, a drug user at the clinic, radiated the most amazing sexual energy. I felt aroused every time I made contact with her. I think she realised and after while kept playing on it. She kindly offered me some free sex in return for healing. I forced myself to decline and it helped me feel closer to Christine for a while.

As predicted the numbers increased and the same chaos began to develop as in England. Stoosh and Marlene came into action promoting my new healing seminar at The Friend's Meeting House. I tried to prepare for the talk but had no previous experience to draw on. I turned to Marlene.

"Hey, honey just tell your story, how you got started, what you learnt, people you've healed. Everyone loves anecdotes, personal stories, stuff people can relate to and think 'that could be me'. Is there anything practical you could do with everyone?"

I thought of breathing exercises, trying to feel ki in their hands.

"That's good and then you might like to give them some of your ideas on food and exercise. Finally you want to end on a high. Some kind of special message."

CHAPTER FIFTEEN

The big day came. We arrived early so Pauline and I sat in a small room at the back whilst people filed in.

"Have you ever thought how most gurus and leaders are male whilst their audience is predominantly female?"

I nodded knowing where this was leading.

"Come on, you tell me, why is it that if you put the most unappealing man on a stage, wind him up and switch him to give a spiritual talk, some female in the audience will want to go to bed with him? Is the female psyche wired to mate with a pair of testicles on a stage talking about enlightenment?"

The intensity of Pauline's delivery made me retract slightly.

"Is this based on personal experience?"

Pauline blushed and stumbled slightly over her next words as her voice wobbled slightly. "I have the good sense to suppress it, but there is always some dope head who is overwhelmed. It does not matter how fat, rude or egotistical the guru is, he will always have someone to share his duvet."

Pauline introduced me. She began in a strident voice welcoming everyone before telling the audience her version of my life so far. She had condensed the first fifteen minutes of my talk into one. To my exasperation Pauline announced me as the greatest healer of our time and dramatically described how she had seen me heal people with her own eyes.

In my state of anxiety I looked around the audience and noticed Brad in the front row, behind were Marylyn and Cheryl. I could recognise many of the customers from Mike's store.

I went straight into the breathing routine synchronising the whole room into inhaling into their abdomen whilst trying to keep all their chakras in a vertical line. I was surprised by the power this had. Two hundred people breathing together turned the whole room into a huge pair of lungs. Moving on, I encouraged everyone to breathe energy into the palms of their hands, ending with them gently moving their palms toward and away from each other to see if they could feel the subtle magnetic sensation of energy. I guided them through bringing their palms close enough to sense the heat field between them where their life-force was more intense. Then they slowly moved their hands apart stretching out the heat field before feeling their palms cool again.

"Awesome, it feels like I have two little magnets in my hands," a woman shouted out.

"Yes, that is the feeling of your emotional energy. How many people can feel it?"

Just over half the audience put up their hands.

"If you can feel it, you can heal. For those who cannot feel it yet, keep doing this exercise and play with the heat field between your hands. If you eat lots of whole living foods with their life force intact, you will feel it too."

Finally in a flash of inspiration I had everyone pair up and place their hands on each other's temples and breathe healing energy into his or her partner's mind.

"Oh, this is so cool, I can feel it! I'm being cleansed, I'm being healed!" a woman at the back shrieked.

She gripped her breasts, stood and made spasmodic movements whilst moaning aloud. I was shocked to see it was the lady with the cell phone from Organic Basket.

I jumped off the stage and picked my way through the people. I managed to embrace her and place my hands on her upper back. She was breathing quickly and writhing around against my body. I matched her breathing whilst trying to spread her energy with my hands.

"Try to let go, big breaths, don't hold on."

She gulped in air. I noticed the twitching subside. I brought the pace down leading her slowly with my breath, focusing my breathing into her back and abdomen. Eventually she became limp and I was able to lay her down on the floor behind the seats.

Stoosh came and knelt next to her. We put a sweater under her head and a coat over her. Stoosh's placed his hand on her forehead and I ran back to the stage.

I resumed showing how to make sounds to move energy up the chakras. I talked about food and absorbing a more natural living energy, about thinking of the environment around us. This part felt very dry and I sensed I was losing them so I wound it up quicker than planned. I looked at Marlene. She entered the stage and managed to whip up a large round of applause. Perhaps they were relieved it was over. Not so, because Marlene pointed out that there was half an hour left and that I would be happy to answer questions.

Actually this part was easy as all I had to do was respond and no longer try to lead the event. Most of the questions concerned my near death experience, Keef and what it felt like to heal people. Finally someone asked what had happened to the woman at the back.

"I'm still here," she piped up.

People turned to see her.

"Sorry if I messed the seminar up but I just felt this huge uncontrollable release. I guess you'll be happy to know I'm much better now. A tightness in my chest has gone and somehow I feel fresher, like I'm making a brand new start."

I thought this might be the high I could finish on and bowed out.

"Well not quite what we planned but that was great honey," said Marlene. "We had drama, interaction, personal stuff and some tips from the great man. You did good. Come on I'll take you home."

I was physically tired but turbulent emotionally, a sort of erratic high. I knew I would not sleep so I suggest we stop for some tea. Talking to Marlene was easy after Pauline. I immediately warmed to her inclusive spirit. The fullness of her cheeks and ease of her broad smile helped me feel comfortable. I felt we'd been friends for years but with the excitement of fresh mutual discovery.

One thing that slightly irritated me about Marlene as the evening drew on was the way she kept trotting out new age platitudes. She apparently believed everything happens for a reason, that the universe will provide everything you need or that if your energy is pure and positive you will get wonderful things in life. I agree that they are all comforting sentiments and can possibly help us through difficult times but is that really how the galaxy works?

Not in my experience. I knew grumpy negative people that had most of what they wanted and chanting, meditating, positive people who had very little. Nor did I think something as complex as our cosmos could in any way work out what we needed and deliver exactly that. I would have agreed that in times of trouble we couild learn and change the way that we developed as a person, if this is what Marlene means by everything happened for a reason.

Although, if ideas are not reality and just another way to perceive the world then who was I to say Marlene's perception was not better than mine. It is just that it seemed rather shallow and poorly thought out. Perhaps it was just that it did not reflect well on her sense of non credo or mental dexterity that annoyed me.

With a sense of déjà vu, reports started appearing of people healing themselves. Brad's blood work took a rapid upturn and Marylyn and Cheryl were off drugs. They didn't have to tell me it showed. A beautiful young girl called Chelsea put her anorexia behind her and was now on a macrobiotic diet. The difference here was that people network a lot in America. Now that my healing was taking off I could see the wisdom of Steve's approach. I remained relatively aloof – just did my healing and the rest happened without me.

I was managing to stay in contact with Christine through a combination of telephone calls, emails and letters. It felt so much better to be holding a piece of paper in my hands onto which her hand had written the words. I needed that personal contact. I kept a brief journal sending it off every few days. True to his word, Steve transferred money into our account.

It was strange living this independent life after so many years with my family, I felt stretched socially and intellectually. Stoosh and Pauline had spent a good thirty years between them in the alternative medicine scene and could deeply challenge my conceptions. They were familiar with a lot of the subjects Sigeyo discussed with me, helping fill in a few gaps. Pauline still had a slightly naive, childlike curiosity. Stoosh was jaded and cynical about people who professed to be authorities on any form of healing.

My second talk was to another full house. Marlene introduced me so I was able to tell my own story. Without the cell phone woman's healing crescendo it felt flat, my delivery was strained and drawn out. It was only when someone asked me what it felt like to be healed that Marylyn waved from the front row. I invited her onto the stage and she told her story from drugs to prostitution, how I refused to have sex with her and her new life free from addiction. I found myself captivated by her description of feeling my hands on her.

"The tingling, the buzz, warmth, nourishing, a sort of filling up and afterwards feeling so much lighter, in harmony, complete again."

I was moved by her obvious dedication to eating her macrobiotic diet.

"Just make most of your food whole grains, vegetables, beans and miso soups and I promise you, you will feel a whole lot better. I did after just ten days."

She ended by giving me a passionate hug, kissing me on each

cheek and finally lips for good measure.

Two women came up to me afterwards and after a shower of compliments asked if I needed a lift anywhere. Marlene came over and led me away in a manner I felt was slightly over protective.

This time I was escorted by Stoosh, Pauline and Marlene to a café near Mike's shop. Stoosh, obviously enjoyed winding Pauline up, winking at me as he encouraged her to open up, be more accepting, a little less dry.

"I think I am perfectly open and accepting, thank you Stoosh."

"Well just a little more moist then."

"Oh I get it, you're trying to intimate I'm not sexy."

"Hey, I just gave you the opening for you to express it. Perhaps a bucket of oysters would help."

"Being vegan means whoever makes love to me isn't pressed up against a sack of rotting animal flesh. When it comes to sexual stamina I would lick you". Pauline put her hand to her mouth. "Oh, I can't believe I just said that. You're probably past it anyway. All this talk is to compensate for a sagging libido." "Well let's put it to the test."

Marlene steered the conversation back to seminars. Stoosh asked me what I really wanted to do, what would be the big dream.

"I guess my ideal would be to do a big outdoor talk, completely free, something that would leave a lasting impression for years to come. A healing version of Woodstock."

"I know what you mean, more like Jesus and less like a new age business seminar. My sentiments completely."

"OK, Pauline but where? I've been in the seminar business for years and there isn't that much choice."

"That's exactly the point, Marlene, business, don't you see it," Pauline countered.

"Hey wait guys, do any of you know Ringing Rocks?" Stoosh's face lit up.

We looked at him expectantly.

"It's this incredible site out in the woods, you come to a clearing just full of rocks. Some of them look slightly charred. If you take two small rocks and bang them they chime, hence the name ringing rocks. It has fantastic energy. A clean river running nearby. You'd love it Adam. Michio Kushi told us it is the remains of an ancient pyramid that built up too much energy and exploded."

Pauline became animated and grabbed my arm.

"I know it, yeah, you're right it would be so perfect, really."

There was a pause whilst everyone looked at Stoosh.

"Hey, let's do it, let's make your dream a reality."

We slapped our palms against each other.

"You know, Adam you would have loved it here at the end of the seventies. We used to have all these massive macrobiotic summer camps where we all came together. I could wander in and listen to people like Michio Kushi, Herman Aihara, Bill Tara, Denny Waxman. I learnt shiatsu with Saul Goodman, studied the I Ching with William Spear discovered the five elements with Michael Rossoff. Some of the lectures just blew my mind. It was so expansive I gave up LSD for the macro buzz."

"And were there any women in this movement," Pauline enquired with a menacing undertone.

"Well Shizuko Yamamoto came and gave these amazing shiatsu classes, Aveline Kushi taught cooking, as did Judy Waxman, Wendy Esko, Marilyn..."

"So all the men taught the intellectual stuff and their wives were stuck in the kitchen teaching cooking."

"Hey, this was the seventies remember. We used to listen to twenty minute drum solos and pretend to get off on it. You're missing the point, that was my age of discovery. Every time I heard a talk my mind was blown by new revelations, spirituality, yin and yang, ki it was truly amazing. Through macrobiotics I discovered miso, tofu, sea vegetables, I even made my own futon. The point is none of it was so commercial then, just a bunch of open minded people hanging out exploring the universe on a diet of traditional rural Japanese foods."

"How old are you Stoosh? I was born in the seventies."

"Oh, he's old enough to be our father, Adam."

Stoosh glared at Pauline.

"So what happened?"

"This guy Anthony Satalaro wrote a book about his recovery from cancer eating macrobiotically and the movement was swamped with people recovering from serious illness."

I could relate to that.

"At this time all the new stuff dried up and after a while I became tired of describing how to make miso soup to people who were never going to be interested in the philosophy. Some of the macro teachers turned into pseudo medical men competing with each other for consultations and dollars, the spell was broken. I want Ringing Rocks to bring some of that old magic back again."

My time in the USA was running out and I felt I had only scratched the surface. I arranged with the team that I would return to England for a month and then we could pick up again.

CHAPTER SIXTEEN

Christine had arranged for us all to go out to dinner at Myama with Aaron and Justine. I felt myself again. These were people who knew the real me, they had witnessed the depressions, the anger, the selfishness. It occurred to me that no-one in America had ever seen the Adam of old, they'd just met the Adam I had metamorphosised into in my role as a healer.

Back home Christine broke the news that Sam, the young boy I had been healing had died. I felt my energy drain away leaving an empty, heavy feeling in my chest and abdomen. The thought of someone so little, so courageous and positive fading out brought tears to my eyes. I imagined his mother crying herself to sleep. Selfishly I let a feeling of failure consume me.

After breakfast I volunteered to get some organic vegetables from the local supermarket. I like to look at the contents of other shoppers' trolleys, to see if I can identify any correlation between the foods they eat and my visual diagnosis of the prospective owner's health. This time I followed an overweight woman with a child to the checkouts. The boy kept trying to reach into trolley for a jumbo bag of mini candy bars. He had a hot rash across his neck and his jerky eye movements indicated a hyper energetic nervous system to me.

"Wait till we get to the car Luke."

The child persisted edging towards an impasse that ended with him rolling on the floor with a full epileptic style tantrum. I surveyed the pile of sugary breakfast cereals, sweets, chocolate biscuits, ice cream, chicken nuggets, crisps, cola that would soon be winding its way down his throat.

The boy's mother was now trying to drag him to his feet, batting him across the back of his head with her free hand. I felt a tremor run from my torso to my fingers and toes, my face flush and my muscles become taut.

"Surely you're not so stupid to feed your son all this crap and then expect him to be able to behave normally!"

They both froze.

"Why? Please tell me why would you want to force this poison into him? It's insane, people like you should be in prison for reducing the next generation to convulsing idiots. I hope he sues you when he grows up, you deserve nothing less."

"Mind your own business. I'm his mother and I'll feed him what I like. Now back off and sod off."

Another bad dream in the cockpit. I woke drenched in fear and cloaked in emotional exhaustion. Christine asked me about it in front of Justin over our morning tea. He had the practical suggestion.

"Why don't we take Matthew and Eleanor down to the RAF museum in Hendon. Maybe there'll be some clues for you there."

Walking around the great halls crammed with warplanes filled me with a sense of awe. The huge black Lancaster bomber looked so sinister, silently watching. How many lives had it taken in its raids? One hanger was devoted to the Battle of Britain and I instinctively homed in on it, although I could not recall any clue to identify when or where my dreams occurred. How childishly naive of me to assume it would be the RAF. I'll never know if it was psychosomatic but standing so close to the planes the smells stirred a primal memory inside me. I watched all the grainy black and white footage of the battles on the museum monitors, observing the lines of tracers targeting in on a wriggling enemy or cutting through the lumbering bombers. I convinced myself I was there and therefore there must be some kind of reincarnation.

The skin on my neck tightened when we stood reading the names of all the pilots who died in the battle of Britain. They were set in stone surrounding a burnt out, corroded wreck of a Hawker Hurricane. Was the name of the soul that haunted my dreams there?

My return to Philadelphia was delayed when a call from

Wendy informed me that Sigeyo had died. She was ninety-one and had died in her sleep as she always wanted. I realised she was much older than I imagined. The funeral was on the following Thursday. Christine and I attended the memorial service. It was held at the Cyril Sharp House on the other side of Primrose Hill. Wendy greeted us both with warm hugs, she kept clinging to my forearm and hand for too long. There were several hundred people there but we didn't know anyone else present. I felt slightly strange seeing so many people from Sigeyo's life, each representing a different strand from a different time. Here we were all together in one room, something that never happened whilst she was alive. I think Sigeyo would have found that amusing. Was she still present, observing us all?

I thought back to my time outside my body, looking down. If I had not come back would I have been able to hang around keeping an eye on Christine, Eleanor and Matthew? I remember the sensation of thinning out and assumed it would not last for long, not for me at that time.

I felt emotionally shaky for a few days, a little numb, missing a tiny part of my soul. It was not that I was very close to Sigeyo emotionally, but she had made the most dramatic impact on my life so far. She had worked and honed me into a man who could help people heal themselves and had a message. Timing is crucial. When I met Sigeyo I was open and ready to change and as a result I soaked her ideas up in a way that would be hard to let go of. I remembered her theory of me absorbing her unspoken thoughts by being together, sharing food, tea and cigarettes. It was so much more than taking on some new ideas, the emotional energy inside me had changed, I believed I was a different person thanks to Sigeyo.

I felt I had been touched by someone so great that just remembering her was a humbling experience. Her theory on the energy of food sent a rush of excitement up my spine. As much as I could heal from the outside, it was using her ideas to change someone's diet that had the lasting effect on people's health. Time and time again I had witnessed the positive change in people's health through macrobiotics.

Naturally I had an incredible appreciation for what she had done for me. I wanted to repay her by showing what I could do with her guidance, how far I could take it all. Was I seeking the same approval I sought from my father all over again? Sigeyo's death cheated me of that. Perhaps I just wanted her blessing, to impress her, gain her respect, to hear her acclaim the great healer I am – all about me again. A wave of self-loathing crashed through.

I got a letter from Wendy enclosing a note Sigeyo had drafted out to me but never sent. I opened her letter. Blue fountain pen on headed linen paper.

Dear Mr Saunders,

I feel I owe you an explanation for terminating our friendship. As our time together progressed I became uneasy. I am not sure you gave the subject and perhaps myself the respect I hoped. My fear was that you would take everything I have nurtured so carefully and for so long and throw it out carelessly into wind.

At first I was disappointed with you but on reflection I began to see that my approach has limitations. I can accept that in your lifetime you may achieve more than I have because you are not constrained by the fear of losing your reputation. As I heard more about your exploits from Wendy I began to realise you had taken whatever I gave you and distributed it as we agreed.

I am not sure either of us can change our destinies and therefore part of me wants to wish you success with your adventure and let you continue the journey ahead, however, I still have a fear that you will rush and meet with great difficulties.

Yours sincerely,

Sigeyo

I read the letter several times but my feelings remained mixed. Sigeyo was encouraging me with one sweep of her pen and warning me of the dangers of following this path with another.

CHAPTER SEVENTEEN

Steve picked me up at the airport, updating me on progress with the big talk at Ringing Rocks. I sensed he felt uncomfortable with the semi legal status of the event but Stoosh had pushed it through with Pauline's support. Marlene had marketed it along the same lines as an English rave.

Pauline took me down to Ringing Rocks to get the feel of the site. Yes, it certainly had a magical air to it. The large clearing filled with the rocks piled on each other had an eerie atmosphere. I knocked smaller lumps together and marvelled at the sound.

"You know, it's so good to have you back. The others have their hearts in the right place but they're not as committed. You have more integrity than any other man I've met. I sense you have greatness in your destiny."

What could I say?

"Do you ever receive healing, who recharges you?"

"Josephine, a young girl in London I studied shiatsu with."

Pauline suggested I lie down on a warm rock near the river. She started to work down my back. It was an interesting contrast. I could feel Pauline breathing deeply, almost forcing her vitality into me. Her movements were precise, brisk and snappy. It had the effect of freeing me up. It was more stimulating than relaxing. By taking in Pauline's energy I got a sense of the nervous power she had. I imagine she would be very intimidating to be in a relationship with. I think I picked up on a rush of sexual energy towards the end, it intrigued me to imagine sex with Pauline. Different and quirky I imagined.

Before the big event Marlene had arranged a mini tour taking in Harrisburg, Pittsburgh and Baltimore. She drove so I could see some of the country and take in the Amish scene. I was fascinated by the Amish people. It was inspiring to see a whole community that had shunned materialism and kept to the basics in the face of rampant consumerism. It amazed me that their children would buy into their parent's natural lifestyle. I couldn't help but wonder what kept them on the straight and narrow – a rush of moral superiority or were the fibres of the community so closely knitted together that each held a fear of the disgrace that a transgression might bring. Of course I didn't know, they may be far happier than I am, but it set my mind on different tracks of enquiry.

Social cohesion and leadership, do we miss them or are we free? Does freedom simply mean we go out and wreck everything we can in pursuit of greater material wealth and self gratification? Those Amish men and women certainly do more for the environment than their materialistic cousins. Who has the most pleasure, who is happier? What if the Amish community was just as content? Surely this would be a model for us all.

I delivered the talk in Harrisburg as planned. The only surprise was that a group of people walked out. I later found out from Marlene it was on religious grounds. My reference to karma upset them. They saw it as a denial of heaven and hell.

As a child I always found the old testament dark. To my childish mind it came across as violent, threatening and even frightening – nightmares about being turned into a pillar of salt. Later much of it simply did not make sense to my analytical mind. Why would God side with one group of his creations and help them kill his other creations?

When Jesus appeared the whole religion took on a loving, caring, healing hue, he embraced everybody. From the story of his birth right through to his early death I felt so much more uplifted. Even at the end there was hope. Having the whole religion personified in a human being made it real. Personally I don't feel there is a significant contradiction between Jesus' teachings and any of my thoughts. God having a part of him materialise as his son on earth for a while and then dematerialising back to the heavens could be said to even describe the process of karma.

Any similarity between my healing and talks and the activities of Jesus was not lost on someone else in the audience. To make the evening more interactive I offered to give a few people some healing – based on those who needed it most. At the end a tall slim African woman handed me an envelope. I thought it might be a donation and thanked her profusely. I opened it in the car. There was a single sheet of paper with 'are you the Son of God?' scrawled across in red felt tip.

After the event Marlene drove towards Pittsburgh. We planned to find a hotel to break the journey. I fell asleep in my seat watching the strings of red lights ahead whilst the oncoming white lights flash past.

Marlene woke me to say she was beginning to fall asleep at the wheel. I kept her company asking every question I could to illicit continual replies. I learnt she grew up in Pittsburgh, her father worked as a foreman in one of the steel mills until its demise. No current relationship. The last ended because Marlene wanted greater commitment and he less. Before that she dumped someone because she wanted fun and he stifled it. She was now looking someone who appreciates the spiritual side of life. My tired mind hit on the thought that she was bouncing from one relationship to another, trying to fill the missing pieces each time.

Had I? Sandy wanting me all to herself, Jackie the good time social girl, Christine for greater stability. Perhaps Marlene is, as she would say, 'seeking closure' on some aspect of her relationship with her father just as I tend to go for women with the same emotional nine ki as my mother.

The bright neon sign of a motel rose from the brow of a hill and Marlene slowed to take the entrance. It looked shabby but by then I couldn't care. They only had a double left. Marlene and I looked at each other.

"I'm so tired I could sleep leaning against this counter, it's fine with me."

I always sleep naked, otherwise I wake tied up in my pyjamas, so assuming I would be sleeping on my own I had not packed for a night with Marlene. Sleep came quick and it was morning when I next regained consciousness. Marlene's body felt warm and soft. She was wearing men's style flannel pyjamas. As my eyes opened fully I noticed she was awake.

"Good morning. How did you sleep?"

I groaned.

I had my morning erection and felt a strong surge of sexual energy being naked so close to an attractive human being. I was touching her outer thigh. I felt her move in a way that ensured I became further stimulated.

"Are you thinking what I'm thinking?"

I couldn't bring myself to say no, which would have been a lie anyway. Being the hopeless weak-willed person I am, we made love. Marlene was bigger than other girls I had slept with. I felt there was more to explore, more to squeeze and hold onto. It's funny how women have embraced the skinny look so obsessively. Women's magazines push the waif image and yet lad's glossies go for more fulsome figures. The biggest turn on was seeing the contrast of our skin colours. The warmth of her character extended to sex. It felt very easy and natural, as though we had been lovers for years.

I felt uncomfortable afterwards. My mind racing, as she drove towards the next talk.

"Is there some way this could be a one off, I feel bad that I have betrayed Christine in this way. I enjoyed this morning and if the situation was different…"

"Hey, I don't want to put you in a difficult situation and I certainly don't want to break up anyone's family. Don't worry, I won't get all bitter and twisted and write to your wife, sell my story to the papers, cook your little girl's rabbit and make sure everyone knows what a two timing bastard you are."

As she said this her voice reached a hysterical pitch. Then to my relief she laughed. I joined in, although not as heartily, in fact with no humour at all, it was just a nervous reaction.

"No really, it's no big deal Adam, let's go back to where we were."

Justifications – it's my body, I feel happier after sex, I need that exchange of fluids, I have no intention of falling in love, life is short…I suppose the big question is would I mind if Christine was doing the same? What if Aaron popped round and was in bed with her now? Yes, I would be upset. I wouldn't feel betrayed? I'm not that hypocritical, yet somehow I can't imagine Christine just having sex, she would need to have much deeper feelings for her mate, sex happens after several barriers have to come down, if she had crossed the boundary of letting another man inside her I think I would have already lost her heart. Would I mind a drunken fumble with one of her male friends after a party?

Terrible double standards all mixed up in feelings of guilt, shame and disappointment in myself. I've gone on the defensive. Perhaps my greatest sense of failure was that I had been here before and nearly destroyed a wonderful relationship with Christine. I liked Marlene and I enjoyed the sex but in the bigger view it was not worth the pain I might inflict on my wife.

My previous incident was a few months after the accident. I wanted to embark on a similar process of healing my karma as I was experiencing with Justin.

Sandy, the girl I enjoyed a three-year relationship with, was on my list. We ended our relationship after months of me being continually accused of spending too much time with my friends, of not being committed and being indecisive regarding marriage. Within days I was sleeping with Jackie. A little later Sandy disappeared and later I heard she had married someone in Manchester. I managed to track her down through a mutual friend and called her.

Her cheery hello fell to a stunned silence when she heard my voice. I made small talk whilst she joined in. Mutual curiosity drove us to find out about each other's current lives. Eventually I broke through the trivia.

"I'd like to meet up. Do you ever come back down this way?"

"Why Adam? Why after all these years do you want to bring it all back?"

"I'm trying to repair my past."

"Have you any idea what I went through? I've had years of therapy and hell after you rejected me. Why didn't you answer any of my calls or letters?"

"Look, I really want to try to mend our past, I would like to think we could go back," and then I dried up.

"So just because you've decided to repair your past after all this time you want me to come all the way to London and help you out."

"I'm sorry, I really am."

I thought I heard her crying and then a disconnected purr.

I felt a depressed sinking feeling penetrate my lungs. There was a flash of a thought that I should fight it and get back into the moment but then I thought 'give up on karma' and slumped on our beige sofa. Matthew must have left some chocolate on it because when I turned over it was smeared across my fawn trousers and the cushion.

When Christine came home I mumbled my disappointments.

"Come on love. You can't expect Sandy to change the way she's felt all these years just because you decided to call her. Don't give up now, what you are doing is really good. Why not call Sandy again in a few days when she has had time to get used to you? What's happened to your trousers? You're binging on chocolate again! No wonder you're so depressed. What's the point of me cooking all this living whole food if you cram sugar into your mouth when I'm not looking?"

I tried Sandy again after a few days and as Christine predicted we were able to talk this time. We arranged to meet up in Manchester the following week.

I took the train from Euston and met her at the station café.

She looked slightly gaunt and thinner than I remembered. A black polo neck and matching knee length skirt replaced the jeans, white T-shirt and leather jacket of our youth. I felt as though I was creeping across brittle ice as I edged our conversation forwards. The rims of her eyes looked a little red and her movements unnervingly jerky.

Her version of events was that I had ruined her life. She was madly in love with me and then for no apparent reason I dumped her. I'd thrown away three incredible years of passion, holidays and the prospects of marriage. All her dreams of giving birth to my children, building a home together and walking through life hand in hand had turned to ashes and scattered in the wind with one irrational sweep of my hand.

My problem was that I could not produce the evidence to prove otherwise. All my character traits she hated and complained of at the time had been air brushed out. Her version even had her in the pub with my mates. Her inability to accept any other possibility began to irritate me. I felt pressure building and pushing against my breastplate. Suddenly the guilt transformed and erupted into a volcano of raw emotion. All rationality receded as my liver raged, exploding into my mind. I grabbed Sandy by her shoulders and hauled her across the table so we were nose to nose. Caffeine and herbs mixed as they ran across the table onto my lap. I trashed my soft feely touchy script.

"Listen we were just two teenagers who loved each other and had a great time. Then you wanted something different and I wasn't ready. It could have worked later but not then. It was you who kept complaining, you found so much to criticise, you wanted me to be someone else. Why do you think a wild teenager like me would want to stay in with you when Jackie liked me how I was? And now you've become some kind of a martyr. Where has it taken you? I mean it. What is the point?"

I slid back into my seat. Sandy looked white and wide-eyed. My heart was racing. I wanted to push her hard, to try and wake her out of this nightmare she had entombed herself in, but it was me who felt the slap.

"You selfish little piece of excrement! You couldn't give a toss about me. All you want to do is get yourself off the hook. Well, it's not that simple Adam. If you want to go ruining other people's lives then at least be man enough to take responsibility for it."

She jumped up and ran off carrying the grotesque balloon of injury and resentment that cocooned her. I desperately wanted to puncture the bubble she lived in and ran after her. We crashed through the leaden commuters as though part of an action thriller. I was still embarrassingly out of shape from the accident and it took an incredible effort to keep up with her. Suddenly she gave up and slowed to a walk. I managed to grab her black coat outside and pushed her into an alley. I swung her around, pinning her up against the brick wall.

I was breathing so hard I could not speak. My fists were clenched as I leant into her.

"What… will it… take to… to move on and get… your life back?"

Instead of erupting in full power, my voice came out in a wheezing, pleadingly desperate thin tone conveying the opposite of my intention.

"I wish you could understand how much I loved you… I really didn't want to hurt you… I was emotionally still a child… I wasn't ready to give up my friends and settle down."

Sandy tightened her fist into handfuls of my hair. She pressed her lips to mine and forced her tongue into my mouth. It took me too long to react – my heart was still in charge of my mind and I found myself shocked by the passion she aroused in me.

Sandy pulled away and for the first time smiled. I felt her fingers on my neck, her lips against my cheek, then my lips against her face. I recognised the smell of her hair. I was there again; lying on our beach, wet and salty, falling asleep entwined.

It was very quick. We were active and assertive with each

other. She grabbed my buttocks as I squeezed and pulled her close. Being out in the open gave it a sense of urgency, daring and madness. On the walk back to the station we were both silent. I expected Sandy to somehow be triumphant but she also sounded nervous.

"I can't believe we did that Adam. Things have not been going well with Randolph but he does not deserve this. Oh Adam, what have we got ourselves into?"

We kissed and then I walked to the train. I didn't want to look round but I did, she was still standing there, she blew me a kiss and turned.

What did this mean? Had Sandy forgiven me? Was she now looking back at our time together with a different perception? I challenged myself with the same question. Yes, I was more receptive to her pain. I flinched remembering the selfish, egotistical youth I was. I let the possibility swirl through my mind that our physical intimacy cut through all the talk and that we had changed each other from the inside, our hearts bypassing our brains.

I felt content that we had somehow reached an understanding but when my thoughts turned to Christine I felt hot acid hit the pit of my stomach. Now what?

Sitting looking at a raindrop streak across the carriage window and the English countryside flying past behind, the birth of a new thought was emerging. It is amazing the capacity humans have to justify their worst actions. Every war wretches up indescribable atrocities and yet at the time the protagonists could always find the justification to carry on. No one is totally evil, or is this just my protected upbringing in middle class England? We might have different views, values, cultures and be in different phases of our journey through life but surely it is the talent for self justification that allows someone to repeatedly perform hideous acts on other living creatures.

Inevitably, as a protagonist in my own drama I did go through a series of justifications, sadly my initial reaction to any kind of discomfort. I have trained myself in this form of defence since I could talk. Fortunately the train journey was long enough for that creek to run dry. I resolved not to tell Christine. Why hurt her when I knew I loved her and would not be seeing Sandy again. When I got home Christine was already in bed.

"How did it go with Sandy?"

"Fine, we made more progress and I think some of the bad feeling has been healed."

"Did you feel attracted to her after all this time?"

"No, we just talked."

"So you definitely were not intimate with her?"

My body and mind seized up. I instinctively said no.

"Randolph just phoned to say Sandy told him you two had sex. He didn't want you making a fool of me, which showed more consideration than you've ever managed."

I felt myself collapse emotionally. My chest caved in, my stomach disappeared, my abdomen weakened. I wanted to shout out it wasn't like that, she didn't understand, but I was unable to find my voice. Christine would never realise that I was in control, I wouldn't fall in love with Sandy. We were just caught up in a moment trying to resolve our incomplete past.

When I thought Christine was leaving, I remember cursing karma. Where had it got me? I should have left my past alone. Later Emily pointed out that it was the incidence with Sandy that led to Christine wanting to leave and me making the effort to nurture and grow the wonderful loving relationship we now had. Emily explained how karma is a process, not simply about ticking off a list of bad deeds. It was true that the extreme fear, panic, anxiety I felt when our relationship was over did propel me into a new phase of my life. Do I need those challenges, difficulties to keep evolving? Do I subconsciously launch into emotional disasters just to go through another period of emotional growth?

Here I was again, caught in the act of infidelity, this time with

Marlene. No excuses this time. Now sitting in Marlene's car I imagined trying to explain it all to Emily. Is it possible that evolution and survival of the fittest has programmed into men the biological desire to try to impregnate as many females as possible, to compete with other men so that it is their sperm that succeeds in defining the next generation? Could sexual motivation spill over into taking on other roles the males would not necessarily want? Protector, provider, companion? How many shelves have been put up on the back of a Sunday morning romp? Quite a few with Christine.

What would Emily say? That I am being analytical, that my behaviour simply reflects my condition and the state of my feelings towards Christine? She would ask whether my treatment of Marlene and Christine simply mirror my feelings about myself?

I don't want Emily to say this, so in my imaginary conversation I cut her off. Now I can make the more rational point that women would have the role of being selective, finding the best father for their children, ideally someone who would help her raise them as well. Whereas the male throws his seeds to the wind with less interest where they land, the female not only wants the best seeds but also the best thrower to herself. This must be a basic instinct wired in for countless generations to increase the chance of survival of her babies.

Now I gave Emily another chance to reply. None of this is a very romantic view. Where is the love? It is all about feelings, Adam.

"So what's going on in that great mind of yours?"

"Oh just looking at the countryside," I lied.

Why don't I express myself more and let Marlene into my head?

"It won't be long now. Are you hungry?"

Yes, but I wanted some real food, straight from the land. The factory food on the run left me energetically empty. Marlene found a diner and I made the best of what was available.

When we walked over to the hall I was shocked to see someone standing outside with a placard asking 'Are you the Son of God?'

"Don't worry Adam, they're some pretty hard core Christians here."

That did make me worry. I didn't know whether it was meant as a question or sarcastically, as though I thought I was Jesus. In the end I decided to take the initiative and started the talk with my thoughts on religion.

"Let me begin by telling you I'm not Jesus, I'm just like anyone else in this room. The only difference is that I worked on the ability to heal through my hands."

I looked around for support but blank faces stared back.

"With the right training anyone here could do it. I can't do miracles, nor do I have any special access to God."

"If you're not Jesus you shouldn't be healing, that's only for those anointed by God," someone shouted from the side, waving a bible.

"Look, it's just a skill, thousands of people do it all over the world, it doesn't make sense for God not to want us to help each other. Surely that was Jesus' message."

"You've no business meddling in God's work, kneel and pray for forgiveness young man."

Now I could feel the anger welling up inside. "What gives anyone the right to speak on God or Jesus' behalf? That book you're basing your life on was written by people like you and me a long time after the events, who's to say they got it right? In fact I think Jesus would be disgusted at what has gone on in his name, the wars, torture, burnings, the wealth, corruption, sexual abuse. And this is by people who claim to be working for God. What did they say about that in your book? No, if I have a message it is to love one another and do what you can to make this a better world for all of us. And yes, that includes healing. I'm not interested in all that hierarchy, God doesn't just speak to the Pope, he's everywhere. You don't need churches or special clothes to feel it."

By now I was worked up. The bible waver and a group of people around her walked out.

"I'm sorry, but to me any organised religion is mental manipulation. All it does is alter people's beliefs to suit the church they serve. Real religion starts here," I put my hand on my chest. "Following Jesus means taking on the work he did. Having a philosophy and living it, helping others and taking on the strong who prey on the weak."

A round of applause broke out from the back, close to the lady with the placard.

"Forget the rest, it's just a distraction from the real work. Live the dream, be a better person by helping others. Give them what they want not what you think they want."

I had lost the point and sunk back on clichés. I remained quiet for a few minutes before inviting a man with a migraine onto the stage for healing.

"I've had terrible headaches and nausea for the last ten years."

"Do you drink coffee?"

"Yup, sure do."

"Cheese, chocolate, meat, sugar?"

He nodded to all of them and smiled. I put my hands on his head. His ki felt hot, acidic, prickly. His blood was pumping around his temples as though driven by a hammer. This man's neck was as tense as a steel beam. I started by massaging and stretching his neck until his blood flow felt smoother and softer. I rested one hand on his forehead and gently probed his abdomen with the other. Here his energy felt thick and sticky.

"Sir, please breath slowly and deeply into your abdomen and then out fast, pulling your abdomen back in as hard as you can."

As the man did this the stagnation started to dispel. It started to clear and I could feel the intensity of energy in his head diminish with my other hand.

"Are you feeling any better?"

"The pain's gone, I just feel very tired."

"You need to loosen up the energy inside you. Heavy, salty, fatty foods are making the situation worse, clogging you up. Why not try going without any dairy food, meat or salt for a few days. At the same time you need to give up coffee and sugar to reduce this hot, acidic feeling."

"What's left?"

"Pasta, rice, corn, porridge, loads of vegetables, fish, beans, seeds, some nuts, and fruits. Do you want more?"

He smiled.

"I can try that."

"Also try drinking a tea made by boiling a bunch of parsley for ten minutes every day. You know how when you look at parsley it grows up and out sharply at different angles?"

The man nodded.

"That is just the kind of living energy you need to break up some of this clump of emotional energy around your middle organs."

I patted his lower ribs and he left. I realised that by bringing people on stage instead of walking out into the audience I could talk to them and give them advice in a way that everyone could share in the process. It became a sort of therapeutic release for the person telling everyone their problems, and the whole audience could benefit from my advice. This form of human interaction brought me to life.

It impressed me how a group of people putting their energy in one direction achieves so much more. I was amazed how frank and open people were, but this was America. I felt everyone willing me on. From now on this would be a part of my talks.

At the end an elderly lady came up to me and held my elbow, "I don't care what you think you are, you're the return of Jesus for me."

I winked and squeezed her arm.

I used the new format for Baltimore. Started with my story, a few warm up exercises, breathing and meditation, and then asking people to come up for an open healing session. I used this format to explain my take on healing.

CHAPTER EIGHTEEN

The Ringing Rocks day arrived. I still didn't have a plan. So far I had just muddled through the previous talks and every time I was in danger of crashing, new thoughts saved me. I tried writing out notes but it looked too uninspiring on paper. The same challenge I'm having writing this book.

There was a huge blue sky, with the sun warming the rocks. The spring air was still cool enough to make it feel pleasant in a sweatshirt.

Pauline was constantly by my side. She gave me a welcome massage a couple of hours ago. Somehow she assumed it would be her making the introduction. I complained to Marlene but she just shrugged. I made Pauline promise not to include my history and keep it simple.

Stoosh had sent out the signals and the location flashed up on a web site and through to everyone who left their e-mails or text details. Scaffolding and planks were erected precariously over the rocks. A pony-tailed monster was sorting out the PA.

Emily arrived with a friend. We hugged and for a moment I felt compelled to tell her about Marlene and I but I could see we would not get the time alone together and anyway after her reaction to my interaction with Sandy this was probably not the place.

With twenty minutes to go people started to arrive. Brad, Cheryl and Marilyn came over and we sat on a rock chatting. Marilyn looked radiant, I couldn't keep my eyes off her. She was wearing a low cut top exposing most of her firm breasts and her pierced navel. Her skirt created the illusion of covering her without enough material. She sat next to me and let her bare knee brush up against my thigh. Although the contact was minimal I amplified it into a teasing caress. Brad had good news from his blood tests, he was in the clear. I gave each of them some healing as we chatted.

The crowd was already bigger than any of us had imagined. The lack of toilets and first aid facilities made Steve visibly nervous.

"We could all lose everything over this. Better keep it short, Adam."

"You mean no toilet breaks?"

"Wait until he hears about the television coverage," Marlene whispered to me.

People kept pouring in, clambering over the rocks to find a good space. I could see people climb the trees at the edge of the clearing. The space was full. This was far bigger than I imagined. Instead of hundreds there were thousands waiting for me to deliver. Deliver what? I sensed we might have taken on too much. I was feeling jittery, the adrenaline was kicking in hard. Despite my efforts to breathe slowly and take one second at a time the excitement was overwhelming. I could feel my abdomen wind up like a steel spring. I wanted to start because I still did not know what I wanted to say, I needed that first step to release the flow.

Pauline's hands on my shoulders were beginning to irritate me, I felt a boxer being warmed up by his trainer. At last Stoosh gave the thumbs up and Pauline walked onto the stage.

"Hello Ringing Rocks! It is my great, great honour to introduce you to the most amazing healer of our time, the man who has been compared to Jesus, the saviour of so many, please welcome the person who has changed my life and so many others, the amazing Adam Saunders."

I cringed, this contrasted badly with my humble, understated expression. Pauline gave me a hug as we passed on the platform.

"I never thought I would have a hero after my father, but here you are," she shouted into my ear over the expectant applause from the crowd.

Where to begin? I began to trot out my story, painfully aware that some people were hearing this for the third time. I then moved into the breathing and meditation routine. This was boring, I wanted to give more. I knew this was my one big chance but I needed that spark of inspiration. Then I saw a sickly looking overweight child sitting on a stone slumped against his father. His big eyes stared back at me. 'Take me out of this horrible body, help me escape this sad life'. I imagined his father dragging him here in the hope that his pale, limp son would be healed. Perhaps he'd argued with his wife, perhaps there was no mother. I genuinely wanted to help the boy, I felt my energy rise, the big wave rose and I was surfing.

"When I look around we are seriously messed up. We have more wealth than ever and yet what do we do with it? Historians will look back on this time as the age when we had it all and blew it. Spent it all on plastic, and not content with wasting our hard earned cash on trash, we kept on spending more, and more, and more. In fact so much that most of you are in debt. You can't stop. And for what? You've become slaves to glittering trinkets. The dollar has taken your soul. The system we created has sucked us to its bowels and we can't escape. It's killing us. So what? Who cares? But there is a generation coming through who'll pay big time. Yes, not only are we ruining the environment for them but we're messing with their bodies, messing with their heads."

I was now pacing the boards with my mike pressed to my lips.

"Here it is. Parents today are killing their kids. Pesticides, cheap fats, sugar, additives, salt – it's slaughtering them. When I see children growing up on a diet of candies, chocolate, ice cream, chips, cola, fries and junk food I have to ask what is happening. A whole generation primed from childhood to diabetes, cancer, heart disease, obesity and emotional instability . We are literally poisoning our own children. And guess what, parents don't want to stop destroying their children because it would deprive them of what their friends are having. How bad is that? Is this a mass murder conspiracy?"

I made eye contact with Marilyn who smiled back.

"Are we witnessing a mass clear out of the human race? The poor and uneducated and those who know better, piling into the very foods that will destroy them. Huge western corporations dumping unhealthy crap they cannot sell here into the poorest countries. Persuading Africans to feed their children on formula instead of breastmilk. You have to educate yourself and your children if you want to break free and survive."

I paused to wipe my brow.

"This will be a bigger puzzle than the collapse of the Roman Empire. Why did such a powerful, rich civilisation implode through ill health and an inability to reproduce? Can you imagine the arguments in a few hundred years when historians try to work out why such a wealthy race killed their children off just because they couldn't be bothered to cook real foods? I can't understand it and I'm living through it."

I was now fully immersed in my rant – running up and down the wooden platform waving my arms out at the audience. My mouth was full of saliva. I must have looked like a raving mad man frothing at the mouth screaming out the words to the crowd who had come to hear a nice healer spread some love and peace. Perhaps it was the energy of Ringing Rocks. I continued on my theme.

"Please, can anyone tell me why we need genetically modified foods? Surely we are trying to reduce pesticides to make the food healthy and stop polluting the land. So why do we have companies modifying foods so they can be sprayed with even more pesticides without killing the plants. It's like living through an Alice in Wonderland dream. The insane have been left in charge of food production and their mad friends are running the country."

I paused to let a new thought in.

"Sometimes when those black moods fill the air I think it's the universe trying to rid us of the very people who are doing the most to pollute it, by manipulating parents to kill off their children and make themselves less able to conceive. The time has come and if we can't change, nature will leave us behind."

After a few deep breaths I invited the child and his father onto the stage. The crowd parted to let them through. It was painfully slow watching the father pull and carry his son towards me.

"Hi, I'm Adam, what's your name?"

"Josh," he mumbled.

"How are you feeling Josh?"

"OK."

"He's got severe asthma and as you said, he tends to put on weight," his father added.

"Do you mind if I try a little healing with you?"

His father nodded and I laid my hands over the boy's chest. I could even feel the mucus stifling each breath.

"So what are your favourite foods Josh?"

Josh shrugged.

"Ice cream, isn't it son."

"Yes, and milkshakes."

I was having trouble projecting my energy through the stickiness under my hands.

"Well, I think you may need some real foods. You're too old for milk products, especially those made for a baby calf. Can you imagine running into a field and sucking on a cow's teats?"

Josh smiled and shook his head.

"I'm talking about foods that still have life in them, whole grains, beans and vegetables."

I began to feel some of the stickiness dissolve.

"If you want to feel better you'll have to get rid of the sugar in your diet. Soon you'll be running around having fun again. Do you like basketball?"

He nodded.

"Josh, imagine you're out there bouncing the ball, running, ready to shoot. Are you there?"

I knew he was because I could feel his ki stirring.

"Stay with it, Josh. You have the energy, keep running. Take deep breaths, suck in the oxygen. You've got the ball, you're ducking and diving, no one can keep up."

His face was beginning to flush. I moved my hands away slightly and felt a prickly heat in my palms. My energy was penetrating. After a minute or so I moved my hands away.

"I can still feel your hands on my chest."

I smiled. "Feeling better?"

"I feel like running."

"Go for it."

Josh pounded awkwardly across the stage, did a little jump, pretended to slam dunk and ran back to his father's arms. I turned back to the audience and blushed slightly as my friends initiated a huge wave of applause.

"We can do it if we stick together, help each other reach a higher plane. But we need to jump off this crazy, consume-everything trip. I know it's hard, but since I've broken free of money and all the unnecessary stuff it can buy, it doesn't mean that much. Now I have the time to do what I want to do and you know what, most of it's for free –friendships, love, sex, walks, holding hands, being with someone close… who needs the rest."

I saw an elderly lady to my left, her hands were knotted and she stooped. I asked Stoosh and Steve to help her up to me. The vertebrae in her back felt fused together, she was in pain from the swollen joints. I tried to draw some of the hot and bitter ki out, whilst dissolving the stagnation in her spine. I felt decades of fats and sugar solidified around her body. As I worked on her a new theme entered my head.

"We all spend so much on the trash around us but so little on ourselves. I bet some of you will spend a fortune on crap you don't really need but try to save cents when it comes to what you put in your mouth. It's insanity to buy anything but organic foods but for a few dollars less people will stuff themselves full of chemicals. You wouldn't put cheap gas in your car if you thought it would damage your engine. Why not spend some money on learning how to take care of yourself, giving your children a better future? Break free of the materialistic conditioning, don't be a slave, there's so many more choices than following the path painted out in front of you."

I could feel Mary's ki flow out of her joints, just a trickle at first.

"My joints are cooling down, it feels very strange. Look – I can open and close my hands better."

I encouraged her to stand straighter. It was like bending steel.

"Dear Lord, I feel a weight's fallen off my shoulders. You really have the magic touch, if only you could make me fifty years younger."

I was beginning to run out of steam, I was flagging. I looked around for Marilyn and saw her leaning against a tree. She jumped up when I waved her over. Letting her tell her story allowed me to walk through the mass of people offering some healing to the weakest. I was surprised at how many children there were. I hoped my ranting and raving had not put them off.

As Marilyn wound up her story with her new work at the rehab unit I picked my way back to the stage. I needed one big theme to end on.

"I beg you not to become a slave to money. Money is a tool, it connects us all as it streams through society, the notes in your pockets will have been through so many hands, the child buying a toy, the father saving for a family holiday, the mother buying groceries, the guy in a suit making an investment. Money gives you the power to make choices. Through the money in your pocket you can determine what succeeds and what does not. Take control and use your money to change the world we live in, use your money to promote healthy natural foods, fair trade with other communities, sustainable energy, organic agriculture. Stop buying meat if you want to free up land for trees."

Although they were ideas I had a passion for, this was

predictable and I felt I was losing interest in my own speech. Perhaps I had heard it too many times in my own head. Help.

"You're too intelligent to be taken in by advertising, packaging and sales gimmicks. Surely we haven't come this far to stumble and implode over cheap gratification. Even the health food industry has been taken over by an obsession with adding value and processing all the goodness out of the foods. Let's join together and exercise our power and create a real world that we can all grow in. Think long term, build a future for our children. Remember we have not inherited the planet, we are only borrowing it from them."

Just as I was winding down another thought popped into my mind.

"We are all connected by our emotional energy, everything you do will have an influence on everyone else regardless of how subtle it is. Go home, clean out the cupboards, make a list of any change you can make, big or small, see how far you can step out of the system. Read food labels and make choices based on your principles. It will make a difference I promise you."

We finished with a mutual healing session.

The site slowly emptied. I felt the usual high mixed with exhaustion. All I wanted to do right now was hang out with those close to me and go into a listening mode. The team, Marilyn, Brad and Cheryl along with some of their friends gathered around as we waited for people to clear.

"That was a... strong... organic message... got to.... health foods ... humous sandwich... pioneer... movement...Africa... organic wine."

I embraced Mike.

The worst that could happen after one of my talks was to be trapped in a situation where people came up and start asking questions, I simply did not have the mental energy. I insisted we walk off into the trees but before I could escape, a monster of a man managed to get through.

"Wow, that was so cool man. Totally bad, you've seriously got the words."

I turned around, standing in his shadow. He was nearly a head taller and surely had half my weight again. He squeezed my hand with a massive black and silver paw.

"Yeah, I'm Seriously Something."

I waited not sure how to respond.

"Seriously Something, rapping into the future."

Seriously started a rap, I so wished I could have recognised or even joined in a bit. I shrugged my shoulders. "Sorry I'm completely out of touch."

"No problem man. It's cool. Listen I heard you out there talking the talk. You ever done some rap."

"No," I was off balance. "No I haven't tried."

"Hey, I think you've got it. Let's lay some tracks down. You have a message man. Look give me your number and we can meet."

I scribbled my number on a scrap of paper. For such a large framed man Seriously looked surprisingly agile as he traversed the rocks.

"Do you know who that was getting your autograph?" Brad's voice bounced off the back of my head. I turned to face him. "He's a big producer in the rap scene."

Steve came over with the news that there was a row of ice cream and doughnut vans doing great trade with the people leaving for their cars. My initial disappointment with not reaching a final high was massaged away by everyone's enthusiasm.

"You're making news man. All those people will spread your word."

"Thanks Stoosh."

I had the feeling that Emily, Marlene, Marilyn and Pauline were vying to take me home. To avoid showing any preference I suggested we all go to a restaurant. I was in a strange state where

I alternated between wishing they would all leave and needing their company.

Stoosh started clearing up the mess with some stragglers. We joined in bagging up the trash people brings to events. Mostly plastic bottles, but I was amazed at how many wrappers there were for candies, chips and chocolate bars. Still better than finding organic falafel and pitta sandwich wrappers and realising I had been preaching to the converted.

As far as I was concerned, Emily, Brad, Cheryl and Marilyn had unofficially joined the team and I invited them along, so now we were ten. Much of the conversation over the spaghetti was how to plan the next event.

After Emily said goodbye, I could feel her pride in me and I wasn't going to sabotage that by mentioning what happened on my road trip with Marlene.

That evening my talk made television news. There were clips of me talking and healing, along with interviews from people leaving. The spin was positive. The next day the Philadelphia Enquirer printed extracts from my speeches. There were more comparisons to Jesus and an analysis of what was perceived as my anti-capitalist message. They didn't understand that I was suggesting people use capitalism, free markets and competition to exercise their buying power and change the environment as well as improve their own health.

I was beginning to feel I had a purpose – to save the planet from human self-destructive tendencies. I did not believed that I was another Jesus but I was beginning to entertain the idea that I might have been incarnated by the forces of the universe to try and change an imbalance that was happening here on planet earth. Perhaps Matthew and Eleanor had brought me back to life for a reason. Were they pulling the strings? Children trying to save the planet through adults? Was this my debt for being given the rest of my life?

Coming to America was no accident. Part of my destiny must

have been to end up in the country that produces more wealth and waste per head of population than any other. It all made sense, Emily, Aaron, Christine, the accident, Nirmala, Josephine, Wendy, Sigeyo, Steve, Mike, Marlene, Pauline, Stoosh, now Marilyn, Cheryl and Brad – all stepping stones, helpers guiding me toward my destiny.

CHAPTER NINETEEN

The rap producer Seriously gave me a call and we met up at his studio. He explained the way a rap song works.

"You have to have a message, a special way to express it, don't make it obvious. Give it rhythm and hook line. I'll lay in the sounds and we'll split it all fifty-fifty. This will reach a whole new cult audience."

Sitting in my living room I tried to write some lyrics. It was harder than I imagined. I started with some rhyming verse.

Climbing into the rolling tread mill,
Poisoning your body with cheap fat,
You'd sell out for bright plastic wrappers,
Eating your way through commercial crap,

You're so commercial,
Wrapped in synthetic,
You're so commercial,
Chemicals in your blood,
You're so commercial,
It's money not love,

I managed to write some more verses and took it to Seriously. I was intrigued to see what he would think of it.

Seriously greeted me with an affectionate, hefty pat on the shoulder. It knocked me slightly. His mouth spread into broad smile.

"Hey Mister Organic, pure cool."

I nodded and sat on the sofa. It appeared that Seriously didn't do small talk so I handed over the paper trying to appear slightly disinterested. Seriously read it through. Within seconds he was grinning and by the time I imagined he reached the second verse he was laughing out loud. He slammed his fist down on the arm of his chair.

"You're torturing me, this isn't for real is it? Please tell me you've got something else, I beg you, I don't want to have take you outside and waste you."

A blaze of indignation rose up through my embarrassment.

"What did you expect, this is all new to me."

"Hey, when you were up on that stage you had the passion, you really cared. This is just so contrived, it's the sort of crap teachers do at school to look cool. Sorry, I'm not dissin' you but I can't do anything with this."

"It's different on stage. All these incredible ideas suddenly come into my head when I put myself on the spot and see all those people expecting me to deliver. I don't plan, rehearse or write it out."

"OK, lets just do it live and raw. You cool?"

I nodded, perhaps the fear factor would help.

"I'll put on a backing track, you to return to those warm rocks in your white trash head, let's just see what comes."

I was fitted with headphones and given a mike. The rhythm track came in and I tried to revisit Ringing Rocks. I pictured the little boy and rapped on my theme of how we were messing up the world for children, suddenly the music stopped.

"Hey, that's better, but when you was on the stage you was pacing those boards, you was into the rhythm, moving your pretty head up and down, that's what we need. You're doing OK, man."

Moving to the rhythm did make all the difference, I could shout out along with the music, and once I got onto a roll it was easier to find the words. Then I dried up and music stopped.

"Getting better, getting better. I'll get you moving in time yet. Do me a favour, rap a line and then miss at least one beat. I need the spaces in your track so we can edit, if you just keep running on we're finished. Try making your tone move up and down, exaggerate it as it goes flat in the process of laying it onto plastic. Like this you'll sound like you're about to sleep on your own thoughts."

The whole day was taken up with trying to record five minutes of me talking in time to the rhythm track delivering my message. Seriously provoked me to the point that I felt my fire rise up and I managed to channel it into my rant. When I finished, Seriously wanted to play around for a while on his own so I made my way to the door.

"Adam Saunders isn't hip. You need a name."

I looked back stunned.

"Who are you?"

I shrugged my shoulders.

"It'll have to be Macroman unless you think of something better."

I nodded.

"Hey Macroman;

I'm macrobiotic,
some say neurotic,
but the food I eat
ain't really toxic."

I laughed and walked off. The next day I had a long talk with Christine, Matthew and Eleanor, and then called Aaron. We started on Ringing Rocks and moved onto Aaron's new lover Annie, only nineteen.

"What is the big deal about her age Aaron. I sense you think the younger the girl, the better. There must be so many women in their thirties that would just love to be in a relationship with you."
"You just don't get it Adam. I don't want someone to be harping on at me about commitment and settling down or trying to enrol me in their problems. A middle aged woman is on a biological time clock and I don't want to be sucked into her program. They

all come with so much baggage, it's just too much hard work, and for what? More grief, arguments, nagging, criticism, who needs it? It kills it for me. Annie is absolutely gorgeous, she still has a bit of puppy fat, those soft, golden, downy hairs on her thighs, we have amazing sex, we laugh, it's an adventure for her. It keeps me young. Remember Manhattan? Well it's like that, only I am better looking but not as funny as Woody Allen. You should try it – only joking."

"What's wrong with getting sucked in and having children, you're missing out. It's what you're here for."

"Not me, I'm basically a selfish bastard who values his freedom too much."

For a moment I was tempted to reveal my adventure with Marlene but I stopped myself. I was still engaged in an internal battle between my mind and body. So far my mind had managed to out manoeuvre my physical desires but I still lusted after her. Aaron promised to come over and stay with me. I sincerely thought Aaron would be happier with someone closer to his own age that he could form a life long relationship with but on the face of it logic was on his side. All I had was a gut feeling. Was it because that was how I was living my life and he should do the same, some sort of safety in numbers? Did I feel jealous? I remembered some of my old values; sexy girls, music, travel, but I had moved on and gained more than I lost. Perhaps Aaron got lost in the ecstasy of one of his early relationships and remained there.

I remember how Christine pointed out that her single friends had such ridiculously high expectations of what they want from a relationship, she could not imagine such a man existed. I certainly wouldn't measure up. Christine used to wonder what they thought they had to offer in exchange for this super male. Perhaps it is being set such high standards that puts Aaron off.

Christine also had the idea that, emotionally there is a sense of completing the circle in being a child yourself, growing up and then bringing up your own children. She believed people who had children when they were young had fewer issues with their parents, as they now knew what was involved in raising a family. They knew how difficult children can be, how easy it is to lose your temper, to shout out hurtful words in the stress of it all. There is an understanding of the way parents become permanently uptight, unwittingly enrol their children in their insecurities, compensate for their deficiencies by asking their children to live the successes they missed. It was only when she gave birth to Matthew that she was able to let go of some of her perceived issues with her mother.

After a few days of healing Seriously drove me to his studio. He played the track as soon as we arrived. It started with a kind of simple kindergarten tune followed by the rhythm track. Next I heard my voice. It wasn't as bad as I imagined, quite deep, powerful, sort of manic. Seriously had added a deep foreboding heavy sound that faded in and out until the chorus came in. Now the tune returned with children singing harmonies, it was quite a contrast. The children brought the joy whilst my adult voice delivered the warnings.

As the track progressed I sounded wilder, my lyrics were more challenging and just as it reached a crescendo, silence save for the children randomly singing and playing. They sounded as though they had been there all the time but had been drowned out by my voice and the music. Seriously had obviously changed the order of my phrases and must have altered my voice towards the end. I was pleased that following a macrobiotic style diet and using money to change the world came though strongly. I was impressed. We hugged and Seriously insisted we celebrate with a peppermint tea. He seemed content to just sit there without talking, I resisted the impulse to verbalise.

"Now you've got the product time for the big one, a stadium. Think about it man, you've got a message, which is more than most in this business."

Seriously slapped me so hard on the back as I left that I

stumbled down the wooden steps from the porch.

"Oh I nearly forgot, Seriously, what is it called?"

"Hey, that's for you to decide."

My mind travelled a convoluted maze looking for a powerful name. "I can't, it's too contrived."

"Organica?" I gave him the thumbs up and left. One of Steve's friends sorted out the contacts for me.

CHAPTER TWENTY

I walk into Portmadoc for a haircut and shave. It wipes five years from my face. I feel more open but a little exposed. This return to my old identity confirms an acceptance of my past. I may even be ready to go back to healing. First I want to complete my writing.

Having become an active father I think it helped me make the transition into middle age. The desire for drugs, alcohol, women and an all consuming social life slipped away easily. I see men my age stressing and ballooning under the strain of their alcohol driven routine. Even Aaron looks to be finding the act of remaining a free spirit in middle age difficult. Hanging around clubs and bars with people ten years younger and bags under his eyes doesn't look so cool anymore. Justin remains a child, lost in those school days, he never matured, stunted emotionally by bullies like myself.

I find it fascinating to see how we can so easily become stuck in certain phases of our life. I know how hard I fought to resist being a father. Matthew was already eight before I finally accepted the change and reinvented myself. I suspect we all have times in our history that were highly influential, inspiring and happy. Once tasted we kick and scream not to be moved on. I struggled to keep my boozy pub life even though everyone else ultimately deserted me. I did not enjoy it but somehow it allowed a tiny part of me to remain in that explosion of happiness I felt after leaving school.

I notice how trying to stay with those flashes of elation, even though they are obsolete and no longer fun, ultimately becomes self-destructive, breaking up the smooth journey through life. Perversely it may be the good times that cause more problems than the traumatic ones. I have always gladly run forwards into a new phase of my existence if it means escaping a period of grief. It is the periods of extreme joy that have tripped me up for years to follow. Writing this book I recognise I was there again, flush with the success of Ringing Rocks, recording and now the stadium gig.

Steve was overly enthusiastic about the idea of a big stadium gig. I assume it was relief that I did not propose another Ringing Rocks style event. Again the team met and I could feel the swell of momentum.

I went home for a few weeks to be with my family whilst the mechanics of setting up such a performance ground forwards. Pauline suggested we go to the west coast when I returned and stay with her friend, the writer and philosopher Lucia Brescatti.

I felt uprooted travelling between the UK and USA so much. Never enough time to plant myself in any one place. Soon enough I was back catching up on progress with Steve.

"Just go out to LA with Pauline and keep promoting your gig. We'll take care of the nuts and bolts here."

As the plane took off Pauline jerked me out of my thoughts. "You know what I like about you?"

"My roguish good looks, my witty charm, my..."

Pauline smiled and hit me playfully across the chest.

"No, it's the way you do not have to surround yourself with females who are infatuated with you. That whole soap opera is so horribly obvious, so predictable and so disappointing. It makes the content, or lack of whatever these people are trying to do so cheap and transparent. You cannot imagine how I hate it all."

I groaned. I had the feeling we were off on another men are crass lecture.

"You don't have any of that. I don't see you flirting, or playing games with us, you just do your stuff, never charge any money and go home. You're even faithful to your wife. You are a real healer, you don't need to prop yourself up. You don't need all that material wealth to believe in yourself. You know the value of what you have because it is for real. You are just yourself. You'll see some real pretentious phoneys when we hit LA. It is a reflection on the depths of human stupidity that anyone can buy into it. I guess you can't blame people for taking advantage of idiots whose wallets are as loose as their brains."

"Yes, but do you think my behaviour is that important, surely the message is what counts." I was thinking of sleeping with Marlene.

"No, when I look at men, they are driven by endless concepts. Look at something like macrobiotics and it comes across as head stuff. A mass of mental masturbation. It should be focused on cooking and eating to feed your soul but instead it's jammed with all these spirals, levels of judgement, five elements, theorems and principles. What's that all about? It's a male trip. See you don't do that. You're direct and simple. Plus most of what you do is real, like the healing. That's why your behaviour is important."

"I know the concepts aren't reality. I know they are just head stuff but don't you think the macrobiotic ideas help explore food more. Even though concepts are just clumsy attempts to describe our universe don't you think they help us discuss life, encourage us to be a bit more objective."

"Sure, but the difference is that you know they're not real. You don't hold them up as though they are set in stone."

"I so wish you could have met Sigeyo, she had such an elegant, simple, dignified way of explaining it all. It felt like she was my grandmother, full of wisdom. To her it was all just energy. Sometimes it moved up or down or out or inward. Compressed in one place, thinned out in another, quick for a while and then stagnant. Even a child could understand it all. It was very much in tune with what you are saying. She felt that by taking a very simple idea and working with it repeatedly you not only master it but develop an intuition that brings amazing insights."

As Pauline talked on I found myself building up an irrational distaste for the LA healing scene.

When we arrived at Lucia's home we were assaulted by a wall of hysteria.

"Oh my angel, you'll never imagine what's happened, Zoe has turned into a bore. She used to be an angel but now she's grubbing around for roots. Oh Paula, it is such a tragedy, I had such high hopes, she's off the team. How can I do all this work on my own. I've been scrambled into the wrong rotten omelette."

Lucia looked to be in her sixties, half a head shorter than me, tanned, beautifully groomed, wearing a white T-shirt and light blue suit. I could detect a hint of an Italian accent.

"Lucia meet Adam."

Lucia didn't take her eyes off Pauline.

"There is so little time and now that stupid whore has exchanged a race horse for a donkey. Where's the vision? I invested so much time in Zoe, what now?"

"Lucia, let's go inside and talk more calmly."

Lucia stood to one side so we could pass. She then looked up and down the street before coming back in and closing the door. We shuffled through to the living room and I flopped into a huge brown leather bean bag. Lucia paced the room.

"Sit down, breathe, relax. What has she done?" Pauline asked, trying to placate. This had the opposite effect.

"What has she done?" Lucia became frenzied. "What has she done? She is working for Stelstack la Ghana, for a few cents more. She's sold out to a punk who peddles NLP. Can you believe it? I'm trying to save mankind whilst he's fiddling with people's brains."

"Let her take her path, Lucia. You have so much to offer, nobody can ever take that away from you. *Life After Life* was so beautifully written and so well received, let your mind do the talking through your book."

The change in her demeanour was astounding.

"Paula, you must move in with me. I need you here."

For the first time Lucia looked at me, pointing at Pauline.

"Look at her, just look at her, she has the poise of a gazelle, the strength of Bodicia, the wisdom of Buddha. Leonardo was the biggest fool in history for pissing on you. Well his sperm's in the gutter now."

Lucia's manner captivated me, I found myself entranced by the display. As she turned her face to me I felt myself change from a spectator to participant.

"I am so sorry, you must let me release all this crazy emotional turmoil that's spinning around my body. It's inherited hysteria. My parents ran a restaurant in Roma and there were constant dramas over the chef leaving, the maitre d' walking out. Even though I hated their ridiculous theatrics at the time, it planted a seed in me that sprouted when I turned forty and now it's in full flower. Now I'm even worse whenever someone departs, rejecting me like a soiled rag. The bitch!" Lucia took deep breaths. "You must have noticed how many people take on either of their parents' dramas as they age, oh to have been born into a family of calm rational souls."

"Let me look at you," Lucia took a step back and put her hand up to her forehead, as though shielding her eyes from the sun. "I have heard so much about you, my dear man. Paula tells me you are a spiritual virgin, still pure, no one has defiled your soul. I have idiotically dived into the depths of human depravity and some of it has stuck. Oh to be clean again."

The way Pauline explained NLP made sense to me. Unfortunately Lucia's introduction was through a salesman who perfected the methods and used them to pick her up in a bar. Lucia has since written NLP off as crude mental manipulation.

One way I test out a theory is to imagine explaining it to my father. Would it have the intellectual integrity to pass his science based logic? Conversely, I also imagine how I would communicate it to someone with little education, living off the land. As a result I have developed a cynicism that prevents me surging ahead from one new theory to another. They are all just opinions anyway. It amazes me how some of the people I have met have built an incredibly intricate illusion of life based on layers of flimsy ideology. Mine have been taken to bits, looked at from every angle and reconstructed again. None are perfect but I feel I can live with the faults they have for now.

In the morning Lucia took Paula and me to a Mind Body Spirit fair. The large halls were filled with white laminated cubic stalls. I could see people selling new age tapes, selling massage, selling shiny plastic feng shui gimmicks, selling, selling, selling. Supply meets demand. Except there was more supply and less demand so everyone was aggressively hawking their wares. Many made more of the price offer than what they actually offered. Ten per cent off all books at the show, half price tarot readings, one hundred dollars off our life training course if you register now.

"Sir, you want to try this massage chair. Guaranteed pain relief."

"Take the weight off your feet, fifteen minutes reflexology only twenty nine ninety nine."

Lucia settled for a reiki session. Pauline dived into a heated discussion with someone selling courses. I wandered over to hear her better.

"How can you justify over six thousand dollars to teach shiatsu?"

Here was a subject I had experience of.

"It's a professional course, fully certified."

"All you've done is raised the standard every year. More classes equals heavier fees. You're are milking those who are taken in by the idea they need bits of paper before they can heal."

Pauline turned to me.

How long did you study shiatsu?"

"Um, just over twenty days with Stephen."

"See, here is the greatest healer of our time and it only took three weeks."

The man in the tai chi style outfit looked at me.

"Listen lady, some people have the gift, but most need years of tuition."

"But not a week of business studies. You're trying to make a natural art into a profession on par with medicine. Thirty years ago my teachers railed against doctors and drugs companies and now people like you are turning each form of healing into a multi million dollar business. You want to become the very thing we were alternative from."

I couldn't imagine that Nirmala or Stephen had been anywhere near business studies. I could see the man had marked Pauline down as an irritant on the smooth march towards filling up his next course. Two women were waiting to talk to him and another prospective student was standing next to me. The professional shiny veneer fell away exposing the cheap woodchip underneath.

"I'm sorry lady but flakes like you give everything we are trying to do a bad name. People want treatments from professionals they can trust, a proper service, someone who knows her adductor from her abductor."

Pauline took a step forward so they were nose to nose. I admired her tenacity.

"Meeting you is like finding out the keys to the temple have been left with a thief. You may think it is a big laugh making money out of people's desire to help others but your karma will catch up with you."

The man took a step back and wiped his eye with a tissue. His expression of contempt for Pauline ignited a fire in my liver. A small crowd had gathered, drawn in by the sound of raised voices. Paula turned to me, her voice was shaking with emotion.

"Look at this man, he has helped hundreds of people cure themselves, some terminally ill, and yet he never charges a cent. And you know why, because he is true, he doesn't need to hide behind pieces of paper to prove himself, he doesn't need material wealth to value himself, he doesn't..."

"Exist?" the shiatsu salesman cut her off, "this man," he glared at me with the same contemptuous look, "is just flesh and blood, he eats, he craps, he wears nice clothes and if he's on some do it all for nothing trip he doesn't know how to value what he does."

I knew my time had come. I could feel the anger elongate my spine.

"Listen I could teach you what I do in a few days. The concept of charging for it is buying into the very system that's corrupting our planet."

The sneer returned. "Everyone has their price and I am sure you don't go without. Please don't hang around my stall posing as some kind of saint with your disciple here dumping your moralistic crap on us."

It started before my brain caught up with my actions. Whack, I kicked a massage stool over, I tore down posters, flung books to the ground, opened his cash box, threw bills into the air, tipped the coins across the floor, finally I turned the display table over.

I turned to storm off, bumping into Lucia.

"Oh by the lightening of Zeus, what have you done my dear. Let's get you out of here."

We marched towards the exit, the crowd opening before me. When I reached the doors a security guard blocked my way. The cops arrived and I was made to face the wall, spread my legs and submit to a body search. Next I was handcuffed and led out. After hours of waiting and form filling my interview began. I think my inquisitor misunderstood the situation but I let it run.

"Look, I've been there, my wife got ripped off by some jack ass selling a cure for candida. She was doubled up for weeks with the powder. But you can't go into him like that, don't you think I wanted to teach the punk a lesson. Go through proper channels."

I nodded solemnly. "We know where to find you and we'll be in contact if the captain wants to take this any further. You're free to go."

Reprimanded I sat tired and empty in the only shade outside waiting for Lucia.

"Well I see you're not afraid to turn against the grain, like a wild boar tearing through the undergrowth, challenging our comfort levels."

Slumped with my head propped up, soaking up the air-conditioned atmosphere I began to rest.

"That wasn't a good idea was it?"

"I am sure you realise more than most that we cling to mutual illusions, because we've all invested so much in the belief of them. You are a threat, my little hawk. You may think you are helping, but to most you are tearing up the very values they have built their lives on. Oh how happy we are to find another soul who shares our illusions, oh how mass belief gives us confidence. But here you come kicking away the supports. You might sneer but to many money is the reason for existence."

My grunt of agreement encouraged Lucia to continue.

"Of course history has been filled by the insane who take a wild delusion and despite mass opposition convince themselves they have grasped reality all on their own. Mostly we hate these poor souls, they are a threat, undermining all the good work that has gone into constructing the mutual belief systems that bind society together. After they die future generations sometimes take his or her mad illusions and use them as a guide for slowly re-orientating mass consciousness. I doubt you will live to see your take on life reach acceptance, but when you die it may be a comfort to think that the human sheep of consciousness may slowly follow your path."

A sobering analysis, that in my current state I fell into agreement with.

"Adam, I too have suffered for daring to speak out and laughed at the king without his clothes. I found out to my cost that attacking people's values, however corrupt, manipulative, unjust, bigoted, judgemental or sexist they may be, invites many difficulties. You cannot turn the tide of a massive common belief."

When we returned to Lucia's home Pauline greeted me with a hug.

"I am so, so sorry, Adam, it was all my fault. I feel terrible."

I pointed out that only I was responsible for my actions. To move the conversation on I asked Lucia about her book.

"I wrote *Life After Life* to help view life now from the after life. It is a meditation on projecting yourself forward into a state where you are floating into the ether looking back over your life."

Pauline looked at me with an expression of concern and suggested a massage. Lucia had a couch in her writing room. I undressed and lay on my front, pulling a white towel across me whilst Pauline mixed up her chosen oils. It felt so good to feel her warm hands squeezing my shoulders, stretching out the muscles beside my spine, kneading my tired buttocks. The unwinding let me fall freely until I began to float, weightless over a deep sleep. I remember being disturbed as Pauline asked me to turn over, for a moment I was in two worlds and then back into the black void.

I could smell years of cigarette and pipe smoke embedded in the green upholstery. The breeze through the window brought smells of burning coal. The rhythmic sway and clatter as steel wheels crossed joins in the rails aided my drift to slumber. I woke to the wail of the steam whistle. Finally the squeal of brake shoes grabbing wheel rims signalled my arrival. I leant out, twisted the metal handle and left my carriage. I heard the familiar clicks of the metal latches springing into sockets immediately followed by the clunk of heavy wood doors hitting carriage frames as I walked along the hot bitumen. Looking up the platform I saw her running, large pink roses on billowing white cotton, with a fawn mackintosh across her shoulders. Dropping the canvas holdall, I opened my arms.

"Oh darling, darling it has been so long. You must be tired. I've such a surprise for you, father has leant me the Austin. I hope you don't mind dearest, I thought we could motor along beside the river, past the mill and have a picnic. I've prepared everything and it would give us a chance to be on our own."

I struggled to make the transition from an airborne killing machine to romantic lover.

"Of course, let's."

We left the car near a wooden style and I carried the hamper over and along the bank. Parting the trailing branches of a willow, I spread out the soft tartan rug and we sat close to each other looking at the river through the screen of leaves.

"How are you darling? You look tired, has it been awful? Can you talk?"

"Not now my angel, but I will, I've been keeping a diary."

I turned to look at her, our heads were closer than I thought so when we faced each other our lips were almost touching. She leant forward and we kissed, tentatively at first and then our tongues connected. She lay back, I followed. As she pushed her right thigh towards me I let my leg slide over and between hers. We squeezed tightly, kissing, consuming the passion of the moment. Then pushing against my left thigh with her palm I realised she wanted me to put my other leg between hers. She pulled up the pink and white fabric, high up her torso. Looking down I could see a band of full curvy white skin, then her cream suspender belt, a sliver of flesh, her lacy underwear, the white of the tops of her legs followed by her beige stockings.

She struggled to undo my belt, her long fingers fumbled with the buttons, I helped her pull my trousers and underwear down, she immediately grasped me. I pulled her dress down off her left shoulder, slipped the strap of her brassiere down her arm, pulling until her breast was fully exposed. I began to tremble, a shiver emanated from my abdomen. I felt her pull the lace to one side and then the tip of my penis being manoeuvred into place with her left hand, her right gripped my buttock.

I looked up from her breast, when I connected with her eyes I knew it all, I knew what love was, the surrender, unconditional openness, willing me to drink from this ocean of emotion, and in that moment I felt myself returning the passion. Pulling me towards her I felt a resistance, she urged me on and I saw her wince, then three firm strokes precipitated convulsions from my loins. My legs felt weak and I shook a little.

Her eyes were still locked deep into mine.

"Anne I love you with all my heart."

We stayed in our embrace, savouring the connection. I began to feel the soft dabbing of wet fabric on my lower abdomen, the contact with Anne dissolved. I cried out.

"Don't worry Adam you had, um, a release."

I re-focused and saw Pauline standing over me with tissues in her hand.

"So who is this Anne that's responsible for such an explosion? Please don't tell me you're cheating on your wife."

In a state of exhilaration, I sat up. She's called Anne. Her eyes – where have I seen them before? In another dream? Surely not, somewhere in my current life. Try to relax, breathe gently, empty mind. Anne, Annie, Anne. And then every hair on my body stood on end as it floated in – Mrs Wadkins, Anne Wadkins I saw those eyes for real all those years ago when she was dying.

"Adam are you all right?"

"Paula, I've just found out who my lover was in a previous life. I must make a call, do you mind?"

"Sure go ahead."

I picked up Lucia's phone and typed in Justin's numbers. His mother answered sounding groggy.

"Hello it's Adam, Adam Saunders, is Justin in... Oh Christ I'm so sorry, I've lost track... Yes please if you think he's awake... Hello Justin... Yes I know I'm sorry... do you have a pen and paper handy?... I may have found the answer to those dreams... Justin could you please find out if there are any records of an Anne Wadkins dying in Welwyn Village in, let's see, 1975, then can you find out who she was married to, and I nearly forgot, see if there is any record of how he died...Thanks I really appreciate this, you know I wouldn't ask if it wasn't important."

Dressing, I explained the dreams to Pauline. I didn't want to make a drama so I persuaded her to keep it between us.

Lucia arranged for me to give an interview, some healing during the afternoon and a small talk in the evening. The interview gave me a chance to rationalise my behaviour at the exhibition. Here after some rest I could express my feeling in words, not physical aggression.

We explored my thoughts on why it is that when some people discover a form of healing their next instinct is to turn it into a business. The packaging, certificates, exams, associated products, services. New expensive clinics give the impression the whole healing movement has been swallowed up by the obsession with consuming. Money has become the drug, the messiah. Measure your worth by the money you earn. Can't even get a few words of wisdom without someone sending you the bill. Why? There must be more to life. I spat out my contempt for the judgementalism that pervaded the healing world, the conspiracy theories, the non acceptance of mass responsibility, trying to inflate limp egos through spiritual superiority, furthering the practitioner's cause rather than the patients, refusing to admit they could be wrong or that what they do is fallible.

The discussion moved on to the language of the new age healing arts and how people create cliques by adopting words that will confuse and alienate outsiders.

I derided the move to dressing up as professionals, playing doctors and nurses, taking healing arts that anyone can do and trying to make it exclusive for commercial gain. Most of all I attacked the charlatans who scare the innocent into handing over their money for some kind of phoney cure. Those feng shui consultants who see homes as full of divine doom, aura readers who see negative energy and un-corroborated illnesses in everyone, the therapists who so readily impose their pet theories on us. The energy rose up in me and I rode the wave ranting about enslaving trusting people in alien belief systems, dogma and rigidity, of leading them out of their own light and truth. It did not occur to me at the time that I was being judgemental myself.

In the morning we boarded the plane back to Philadelphia. I felt playful and turned to Pauline as we took off.

"I must ask you this, did you, you know, play with me whilst I was asleep to make me come. It's never happened during a massage before."

Pauline reddened slightly, looking shocked.

"I can't believe you just said that. Really, Adam, I was just massaging your leg and thigh when I did notice you became hard, then you became restless. You had this massive orgasm and I heard the name Anne. I'm shocked you would even think I would have taken advantage of you."

I smiled and winked at her. Pauline mocked horror and then smiled.

"No really, you're kidding aren't you?"

I laughed, why did she need a double take when I had just given her enough clues. I changed the subject.

"So how come you're not in a relationship?"

"Here's my take on relationships. You put ten young heterosexual men and ten young heterosexual women on an island and at the least half the women will want to have a relationship with the same one or two men. Inevitably there will be some men left single because none of the women want to be in a relationship with them and some of the women will remain single because they cannot bear to give themselves to someone they do not love. For me it is better to be single, on the off-chance that the one I love will become available again."

"An interesting differentiation between men and women. Wouldn't the men hold out for the ideal mate?"

"A few might, but in the main I think if there is good sex on offer along with domestic stability most men can re-orientate themselves to a second or third option. I think you need the sex more. It's harder for a woman. There needs to be the respect, admiration, trust; after all this is someone who will plant his seeds inside my womb. Of course it changes when the time for having a baby runs down."

"OK, go on."

"Well, I am one of those women who only falls for the one or two men in demand. If I succeed the relationship becomes unbalanced because he is in demand and by my own selectiveness I am not. If we go through a rocky patch he knows Chelsea, Ruby, Marlene or whoever will welcome him into her bed. For me there is no back up, no second option because I've written them all off, so it is me that has to find ways to make the relationship survive."

Pauline's eyes reddened around the rims, watering slightly.

"And despite all the giving in and compromises he can still go off and love someone else behind my back. So that, Adam, is why I am single and lonely. I don't want to compete, I don't want to play a game where the odds are stacked against me and I'm destined to fail."

"Come on Pauline, that's only one way of looking at it. I understand your point and of course there are fundamental differences between the sexes, but I don't see why you could not meet someone you love and someone who loves you so much that the competition becomes irrelevant."

Pauline turned and looked out of the aircraft window. I gently placed my hand on hers. Then turning back she began again.

"Maybe I'm just attracted to the wrong men. In my limited experience, men have an in-built need to chase women, to have an ongoing supply of sexual partners and of course that kicks me back into the arena of competing to keep my man. I'm too drained to go through all that again."

"I know what you mean about being in demand. I cannot say that has happened with women, it's usually one at a time," I felt a pang of guilt thinking of Christine and Sandy, Christine and Marlene, "but some of my happiest times have been when I have been in demand for work or for my friendship. It may be that the only reason I perpetuate this healing phenomenon is because I'm in demand and being in demand makes me feel so good about myself."

"Yes, but how do you feel happy when you're not in demand?"

I did not know the answer so I shrugged my shoulders and took a philosophical tack.

"It must be an in-built mechanism that ensures survival of human kind, wired into our DNA so that we try to be useful, wanting to be popular, work at becoming indispensable. I suppose it is our motivation for putting in the work required to create a society. Having something to offer equals happiness. It must also mean that evolution tells us that humans depend on having communities to survive."

"And for those that have zero to offer?"

"You're just feeling down. You of all people have so much to offer. Apart from your bodywork, your integrity, your philosophy, just a smile is enough to touch my soul. I have known you long enough to see how people gravitate to you, respect you. Your problem is as you said, you focus too narrowly on one or two people and miss all the opportunities to be in demand that exist around you, not just for a relationship but for a whole range of reasons. Have you read Dale Carnegie's *How to Win Friends and Influence People*?"

Pauline scowled at me.

"It's much better than the title. It shows you how to make other people feel better through very simple interaction. When we land I'll buy you a copy."

"Thanks."

"That sounded terribly insincere."

She smiled.

"See now I feel happier too. You should go around smiling and laughing insanely all the time – all your problems would be solved."

"Ha, ha, ha."

"Honestly, don't you think you take life a little too seriously at times? Perhaps if you saw the funny side more often, let go, drop your expectations a little, you would be happier and your magnetism would increase."

CHAPTER TWENTY-ONE

I am now listening to *Ezy Rider* and I feel my outer energy field being blown away by the power and lift of the music. It starts with a drum and lazy guitar riff with an incredibly long feedback driven note on top, then a wailing guitar melody crashes in. My emotions soar as Jimi begins singing and a new pounding, rising, distorted rift kicks in. Sounds like thundering horses, the wind whistling through the trees above, waves crashing to the shore. I am leaping onto the sofa, jumping around the room as I ride the exhilaration.

Hendrix's ability to create beautiful music out of a collection notes, changing riffs or flashes of instrumentals instead of strumming out predictable three chord songs with a middle eight, marks him out as one of my musical heros. Sometimes I am so in awe, so overwhelmed and astounded by the creativity of members of the human race that it is enough to restore my faith in mankind.

It also makes me question Lucia's asserting that we are no longer producing future classics, that we have degenerated into a grey mulch. It is always easier to go back in time, to be selective and hold up the masters from any period and point out that what is happening now falls flat. I make a note to work this into my book.

Back in Philadelphia I found out that Organica had been released to the radio stations and was due for general release. My huge stadium gig was less than a month away. I made the most of this time to keep in contact with my family. Christine sounded a little flat at times. Aaron was due to come over and I tried to persuade her to come with him.

"Don't worry darling, I'm just feeling very tired. You're so busy and if I was there I would want all of you, not to be hanging around on my own waiting to see you at night. When you come back I just want us to have a month to ourselves, no distractions, you and me and our bambinis."

I felt disconcerted. Not by her words but by the delivery. It sounded as though all her energy was on the surface, as though the foundation had fallen away. I resolved to not make any commitments. I would spend that month with her.

The news from Justin arrived. "You really owe me this time Adam. She wasn't buried in Welwyn but in Woodbridge in Suffolk. You were right, she was married. To George Wadkins from the same place. It all fits in with your dreams. He flew for the RAF during the Battle of Britain, survived it but then crashed over East Anglia a year later. They are buried next to each other in the village church. If it helps, there is a train station, mill and river."

I had to breathe deeply and slowly to contain the rush of truth to my head. Here was proof that I had knowledge of another beings life who died before I was born. I broke into a cold sweat as I remembered that look in Anne's eyes as she died holding my hand.

"As soon as I return, I want to visit their graves."

"I'll come with you. After all the research and your dreams I feel part of the family."

I called Christine with the news. Justin had got there first and again I thought she sounded strained, as though she was forcing herself to sound cheerful and interested.

Aaron turned up. Being the gregarious soul he is he soon integrated himself into my US social scene. I could see he was mesmerised by Marilyn, I suspected a romance on the horizon and experienced a twinge of jealousy.

Whilst I worked through my daily healing sessions he was entertained in various cafés by members of the team. I could see Aaron and Stoosh recognised a kindred spirit in each other. They assumed that Aaron, being my closest friend, was part of the group and included him in any meetings we had. Now we were eleven.

I was pleased to see Pauline had finished reading my gift of Carnegie's *How to Win Friends and Influence People*. She did seem more ready to smile and take greater interest in the more potentially mundane side of interactions. I even caught her paying Stoosh a compliment.

I heard my song on the radio for the first time today. Once the initial crash of excitement gave way to a feeling of contentment I called Seriously to find out what was happening.

"The brothers are giving Organica the big up, Macro-man."

Seriously wanted me to write for the website he was putting up. I realised there were little glimpses in my life where it all comes together. The place, the people, my mood and suddenly the world opened, my spirit soared and I had the ideas, the messages and the means to express them.

The biggest challenge I still have is to write. Occasionally coffee is the drug that helps. Kicking my nervous system into a state of electric frenzy I am able to spark the creative process. It is a delicate balance as too much coffee too often and I become erratic and then over time, immune to it. I need general abstinence to feel the required buzz when I need it. Coffee must have had an amazing impact when it was first introduced to society, a legal drug that smelled divine and had the taste to go with it.

Emily arrived in a hire car. For a moment as we sat around drinking cups of kukicha with Aaron I felt transported back to our parents' house and the three of us sitting in my room listening to Primal Scream.

I felt the bond of time with them. In that moment I felt free from the expectations. I took off my healer clothing and felt myself with them. Having Aaron and Emily mix up with my new friends did confuse the old me and the barefoot guru I had transformed into in Philadelphia.

Steve organised a meeting for the big gig. The whole team and Seriously made it. This time it was agreed that Marilyn would start the ball rolling. For the first time I voiced my desire to give it a more spiritual, even religious tone. There was resistance to letting religion in but an inexplicable force was driving me. The general consensus was that Ringing Rocks was a great success, I had my rap out and more of the same was the logical path. That way everyone knew the score and could play their part.

It started after the LA trip, a feeling that rather than condemn I needed to create, to put myself up to be knocked down rather than be so critical of the people in the religious, new age or healing scenes. My actions at the exhibition and subsequent interview won me many enemies, just as my earlier attacks on the food industry and some aspects of established religion had. It is far easier to trample down someone else's sandcastle than build your own. I could see the others were not going to understand so I dropped the argument but deep down I knew my desire to give our movement a more spiritual dimension would resurface.

Marlene began pumping the media with press releases on my big gig using the Ringing Rocks event, my healing successes, kicking over the table and my controversial interview to keep my name and the event alive in the media. The hype began to gather momentum and little by little, I began to believe it. I felt the power, the sense of destiny, the opportunity there for the taking. I asked Pauline to drive me out to Ringing Rocks one night so I could stand under the stars and soak up the cool, dark atmosphere of the night. I wanted to come back here for the atmosphere.

For the first time I could imagine myself sparking off a new religion. I could feel the words in my head. The timing would be perfect. The gig was on the full moon and it was spring.

Organica made a slow start in terms of sales. Seriously and I met to rehearse, create new songs and most importantly develop a medium for me to rant freely. Seriously worked on a range of sounds and rhythms that could form the backdrop to what I wanted to say. It was down to him to anticipate where I was heading and create the sonic vibration. We worked out a series of signals to help. I practiced a number of new rap lines, trying to anticipate my mood and incorporate all the new messages I wanted to express.

Stoosh and Brad were working on the lighting and big screen images. They were bringing together photographs of nature, natural foods and cutting them with junk food wrappers blowing through desolate streets. Brad had put together shots of children from around the world and these were contrasted with footage of manmade pollution. They included pictures of obese children, children in hospitals, deformed infants, young corpses from Rwanda. I was about to deliver an emotional message.

I felt I was slowly limbering up for the big event. Aaron insisted we join a gym and work out together every day. Mentally I was trying out different parts of what I wanted to say on different members of the group. Letting them help me hone my ideas informally, challenge me, stretch me a little. Aaron was the best company for this as he knew me from old and did not hold back from telling me if he thought an idea was crap.

CHAPTER TWENTY-TWO

When I woke on the big day I knew the countdown had begun. I tried to pace myself, but my mind sped up too quickly. I couldn't find my inner peace, my nervous system tightened, pinging with raw excitement. I didn't want to peak too early. We sat around talking, Marilyn tried out parts of her talk, I ran through some last minute ideas.

In the late morning Seriously appeared and led me out for a sound check. Here I could feel the enormous stage, see the huge screen behind, familiarise myself with the lighting. We watched the stadium fill up.

One last call to Christine, she was out so I left a message, then I got ready. As the final minutes passed Pauline suggested we stand in a circle and put our arms around each other. It was good to feel the sense of togetherness. Pauline was on my right and Emily on my left. I soaked up their warmth and felt a greater power in my abdomen, solid and substantial. My last act was to change into a clean white T-shirt and jeans.

Marilyn held her nerve to deliver an incredible warm up. I knew she had rehearsed her speech but it still rolled out very naturally. She wore a short red skirt and yellow sleeveless shirt, just buttoned across her breasts. No jewellery, bare feet and long wild hair. Her body language radiated out into the crowd, I found myself absorbed with every detail, the tilt of her head, the way she tipped one foot resting on her toes, the casual look of her hand on her hip. I liked her style and also removed my trainers and socks. I suddenly felt a great attraction to Marilyn, I wanted to rush out and hug her.

My thought must have reached her because Marilyn ran over to me, pulled me onto the stage and gave me the big warm hug I craved. Her enthusiasm was infectious, and without realising it I was out there, centre stage.

"Please welcome, Adam, the amazing Macroman who…"

A roar from the crowd drowned her out.

As Marilyn left the music came crashing in, the power of the sound waves swept me away and I let it run longer than planned before coming in with the words to the song. I could see a mass of heads bobbing up and down, hands waving at me. The music and familiar song sheet allowed me to launch into a powerful rant. I leapt across the stage surfing on a wave of adrenaline.

Once the sounds died down I paced myself launching straight into my message about food and health. Whenever I found a meaningful line I repeated it over and over to the beat, occasionally I managed to return to a previous line using it as a chorus. This had the effect of sparking off waves of clapping. When a line became familiar, people chanted along with me.

Whilst Seriously accompanied the big screen imagery I walked into the audience and began healing. The cameraman followed, sending the close ups onto the screens. People pushed children with string tied around their waists to me on a wave of hands like a human conveyor gently letting them down into my arms. I tried to seek out those who needed me most. As before I used the healing to educate everyone in the audience. My mobile mike ensured my voice boomed out of the PA.

It was hard to turn anyone away but eventually I felt it was time to climb back on stage. I ran through my familiar routines until I felt I was entwined into the soul of the crowd in front of me. Now it was time to deliver what I felt my life had been leading up to, I breathed in the moment.

"Brothers and sisters let's start a new religion. The time has come to let go of the religions with blood on their hands. Let's dispel the torturers, women haters, sadists, perverts, control freaks and judgemental moralists. No more fighting, no more religious hatred, no more persecution."

If religion was simply a means to change our perception of the world I wanted to give people one that would save them from this life of slavery to money, addiction to poisonous foods, from this shallow, superficial existence. I wanted to lead everyone to a more natural healthy land.

"I want to build a religion with you where men and women are equal, where we are content within ourselves to let people choose their beliefs, a movement that encourages its members to find spiritual inspiration within themselves, not through buildings and imagery. Let's create a space where we can heal each other."

Seriously managed to adjust to pure, gentle, melodies rising and falling. I fell to my knees emptying my mind as I reached out with my hands for inspiration.

"No coercion, no pressure. Rather than preaching, rather than using religion as a means to manipulate society, rather than make people feel bad about themselves, let's be receptive, ready to help, reaching out when needed, a passive religion where there is always a warm heart, open arms, a kiss on the cheek. No guilt, no sin, no beating ourselves up, just a pure and simple worship of ourselves and the world we live in. Let's recapture that sense of appreciation, marvel and curiosity we had as children and keep it alive. Help me build a community that will give each of us the power to live life to the full. A real life, not synthetic and superficial.

"Now, more than ever, our planet needs people who can take the initiative and lead us away from the black pit of manic consumption. I want to eat well, to build a healthy body and active mind but it is so much easier to do it together. Do you want to join me?"

A cheer ran through the crowd. A spontaneous chant of 'new religion' rang out from the audience. After the shouting died down I led a mass meditation. Breathing together we emptied our minds. Once I sensed people had cleared their heads I expressed the thoughts floating through my mind on religion. I relied on my trance-like state where I soaked up inspiration and simply verbalised the waves of energy. I felt as though the vast energy of the universe was speaking through me. Is this what religious leaders felt when they claimed to be God's messenger?

"Can you commit to treating your body as a temple, a holy vessel where you resonate with the beauty of the universe?"

A roar came back.

"That means doing your best not to pollute your body with crap, I'm talking junk foods, sugary drinks, commercial processed poison that insults your intelligence. I'm talking about eating real whole foods, natural organic produce, full of life. Foods from the land, not a factory."

A more muted acceptance returned.

"Can you commit to improving yourself everyday? Exercise, study, sports, learning new skills. When you put your head on your pillow you should be able to list at least one way in which you have developed. Invest in yourselves!"

Applause.

"Can you commit to supporting those people around you to do the same? Reach out for help when you need it and give unconditionally when it is needed from you. Just doing what is required to help your friends, without letting yourself assume a position of power. Simply listen and give them what they ask for."

Another buzz of approval.

"Can you commit to loving those close to you just as they are? Opening your heart to them, letting them under your skin, sharing your joys and fears.

"Can you bring up your children so they embrace a new understanding of the world and break this spiral of self destruction?

A rising tide of approval rang back.

"If you can do this you will live a life to die for, you will leave this world happy and content knowing you have taken yourself as far as you could go.

"I want to go there myself, but I am weak and need your

support, because I know the challenges I am also ready to help, I want to walk through this life, hand in hand with all of you. Face it together and see where it takes us. No regrets at the end, just a love of the substance of life."

Now there was silence broken by a solitary female voice.

"I love you Adam, and I will follow you to the end of the world."

Another cry of excitement.

"No, no, that's not my message, please don't follow me, walk with me, guide me, be my companion. Let's enjoy the journey together."

I signalled Seriously to start into a rap rhythm leading me back to my original radio release. The girls, Brad and Aaron joined in.

We finished with a mass healing session where we breathed our life-force out into our hands and then laid them on each other. I jumped down into the audience feeding my energy into the knotted web of people laying their hands on each other. Waving to my friends they joined me and spread out into the mass of people.

I used my radio mike to maintain the breathing and healing rhythm as I laid my hands on people, wading through the warm colourful bodies. When I reached one of the exits I cried out, "Goodbye friends, I love you."

I met a security man who took me through a maze of corridors back stage. Marlene had arranged a media session immediately after the show. Meeting outside the dressing rooms she grabbed me and led to the awaiting press. A woman with dark curly hair started. "What is the main difference between your new religion and all the others. I mean do we really need another?"

"The difference is that this religion is devoted to making you a better person in every way. What I am proposing focuses on you. Spiritual wellbeing is linked to creating a clean, healthy physical body. This means eating real living foods straight from a farm, exercise and stretching. I am not aware of a current religion that aims to build up the individual, from the inside. From the little I know most are designed to mould people into a common belief system."

A deep male voice broke in. "Doesn't that sound more like the beliefs of the east, is this the result of studying with," he looked down at the press release Marlene had prepared, "Sigeyo?"

"Yes, it's true that she has had a great influence on me but I think it is more of a common sense spiritual ideology. I am sure that anyone here would design a philosophy based on similar principles if you wanted to extend the life of the members and the planet."

A new accent. "How do you intend to spread your message? Will these big events become a regular feature?"

"For a start I don't want it to be focused on me. I can accept I have initiated the movement but it will gain its own momentum. As long as people do not try to assume positions of power, we can grow organically. The whole point is to empower not enslave."

When we reached the dressing room Seriously, Steve and Mike were already there, it took another twenty minutes for Brad to arrive and complete the team. I sensed a mutual flush of excitement. We arranged to go out to eat together. Steve found somewhere private where we would be free from interruption. There were thirteen of us now; Marilyn, Marlene, Pauline, Brad, Steve, Mike, Stoosh, Seriously, Aaron, Cheryl and Emily. I included Christine, although she was not there in person, I felt her presence. In fact as we sat down I felt it very strongly.

We toasted in the new age of freedom through our religion with a bottle of spring water.

Just as my energy crashed Emily said she wanted to leave. I dozed in the car and just managed to stagger up the steps to my apartment. I cleaned my teeth whilst listening to my phone messages. It was Justin.

"Adam, Adam, are you there? Bad news mate. Christine's been taken into hospital. She has a blood clot in her brain. Started throwing up an hour ago. Sounds very serious. You need to be here. Give me a call on my mobile when you get this. I'll check out flights."

Emily stood in the doorway looking white and frozen. I started to punch Justin's number into the phone. He left a message for me on his outgoing message. Flight times from JFK. I could just make the American Airlines flight at 11:55pm.

We ran down the stairs into the car.

"Passport Adam."

I ran back, emptied drawers onto the floor, checked it was mine and ran back. Emily drove to the airport, she did not attempt to make small talk, just reached across and held my hand as we cruised along the expressway.

I felt sick as I ran into the airport. We found the American Airlines counter and Emily paid for the ticket with her card.

"Do you have any money?"

I pushed my hands into empty pockets.

"Here take this, she pressed folded dollar bills into my palm."

One long hug and kiss and I was gone. No luggage just the clothes I was wearing. Sitting on the flight I thought through all the possibilities. What was it I'd sensed when we spoke on the phone? Now I could take that month off and dedicate it to Christine, I would take the rest of my life off if that was what was required. By the time we landed I was seeing the world through tired red eyeballs. Numb, wired, I felt I would snap. Once I had pushed my way off the plane I waded through Heathrow and onto the Express.

CHAPTER TWENTY-THREE

More phone calls revealed that Christine was in the Lister hospital in Stevenage. Taxi, train, taxi. My mind was spinning so frantically I could not hold any thought, my emotionally energy had spread out so much I was worried I would not find the stillness to heal.

When I arrived, Justin was waiting at the entrance and took me up to the ward. Christine's parents were in the room sitting on the metal-framed bed. Walking round them I saw my wife's pale face, limp on the pillow. John hugged his wife, holding her head to his chest.

"I'm afraid she is dying, Adam. She had a massive haemorrhage in her brain."

I sat on the bed placing my hand on the sides of Christine's head.

"Where are Matthew and Eleanor?" My voice sounded strained and broken.

"With your neighbours, Angela and Martin."

My mind switched out of the world around me and into Christine's. Through my hands I felt a city of lights, tiny pin pricks of energy filling her head. I tried to breathe my life into her, I tried to precipitate a crescendo of healing energy, I tried to feel my hands pass though her skull and repair the broken tissue. I connected but I could not initiate any change. I pressed my lips to her forehead, wiped a tear from my eye on her eyebrow. Feeling my lips against her soft cheek I whispered into her ear.

"Christine darling, can you hear me? I love you so much, please don't leave us. Remember how I came back to you, you can do it too, please turn round darling, come back to us. You can do it darling."

I could not feel any response. I willed with all my heart for her to show some sign of reviving. My mind ached with the force of concentration.

"Christine, you know I'll always love you and the children, you know I'll always look after them. I promise you, I'll be the best father they can ever have."

Naked fear spread from my pelvis as I felt the pricks of light fade like a city falling asleep. Her breathing faded. I willed all my energy into the fading sparks.

"Please darling, I beg you not now, please stay, please."

A continuous sound filled the room, the door opened; a nurse came in and took Christine's wrist.

"I'm sorry she gone."

"NO, NO, NO! Please God, don't do this to me. Please give me another chance." I lay my head on Christine's chest and wept. Mary put her hand on my hair. John spoke softly. "I think she was hanging on until you came. I'm sure that once you were close and you told her how you would look after Matthew and Eleanor, she was able to go peacefully. There was no more you could do."

Part of me still believed it wasn't true, she was playing, she would make an amazing recovery, it was all another nightmare. But I was still in the hospital room, still lying with my head on the body of my wife. I could hear Mary softly sobbing, asking her husband why, why her little girl, why now.

I remembered floating away after my accident I looked up wondering where Christine was. In my mind I begged her to come back. Part of me felt rejected that she was leaving me but those feelings were drops in my ocean of sadness. I felt so sorry for my dearest lover, sorry that after all her hard work, all her attention and devotion to her babies, she was not here to continue her journey with Matthew and Eleanor. I knew she would not have left them without a fight.

I wanted to carry her with me, hold her tight, keep her warm. We must have stayed in the room for another hour, too numb to move, wanting to be there just in case life returned. I wanted to sleep, fall into a big black void next to Christine, let my soul go and merge with hers.

Mary broke the silence. "We'd better go and collect Matthew and Eleanor."

I gave Christine one last kiss and held her close to me before I willed my lifeless limbs out of the ward, out of the hospital and into John's car. I've lost a wife, they've lost a daughter and Matthew and Eleanor have lost a mother, how sad, how very sad.

Justin squeezed my shoulder as we walked out of the hospital and wandered off to his car without speaking.

"Daddy! Daddy you're back!"

I hugged the children, holding their faces against mine. I could hear John talking in hushed tones to Angela. How I needed his strength now. We walked across the front garden to our house. Back on our old sofa I sat Matthew and Eleanor on my knees. How could I say it?

"Where's mummy? Did she have to stay at hospital? Is she not feeling well daddy?"

"Darlings, mummy's gone to heaven. She loves you both very much and always will, but," tears streaked down my face, "but she had something wrong with her head and couldn't live anymore."

Eleanor looked up into my blurry eyes. "But daddy, you could have healed her with your special hands."

"I tried, I really tried but it was too late."

"We'll never see mummy again."

"No Matthew, at least not in the same way."

My son began to weep, his sorrow spreading to Eleanor.

"But daddy why didn't she come and see us, like you did when you had your accident."

"I just don't know Eleanor, perhaps she didn't know how. I don't even know how I did it."

Matthew turned to me shaking.

"Who will tuck me up and cuddle me in bed, who will make my school lunches? I want mummy to come back, daddy."

"I'll do everything for you now, darlings. I may not be able to do it as well as mummy but I'll try my best for you and I promise you both I will not go away again."

Mary made some tea. Nothing interested me now, I wanted to disappear, but for the sake of my son and daughter I fought to remain in the room acting out the motions of normality.

Christine had disappeared so quickly the house was littered with the evidence of her last acts. Brown rice, barley and wheat berries soaking in a pot, Matthew's homework waiting to be checked, a half read copy of *Any Human Heart* and cup of cold tea on the table, it all felt so incomplete.

At least it was just the five of us, all brought together by the loss of Christine. I didn't want to talk to anyone, not to explain nor to deal with sympathy. I just wanted to lose myself in the feelings.

With a great effort I managed to carry on reading to Matthew and Eleanor in bed. Christine was nearly a quarter of the way through the book. I could imagine her lying here, laughing at the funny parts, giving the characters special voices. This reading was flat but I wanted to persevere. Keep a part of mummy alive.

That night Christine came to me. I could feel her in the room, snuggling up to my back, putting her arm around me, her hand on my tummy, resting her face against my neck; it was all a nightmare after all, she was here for real.

"Christine is it you? You're here, I thought you had died darling."

I turned to a cold empty bed, alone. I lifted Matthew and Eleanor one at a time into my bed and lay between them, hoping she would come and visit us, but I couldn't sleep and she didn't.

The next morning I was surprised at how I still engaged in my normal routines, taking a shower, eating breakfast, cleaning my teeth. My life had disintegrated and yet here I was functioning, the difference was that I had switched off my emotions.

Turned off the answering machine, walked in the woods, thought a lot. What would have happened if I had come home earlier from America? Why did Christine die whilst eating such a healthy diet? Surely the macrobiotic foods would have protected her. I used to think of my diet as the best health insurance policy. Eat well, exercise, avoid stress and live a long life free from illness.

Did she cheat? Sneak out for colas or ice creams. She used to take a lot of aspirin for headaches before macrobiotics, could they have thinned her blood too much? Perhaps she piled loads of salt onto her food whilst I was away. Not Christine. I don't think she felt as strong about it all as strongly as I did but she seemed to enjoy the foods. She wasn't the bingeing type but who knows, perhaps she hated it all and just did it to please me.

A rational voice came from the back of my head. It's all percentages, subtle shifts. We live in a world made up of different shades of grey not black and white. More people do go to Accident and Emergency wards, have car accidents and commit crimes during the full moon but it is only by a few percentage points. Eating well leads to better health and reduces the risk of serious illness, but by how much? Certainly not a hundred percent. In scientific terms even twenty five percent would be a lot. Would you change your diet for those odds?

Alternatives. Was it destiny? Karma? Not really wanting to be here? Negative emotions? Bollocks, I always thought they were just pathetic excuses to help humans come to terms with the hell life can be. I'm part of a civilised world that is so removed from death that there have to be reasons to try to quell the spread of fear. Don't worry you'll be all right. Christine died because she didn't want to live enough, because she ate too much cheese, because her husband didn't nourish her. I felt anger surge through my body, picked up a large branch and repeatedly whacked it against a tree trunk. As my rage consumed me I let out a long howl of despair. My foot became entangled in brambles and I fell into the soft leaves, my body shaking with grief.

I've never been close to someone else's death. I've never killed an animal with my bare hands. Death comes neatly wrapped in plastic with a bar code across it on supermarket shelves. Where did that thought come from?

Read Matthew and Eleanor stories, ate a little, discussed the funeral with Mary and John, slept after lunch, found one of Christine's old T-shirts, held it to my face. I breathed her scent, tears flooded into the fabric. Later made a Brio train track, played Uno, fell asleep putting Matthew and Eleanor to bed. Waited for Christine but she did not return. Not that night.

Compiled a list of people to invite to the funeral with John and Mary. John made the arrangements, a church funeral in the village. The same church we vowed 'til death do us part'.

"Do you want to speak at the funeral Adam? Only if you feel up to it."

I agreed.

I looked through all our photograph albums after Matthew and Eleanor were in bed. More tears, more pain in my chest, more emptiness. I still cannot believe I will never see her, touch her, hear her, smell her, taste her again.

The effort to pull myself up from sinking into despair was proving too difficult. I had a deep fear that I would not cope, that Matthew and Eleanor would suffer, no mummy and a miserable father. I felt alone, left behind. I remembered how she wanted to spend more time together. Thank God our relationship changed after the accident. If I could cling to one comfort it was that we had been so close during our final few years together. How could I live without that loving look in her eyes, without her playful smile, without her soul.

I recognised a part of me wanted to punish myself, to increase the pain, to never smile again. Was it that I felt betrayed by nature, the injustice of it all? My wife ate a healthy macrobiotic diet for the last few years and yet she was taken from me. Perhaps but I also felt guilty. Why didn't I recognise the signs in her voice? I should have rushed back immediately. Christine was more important to me than anything that happened in America.

I dreamt of Anne looking at me, she had been crying, reaching out but not able to touch me, mouthing words I could not hear. I was being taken from her.

Emily came back from Canada and stayed with us. On the day of the funeral Emily drove me to the church, I was suited and sallow. People I didn't know arrived. Then Justin approached. He appeared embarrassed, awkward and distant. I assumed he didn't know how to relate to me in this situation.

My eyes blurred and I lost focus as I saw Aaron walk through the gate with the Americans. They were all there. I didn't want to cry here, I wanted to be strong but just the sight of them brought it all flooding to the surface, I melted into Aaron's arms. He didn't talk, he just held me.

They took it in turns to hold me, pat me on the shoulder, squeeze my hand, pass me from one to another like a broken doll.

"What can I say, I am so sorry."

"There is nothing I can say that will make you feel better but I just want you to know we are all here for you, really."

"It's OK, it'll be all right, you have to grieve, take all the time you need."

"Tragedy happens, man, but we're here for you just as you've been there for us."

"I've been there, my wife died five..." Something I didn't understand. "It doesn't get any better or worse but it changes, believe me it will change, sometimes you'll miss her so bad," a mumbled sentence I couldn't decipher. "Sometimes you'll feel warm just thinking of her, sometimes you'll feel proud talking to people about her and yep sometimes it'll feel like you can't go on." A few incomprehensible words petered out.

"I love you Macroman."

"You mustn't blame yourself for this. There are powers so much bigger than any of us, we're just specks of dust blowing in the wind. You can't always change destiny."

"Although I never met Christine, I know she was very special to you, she must have been an amazing person."

"We're all here for you, please, if there's anything you need."

I made up the team that shouldered Christine's coffin into the church. To be so close, my head inches from hers, if only. After we set the casket down, I sat between Matthew and Eleanor holding their little hands.

"This is where we say goodbye to mummy, darlings. Let's pray that she is happy and tell her we'll be all right. I don't want her to worry."

The vicar invited me up to give the eulogy. Unprepared I walked over to Christine and laid my hand on the case looking up at our guests.

I reached into my pocket and unfolded a page from *A Prayer For Owen Meany:*

"When someone you love dies,
And you are not expecting it,
You don't lose her all at once;
You lose her in pieces over a long time –
The way the mail stops coming,
And her scent fades from the pillows and even from the clothes in her closet and drawers.

Gradually, you accumulate the parts of her that are gone.
Just when the day comes – when there is a
Particular missing part that overwhelms you with the feeling that she is
gone, forever – there comes another day,
And another specifically missing part."

I paused letting the feelings rise to my throat. As I looked up I saw Josephine sitting at the back looking straight into my eyes. Her serenity helped me carry on.

"Christine my love I feel you close, you will always be in my heart. I can still feel you inside me. I can hear your voice in my head, I can feel your warmth when Matthew and Eleanor need a cuddle. Now you are leaving you have also taken a part of me with you. I feel empty, there is a hole in my chest, we have been pulled apart at a time when I could finally give you my love."

I remembered seeing my father with the black haze across his chest in my dream. Did mum take his heart with her when she died? Poor dad, how did he cope? I took a deep breath in, shaking slightly, letting the tears flow freely.

"Christine, I know I caused you much pain at times and you must know I am truly sorry for every time I missed the opportunity to make you smile and laugh. I don't think I really knew how to love, but you showed me and since my accident I have loved you. Thank you for that, because when I love you, I can feel your love."

Eleanor ran over to me and I picked her up, squeezing her to my chest.

"Christine I know you devoted yourself to Matthew and Eleanor and I promise you, darling, I will step in and for the rest of my life give them both all the love they can take. Please have no regrets. You did everything you could, you led a wonderful life, you gave so much. You gave something to everyone, you enriched the world you lived in and I think you should be very proud of your life here, because I am truly proud of you."

I leant onto the coffin for support.

"Christine you are my lover, my guide and when I'm afraid, alone or cold I will think of you, I will find that part of you inside me."

I walked back to my pew and put my arm around Matthew. John gave my shoulder a squeeze.

I shook with fear as Christine was lowered into her grave, gone forever, left in the cold damp ground to rot away. I wanted to take her body home with me. How could somebody that exuded so much fun, love and energy end here?

After the funeral everyone was invited back to John and Mary's home. I switched onto autopilot. Shaking hands, hugs, taking the sympathy, hearing offers of help, listening to someone reminisce about Christine picking flowers as a child. I let it all wash over me because I didn't want any of this. It was all wrong, I wanted to be on my own, I wanted to hide and preserve my feelings. A little oasis of peace surrounded Josephine and I felt comfortable standing next to her.

To my surprise Josephine took my hand and led me out to Justin's car. Justin opened the door for me.

"You're dying in there, Adam. Let me take you to Anne and George. Perhaps you will find solace there. I'll go and tell John and Mary and say goodbye on your behalf."

Without replying I sat in the passenger seat and Jo climbed into the back. As Justin drove off I closed my eyes. I felt so tired.

It was a long drive and by the time we parked outside the church gate I was feeling more settled. English churches can be so similar. A portico, gravel path, flint stone belfry, dark wooden door, notices photocopied onto faded coloured paper pinned to a board, mossy stone graves, it could easily be the church where we buried Christine.

Justin, Josephine and I split up looking for the gravestones. Some were so faded it was hard to read them. I tried to trace the shallow lettering with my fingers. It was Justin who found them side by side, on the higher ground close to an old red brick wall. I pictured Anne as I knelt laying my hand on the long grass growing over her. I thrust my fingers deep into the damp soil and was surprised at how tranquil I felt there. I leant forward onto my knees and lost myself in the atmosphere.

Justin lay on his back looking up at the clouds and fell asleep. I lay between the graves pulling at the grass, rolling soil between my fingers. Josephine sat next to me in silence.

The clouds were moving fast. Was it Sigeyo who compared clouds to emotions, ever-changing crossing the sky? There was no resolution, no sense of completion, no flash of enlightenment, nothing to enable me to go back and face the world, just a sense of peace I had not experienced for a long time. Before we left I took some stones from the soil over Anne and George's graves. It felt reassuring holding them to my navel on the way home.

When I returned everyone except Emily had left. I registered the look of concern. Did I look that bad? I had a sudden urge to lie on the sofa and cuddle up with Emily, as we did as children. We had put on adult moral clothing now, confined ourselves within the straight jackets of normality and in any case, how would I begin. Justin drove Josephine to the station.

That night I fought off my natural reservations and crawled into Emily's bed.

"You can't sleep either? It has really shaken me to see you so upset. Do you remember when dad died? My world fell apart. I never want to experience that again and I feel so bad that it is happening to you."

I remembered how Emily had looked after our father after mother died how close they were towards the end. How terrible not to make the most of all those important relationships, how I wasted my time in pubs instead.

We lay in bed reminiscing; mum, dad, Hugo. We laughed about our curly haired uncle, giggled at the childhood church services, remembered some of our made up stories. That night broke any unease between us and for the rest of the week Emily and I stuck to each other in the way we did during those summer holidays in Salcombe.

"I so wish you could come to Canada with me. Promise me you will visit us soon. You would get on really well with Pete. Matthew and Eleanor would love it. Don't just say yes and then forget us."

I didn't want to commit and then let her down so I just kissed my sister and waved goodbye. Thank you Emily.

I developed a routine of visiting Christine's grave after lunch.

One day the rain forced me to sit in the church. Sitting there I felt a sense of peace alone in the big empty space. Without thinking I fell into a prayer. Reaching out was easier here, my emotions resonated around the old stone walls.

Out of the atmosphere a guilt arrived. How I could I have attacked religion, a force that has brought comfort to so many in their time of grief?

CHAPTER TWENTY-FOUR

My spirits sank after Emily left but I forced myself back to the routine I had used to recover from my depression. The gym, walking Matthew and Eleanor to school, cooking macrobiotic food, playing football, reading, anything to keep my head above water. The slow, careful attempts to become a real functional human being ended when I received a call from a Mr Phillips.

"Hello Mr Saunders?"

"Yes."

"Adam Saunders."

"Yes."

"I am just following up a story that has come from America alleging you had an affair with a Marlene King. Can you comment or give me a quote?"

I was stunned into silence.

"Well, would you like to deny it? We are planning on running the story tomorrow."

I slammed the phone down in shock. I tried calling Marlene but the man was still there.

"Look, I am sorry about your wife. You once helped a friend of mine. Couldn't you just give me an exclusive, get your version out first?"

Marlene's phone rang on, she must have turned her answer phone off. Justin wasn't any help and Aaron had disappeared. I couldn't face calling John and having to explain it all to him. I imagined my father's reaction had he still been alive. He was always so correct, so dignified. What would he think of his son now? For the first time since my accident I drank myself to sleep.

My worst fears hit me in the face when I checked out the next morning's papers on the internet.

'The self proclaimed greatest healer of our time was too busy having an affair to save his wife claims close friend' screamed off the front page of Tuesday's tabloid.

'Adam Saunders (thirty-six) aka Macro-man and self styled healer was allegedly so engrossed in a passionate affair with devotee Marlene King that he couldn't be bothered to come home to save his wife. Christine Saunders (thirty-five) died of a brain haemorrhage leaving two children'.

It continued describing my healing activities and how people thought I was the return of Christ. Apparently my rant has made the top ten in the US. It noted that both Marlene and I had refused to deny it.

When I looked out of the window I saw a group of photographers huddled under umbrellas outside Angela's house. When Martin came out a battery of flashes caught him setting off for work. There were shouts for a comment but thankfully he just drove off. No school for Matthew and Eleanor today. My phone kept ringing. At first I let the answer phone run hoping it would be Marlene or Aaron but after an hour I couldn't stand it and unplugged the machine.

Other sites followed up the story, each trying to add their unique spin. Keef pleaded that I be allowed to grieve in private. I had become a guru and the rest of my team, followers or disciples.

Finally I managed to talk to Aaron. He was assertive, persuading me to pack for an escape. He came round in a rented people carrier at two o'clock in the morning. We threw our bags into the Toyota in seconds, carried Matthew and Eleanor into their seats and left. No flashes, I did not see anyone following us.

"Listen, you might be big news today but in a few weeks you'll be forgotten. Good you didn't deny it. Let's hope another woman accuses David Beckham of sleeping with her or the Royal Family suffers another scandal, taking the focus away. I found a cottage you can stay at in Wales. You'll need to keep a low profile. Have you thought of growing beard and letting your hair go wild? It'll suit you."

We arrived at seven in the morning under the cover of the

biggest storm I have witnessed. There was no human, or any living creature visible. Running out into the torrent of water washed off some of the emotional pain. As I opened my chest to the heavens and walked towards the grey, foamy turbulence, emotions I had clung onto moved out from my heavy chest into the wildness around me.

Once in our little cottage I felt lighter, freer, cleaner, refreshed. The storm subsided and we explored the village. No one took any interest in me. Just two scruffy men with a couple of children.

Aaron managed to reach Cheryl. The news was that Marlene, in shock, was now staying with Stoosh. Steve wanted to put out some kind of statement. After the children had gone to sleep Aaron started the inevitable.

"So, you and Marlene. I thought if anyone it would have been Marilyn. Every time I saw you together you had a mouthful of saliva and a new shape to your trousers."

"It was on our travels, you know, a moment of weakness."

"Hey, you don't have to explain to me. It's cool if that what makes you happy."

"It doesn't make me happy, I'm disappointed with myself. How can I face Christine's parents, what will I tell Matthew and Eleanor? How did the papers find out anyway? I can't imagine Marlene would tell them."

"I think the other women knew. You know how it goes, someone tells someone else and then before you know it someone cashes in and it's on the editors desk."

"Who would have thought."

"All we can do is take away the fuel for the fire by keeping you and Marlene away from the media and make sure no one else talks. I don't see what Steve can say that will help. It'll just draw him in. Do you want me to tell him to wait?"

I nodded.

"You must get a grip. Remember you promised Christine you would be there for Matthew and Eleanor."

"What do you mean?"

"I mean come back to reality. Reconnect with the earth. You're not Jesus or Macroman you're Adam Saunders as of now residing in North Wales with two children and no visible means of income."

"Whatever gave you the impression I thought I was Jesus?"

"You changed back there in America. Where was the empty, humble man ready to listen, to take in new ideas? You laid into a lot of people who would have been on your side. You became self indulgent, trying to start a new religion without properly discussing with us. No plan, no consideration, just blundering ahead. What happened? Did it get to you so much, all the hype and everyone telling you how great you were? Did a part of you begin to believe it all?"

Christ, I did.

"It was the rush of momentum, I was riding the crest of a wave, I didn't have time to get off and look around. I thought most of you thought the religion idea was OK."

"Pauline supported you but she would support you if you claimed you were Cleopatra. Most of us wanted another Ringing Rocks. When you talked about being more spiritual no one imagined you would try and start a religion right there. And what was with the kneeling down praying on stage?"

"It felt right at the time. It gave me inspiration."

"You used to talk. The Adam I knew made mistakes and laughed at himself, he needed the people around him, you used to be open, approachable. Why did it all become so serious? You withdrew and just did what you wanted. I don't think you ever thought about anyone else's opinions. It was all you."

When Aaron recounted these events I began to cringe. Had I believed I was Jesus? Had I gone that far? When you take events apart, when you take actions out of their context to examine them, suddenly it all takes on a disturbing new perspective. Listening to Aaron go on to regurgitate some of my claims of spiritual supremacy left me feeling uncomfortable. Now it was hard to understand what I thought I was doing. Strip out the emotional energy of the moment and it all felt absurd, ridiculous, embarrassing. To think that if I had still been in Philadelphia I would now be plotting my world tour.

That night I could smell my father in my bedroom, I could feel his presence. I felt ashamed, embarrassed to see him.

"Adam darling, ever since you were born I have treasured you. I have always loved you and it would be hard to imagine what you would have to do to spoil it. I should have told you before but I assumed you always knew."

I woke briefly. I did not love Matthew or Eleanor when they were born. I found them irritating. Love drifted in slowly, later, it is still growing. But now I can see that I would forgive them, love them as much if they made similar mistakes. I still don't know if it is my father's soul I sense or my own projection but through loving Matthew and Eleanor I feel better able to accept his love. With this realisation I felt a great constriction unwind.

I kissed my children before falling asleep.

CHAPTER TWENTY-FIVE

I would love to be able to take human beings apart. Not physically but spiritually and emotionally, pare them down to their naked soul. We have evolved to become the most successful species on the planet and yet I am fascinated by what makes us function. I can understand having the drive and desire to reproduce, the hunger that motivates us to find food, but why the rest? Why the self destructive desire for material wealth, why want so much that we destroy the planet we live on and ourselves in the process. Is it an innate part of our make up to compete to the death or is it learnt, a product of the society we are born into. Will we just consume all that's in front of us or does another characteristic kick in helping us find restraint, the sense to conserve.

I suppose it might be possible to examine the human make up if we were individual beings living in isolation but the fact is we are so closely integrated, so entwined by our emotional energy, that I would need to take whole communities apart.

How would I account for the forces of nature, the food, the weather, the alignment of the sun, moon and other planets? No wonder so many psychologists and philosophers have struggled in vain. The number of variables must make consistency impossible.

It makes me think of Sigeyo's idea of humans just being a concentration and expression of universal energy. In which case we are being driven by the cosmos rather than society. Does our behaviour reflect a patch of the cosmos that is out of balance? Is it that certain stars have aligned in a way that the force coming into our planet is too intense, too fast and we are simply responding to the energy pouring through our chakras. The problem with this line of thought is that it implies it is all beyond our control. But then understanding is the key to taking conscious action and learning from it. Knowing how forces ebb and flow through the universe would unlock all kinds of ideas on how to create a better world.

I decided to make a shrine to Christine in my bedroom. I put my favourite pictures of her on a small teak table. I placed her wedding ring, necklace and earrings on the surface. For vitality I placed a bowl that I filled with fresh water every day. I put a plant next to water for life and finally two candles symbolising Christine and me. Before going to bed I lit the candles and talked to her. It didn't bring her to me in the night but it did make me feel closer.

Justin came down with an old laptop and helped me set up an internet connection using his identity. Justin is the only person I spend any time with who has not travelled my spiritual journey with me. He still finds my insane, crazy ideas amusing. In a way his stock attitude to life keeps me more centred.

My laptop and internet connection were my sole means of contact whilst hiding out. I felt safe and anonymous as my messages dropped into my server devoid of any geographical identity and onto the world beyond. I didn't risk the phone. I was able to keep in contact with all my friends in the USA except Pauline who had gone back to LA without a connection. Another person I could not reach electronically was Josephine.

I was amazed to find that a whole conspiracy theory was developing on American sites. The basic theme being that Christine had been killed to keep me quiet. Drug companies, organised religion and the food industry were the main suspects. I had gone into hiding to protect my children. Chat rooms and bloggers pored over apparent inconsistencies in her death, speculating on what drugs would cause her brain to haemorrhage. It was both addictive and destructive. I knew I was not stable enough to expose myself to thoughts of being persecuted and yet the intrigue was captivating. My first waking action was to log on and check through my favourites listed under Christine.

I wrote down the phone conversations we had, the feeling in

the room, the doctors comments to try to preserve my experience of her death.

I forced myself to write a letter to Mary and John. I explained how I understood if they hated me, and explained my reasons for hiding. I also assured them I did not want to deny them the opportunity of spending time with Matthew and Eleanor. I suggested they contact me by email if they wanted to meet up.

A few days later my face was spread over the front page of a tabloid again, with the headline 'Health Warning This Man is a Fraud.' I consciously folded the paper to hide my picture, hoping my beard had grown sufficiently, as I handed over the coins and rushed home.

'Adam Saunders has been exposed as a fake as hundreds of people from the UK and USA have come forward to claim they were not healed.'

The story ran on to claim that people found their illnesses returned or that they received no benefit. In a sidebar a nutritionist showed how the foods I recommended could be deficient in the vitamins B12 and D, describing the symptoms of the pernicious anaemia, one of the possible results of low B12.

Another so-called expert explained how my healing was just a placebo and that a third of my clients would be fooled into thinking they were cured, however, this could be short lived and dangerous if this encouraged them to forego proper medical treatment.

No mention was made of me not charging money or questioned how the placebo theory worked with the babies that had recovered. Nor did the article discuss those people whose medical records documented an improvement. Even my ideas on diet had been turned into a purist vegan style gleaned from other people's macrobiotic books. The fact that I recommended eating fish occasionally and even some eggs or wild meat was ignored. The lasting impression was that I was a fraud, peddling an unsafe diet.

This precipitated another rush of emails between Borth-y-Guest and Philadelphia. Steve was logical and reassuring, he had begun to organise a list of people who had documentation of benefiting from my healing. His belief was unshakable. Stoosh had become immersed in the conspiracy theories to the point of paranoia. Marlene distanced herself from the drama, wounded by the initial assault.

Seriously was mixing a recording of my stadium gig with new sounds of his own, working on the principle that whilst my name was still pinging through the wires people would be interested in hearing what happened at the infamous gig.

"Let's give 'em the message everyone's claiming they're trying to suppress Macro-man."

Immersing myself in my electronic link to the outside world everyday allowed the opinions to invade my being. I began to lose confidence. It was hard to discern whether my memory was true. The sickening thought that I had deluded myself into thinking I was a healer, or worse some kind of spiritual guru, began to take hold. My work was all based on feelings, emotional energy and now that had gone where was the solid evidence? I could feel the results of my efforts in my hands, see it in people's auras, sense it but not measure it, not record it.

My work was not like writing a book where you have your physical creation to show for it at the end. All I had to show for those years was other people's experiences and if they were critical then I had nothing. I had just come and gone making a temporary splash, the tiny ripples soon consumed by bigger storms.

Questions were being asked on the macrobiotic and healing websites. If the macrobiotic diet is so good for healing why did Christine die? There was speculation over whether she really followed it anyway. Another theme developed claiming the macrobiotic diet was too high in sodium rich foods and that this could have resulted in high blood pressure.

One woman thought my affair with Marlene killed her. Another put it all down to the strains of bringing up children without support.

A man I met in LA wrote a long list of all the variables that influence our physical and emotional condition and reasoned that food was only one part. He claimed even eating the best diet in the world does not guarantee everlasting health.

Why was I torturing myself like this? I kept feeding a masochistic streak in me. Perhaps I was feeding my depression, trying to keep it alive, punishing myself. I think I chose to be miserable because without Christine I didn't want to feel happy again.

On a shiatsu site I read an article pointing out how contradictory my claim was that we should use the power of money to change the world on the one hand and then attack people who make a living out of alternative health on the other. Surely I should embrace all those people who instead of working in offices on products or services that contribute to pollution and consumerism have carved out a career improving the quality of life for others using nothing more than their hands. These people are the most likely to spend their earnings on organic food and green energy.

Yes, I agreed wholeheartedly. I wrote an open email to the administrator of the site apologising for raging against the LA shiatsu school and expressing my agreement with the sentiments of the article. I had become narrow minded and had lost sight of the big picture.

I had to force myself out of bed each day, struggling to find the energy to look after Matthew and Eleanor. Was this the self-sabotage that Sigeyo predicted? No I think my self-destructive gene became active in Philadelphia.

John and Mary came to stay and helped out with the domestic chores that had been piling up. Marlene was not mentioned until John confided to me that he once had a brief affair with someone at work. It didn't make me feel better about my infidelity but it did take away the fear that John despised me for cheating on his daughter.

The internet was still full of speculation on my healing abilities. Some of the people who felt healed were actively trying to turn the tide. Aaron's words rebounded into my head as I read a scathingly critical judgement of my work by a macrobiotic teacher. The basic theme being that I didn't build any structure into what I was doing, just wading in waving my arms around making a lot of noise, kicking other people's structures over and then when I faltered there was no foundation to fall back on. He coldly reasoned that I had done more damage than good.

In a state of despair, I phoned Aaron. "Stay with reality. Christine died, you feel sad and you miss her. That's all, the rest is in your head. You've made it all up or you're believing other people's opinions. How does all this mental turmoil make you feel?"

"Like I want to die."

"So why bother? What is the point in putting all this energy into collecting and developing ideas that make you feel like you want to die?"

"It just feels like a slope I slip down and once I'm sliding, the best I can do is slow it down."

"That's crap and you know it. It's just another delusion you've chosen."

"Hmm, I'm not sure."

"Go back to your breathing, find that gentle state inside where you can listen to your soul again."

After I put the phone down I felt resentful. Aaron didn't understand what I was going through. Who was he to give me a Zen lecture when he had never had a wife. I'm not sure he had really ever loved like I had.

Deep down I knew I was being defensive, he had shown me a way out of this self-made mental chaos but I resisted consciously.

Unconsciously the weight of my thoughts had been eroded I could see through the game I was playing. I knew there were other options.

I persevered for three days and then left the cottage to climb Tryfan. The extreme contrast, from being caved inside small low ceilinged rooms, to this complete openness expanded my mind. The exertion had stirred my blood and helped stabilise my emotions. Standing still on the peak gave me a new connection to the world around me. I felt open, exposed to the elements, nowhere to hide. To increase the sensations I took off my clothes and stood on the peak naked. No one was around, just me and nature, no barrier between us. My feet felt earthed. Some kind of electrical smog drained into the rocks below. I was still hot from the climb but the wind cut through my skin, quickly blowing the heat from me, stripping out my superficial emotional energy. I stood in the wind, gently breathing with the world. Concentrating on initiating my in and out breath, I experienced the connection to my soul that I had lost. I realised that in my healing journey I had lost myself.

As I stayed with my soul the idea of writing a book floated up into my mind.

I felt I had regained my truth, winding my way down across the rocks and scree, crossing the bubbling brooks. I just want to be myself again, to let go of all the ideas and theories. Perhaps writing would help me find out who I really am.

After all the discussion about the cause of Christine's death and the claims that the macrobiotic ideas on food did not work for people, I asked myself why I still bothered with it. The first part was obvious, I now prefer the taste of real foods to anything else and I genuinely feel better when I eat this way. I no longer think it will guarantee freedom from illness but I do think it increases my chances of getting through life without any premature disease. I feel that I have some biological control over my body. By how much I have turned the odds in my favour I have no idea, but unless something better turns up I will continue with my macrobiotic eating.

When I got home there was no one to talk to so it was going to have to be me and my computer.

I wrote to Josephine to tell her of the book but again no response came.

George Wadkin's diary played on my mind. I had once harboured hopes of finding it but now I saw my book as being a continuation of my former self, another tiny piece of completion. Is this what life becomes as we age? Filling in all the gaps so that we achieve a sense of completion, letting us die in peace?

Today when I did my trawl through the internet sites after taking Matthew and Eleanor to school, my heart raced and my breathing quickened. The news was breaking that some of the people who claimed they had had healing sessions with me and experienced no benefit, admitted they had never seen me. They alleged that they were paid to expose my healing as ineffective. More stories entered the murky world of paid informants. An employee from a PR company called Global Influence with its headquarters in the Bahamas had fronted the operation. They were now closed.

These claims sparked another explosion of internet fervour, speculation about the usual suspects; food companies, pharmaceutical industry, religion and free marketers. My suspicions leant towards the food industry as they potentially had the most to lose if people ever took my advice seriously. I reasoned that it was the food industry that was doing the most harm, not only to people's health but also the environment through intensive farming, meat production and genetically modified foods. They were contributing to world poverty as a result of their trading practices so they must have felt the most vulnerable.

The story ran for several days and gave people who supported me the forum to come out and say their piece. It intrigued me how a newspaper that only weeks ago had tried to crucify me was now claiming to be leading a fight to clear my name. Steve wrote with the news that he was involved in a documentary looking into what I really said and why someone would have paid people to discredit me.

I sensed that a popular backlash was building up. Some of the pride came back and yet it saddened me to realise how dependant I still was on outside opinion.

I felt I was still miles away from that inner self-belief, there was no steel at my core. I was blown off course each time the wind changed. I tried to console myself that at least I had dissolved the arrogance and egotism that must have taken hold towards the end in Philadelphia.

Seriously sent me a DVD of the big gig. He had mixed in new sounds where I was healing and talking so that there was a fuller musical backdrop. He must have broadened his repertoire as I heard choral singing blending with a loose metallic rhythm, a haunting violin piece whilst I touched the children and southern spiritualist singers overlaid on my ranting. Seriously spliced in some of my food mantras, fading in and out so my message was loud and clear. This was all mixed in with interviews with people who had seen me for healing, with parts of the Ringing Rocks event and my UK shopping centre news reels. The quality, pacing and vibrancy was impressive. Here it was all fresh and new but events had already pushed phrases back down my throat. I now felt embarrassed by some of my words.

Royalties started to come in for the song. I recognised the hypocrisy given my speech on the DVD claiming not to be a slave to money. I was tasting the drug I ranted against and I am ashamed to say it felt good.

It allowed me to dream of a different future, taking Matthew and Eleanor away from here, finding a different life. I fantasised about living on a sailing yacht, visiting various Mediterranean ports, owning a small Chateaux in southern France, growing my own organic food.

CHAPTER TWENTY-SIX

Writing the book is therapeutic. I am at a point where I feel more comfortable reliving my journey, it has softened the sharp edges, smoothed the highs and lows. Each pass through the book to tidy the language or refine my expression has enabled me to go back to the most painful sections of my story without falling into the old traits of self loathing or depression. In a way it strengthens my connection to Christine, helps keep her alive. I dedicate my book to her.

I decide to take the manuscript in person to my new agent, Sophie. It is an excuse to get out of the village, no risk of losing the manuscript in transit, but mostly I like handing over the pile of emotional energy face to face, I want it to be tactile.

On the train my mind drifts. What have I learnt so far? I went in as a motor cycle mechanic who spent a lot of time in the pub and came out a partially broken man but one who knows how to love, who can express his emotions and who has connected with his children.

Did clearing up my karma make any difference? Yes, it has with Christine and it has with Justin. I feel my efforts were too late with my parents, it should have all been said whilst they were still alive. Perhaps the most significant change is that by returning to the messes I made I have altered my current behaviour. I think I am now less likely to upset people in ways I will regret later and I am not sure if that would have happened if I had not tried to clean up my past.

Do I believe in being reborn? I thought back to my conversations with Aaron.

I believe I have an emotional energy, and I can accept that this will not die with my physical body. I know from my own experience that when I die I will experience my spirit float away into the universe. I don't know what would have happened after that. Would my energy just spread out and merge with the surrounding atmosphere? Perhaps it is as though our soul is a cup of water and when we die that water is poured back into the ocean. For a while it remains contained in one place and here we might choose to return intact but we can also let our energy merge and dissolve in the universal energy of the cosmos.

It is confusing that since my accident I have all the memories of being George Wadkins. Did he die and then his spirit become mine or is it that certain events, memories, packets of energy were out there and somehow became muddled up into my energy as I came back to life? I prefer to think a segment of his life force partially merged with mine.

I need some kind of conclusion to the book. I take out my note pad and write:

DEPRESSION IS WHAT STRIPS YOU OF EVERYTHING THAT PREVENTS BRINGING ABOUT MASSIVE CHANGES IN YOUR BEING.

NO PRIDE, EGO OR SELF ESTEEM EQUALS A STATE WHERE YOU CAN REINVENT YOURSELF – NOTHING TO LOSE.

I am convinced that without the depression I suffered after my accident I would still be working as a mechanic. None of my school friends have changed much. Without the despair I am not sure I would have been as open to Aaron's ideas. I also recognise that depression can become a habit. Once you are up to your neck in the swamp the effort to climb out and live your new life may be overwhelming. Christine helped me, I couldn't have done it by myself. Now I am on my own I am struggling to move forward again. I have tasted intimacy and independence, being on my own does not suit me. Thankfully I have Matthew and Eleanor. I might not have been the most responsible or reliable father before but recently there have been more and more patches when I give them everything. I hope these moments when we are as one will mean more to them than a lifetime of correct parenting but never really connecting.

ONCE YOU STOP FEELING YOUR EMOTIONS YOU ARE DEAD. EMBRACE THEM AND LEARN TO LOVE THE EMOTIONAL LIFE FORCE SURGING THROUGH YOUR BODY WHATEVER IT BRINGS.

Trying to be more specific I make a list:

DO NOT RIDE MOTORCYLES FAST.
DO NOT LEAVE YOUR CHILDREN.
DO NOT HAVE AFFAIRS.
QUESTION EVERYTHING – MAKE IT YOURS BEFORE BELIEVING.
KEEP AN OPEN MIND – CONCEPTS ARE NOT REALITY, JUST PART OF MY PERCEPTION OF REALITY.
STAY CONNECTED – PEOPLE, FOOD, THE PLANET AND MYSELF.
DO NOT ENSLAVE PEOPLE INTO MY BELIEF SYSTEM, HELP THEM FIND THEIR OWN SOUL AND OWN TRUTH.

I rip the page out of my notebook and add it to the file for Sophie. Leaving Sophie's Covent Garden office I take the tube to Camden Town. I walk to the high street bookshop Josephine worked in. There she is stacking books in the autobiographical section. I walk up behind her and put my hands around her waist.

"I've missed you."

Josephine turns sharply, mouth open. I watch the blood slowly return to her face.

"Adam, what are you doing here?"

"I've just dropped off my manuscript. Didn't you receive any of my emails or letters? I even called you from a phone box and left my email address on your answer machine."

"To be honest I didn't want to hear from you."

"Excuse me, do you know where I can find *Alan Clark's Diaries*?"

Josephine reached for a copy of the book.

"Look this isn't the right time or place. Let's leave it for another time."

"Sorry, is this the original diary?"

"Yes."

"Josephine please we must talk or at least tell me why you don't want to talk."

"I finish in half an hour. Wait for me at the Polish Café in Primrose Village."

I walk to the café and I am amazed to find Wendy there. She is so loud, so colourful, so dramatic, such a contrast to my village.

"Oh my God, Adam, Adam Saunders, Christ you've come back from the dead. Wow, you look good, it's been so long."

Wendy stops waving her arms around and puts them around me, pulling me hard against her. I respond with a kiss and squeeze. This is my closest encounter with a female for nearly two years. I feel a buzz as the energy in my most primal chakra stirs. The stimulation of London is hyping me up. I feel a wave of excitement as Wendy smiles inviting me to join her.

We sit and I order a peppermint tea, coffee would have sent me into outer space. Wendy bombards me with questions. She has been following the whole story. I assure her it is all in my book. What can I say in a few minutes in a café? To turn the tide I question her about our shiatsu group. She is still in contact with Stephen, now living with Jane of all people.

Sigeyo left her the house and enough money to pay the taxes and feel comfortable for a while. She works as the editor of the new age magazine Free Spirits. Somehow I do not feel comfortable asking her what her relationship with Sigeyo really was.

"It would be so incredible if I could interview you. Get the real story. It would be such a scoop and I would be so, so grateful. Please say yes."

"Yes."

"I love you."

Wendy cups my head and pulls my face to hers so she can plaster me with kisses. I look up to see Josephine standing to my side. Wendy speaks first.

"Jo, how fantastic to see you. We were just talking about our shiatsu class."

"Hi Josephine, I'm glad you came."

Josephine sits and gives minimalist replies to Wendy's questions. After a while Wendy realises she is late for an appointment. We exchange emails and I flirt with the idea of inviting her up to Borth-y-guest to interview me. Now that Josephine and I are alone I pull my chair closer to hers.

"So please tell me, why have you been avoiding me?"

Josephine looks into my eyes for an uncomfortably long time. I find it hard not to flinch. I feel she is searching through every corner of my mind, looking for a clue that would tell her it is the right time to talk.

"For a while my life revolved around you. I knew you had a family and I didn't want to have sex with you but I wanted to be a part of your life. Then you ran off to America and just abandoned me. Couldn't you have invited me over for a week? But what really hurts is to hear you were having an affair with someone else all that time."

I try to speak but Josephine holds her hand up.

"No wait. I know none of this is your fault, you can fall in love with whoever you want, do what you want but it just isn't good for me to be around you. I need to live my own life, find my own strength not exist off yours. I am too weak to be around you and I don't want to be sucked in again. Just seeing you will start it all off again."

Josephine looks down.

"Jo, look at me, please. That is just how you perceived our relationship at one particular time. It is not that I am strong and you are weak. I can't tell you how much I relied on your support when I used to see Sigeyo, it was giving you a shiatsu at the Healing Centre that made me want to take up healing in the first place, it was you that gave me the confidence to go to America, you who helped me at those shopping centres and it was looking into your eyes that gave me the strength to go on at Christine's funeral. I needed you these last two years. Of course I don't want to do anything to hurt you but please, it is a friendship of equals. I am sorry about America but perhaps it is just as well you didn't come, in retrospect it wasn't my finest hour."

I want her to sit on my lap so I can cuddle her, stroke her long hair, wipe the tear from her eye but I sense this is exactly what she is afraid of. She looks up at me and turns the palm of her hand upward. I let my hand rest on hers. My smile is returned.

I suggest we go out to eat. There is a vegetarian restaurant called Manor close by. I do most of the talking. Borth-y-guest, my book, Matthew and Eleanor flow easily. Finally I describe my despair, loss of self esteem. It was so much better talking to Josephine than typing into my computer, looking into her compassionate eyes rather than a flat screen.

Afterwards we walk back to Jo's house and return to our old routine of swapping shiatsu treatments. I was surprised to feel Josephine giving me a more sensual, warm treatment. I felt her mouth close to my ear. She sat on my back whilst squeezing my shoulders. Jo slipped her hands under my sweatshirt to palpitate my abdomen.

Then I leave to rush round to Euston station and return to Matthew and Eleanor.

On the long train journey back, my mind twists and turns thinking through my encounter with Josephine. Does she want to be in a relationship with me and do I want to be in one with her? If she wants to be in a relationship with me but I do not, how would we avoid a situation where she feels rejected or hurt?

I think Josephine is someone I could love in time, she does not exude the natural passion and fun I usually look for but she is different, special. I do not sense any sexual chemistry between us, an important ingredient for me, but who knows. I try to imagine making love to her.

CHAPTER TWENTY-SEVEN

Back home I find an email from Marlene describing her new life working with Steve. She invites me to stay with her. My friend signs off with love and a kiss. I call her and we talk through the night. My spirits are lifted just hearing her voice. There is something so positive and 'let's do it' about Marlene. She does not analyse or procrastinate, if it feels right just launches off. Whereas I have tried so hard to rid myself of beliefs and be more instinctive she appears to live off her intuition more easily.

As we talk I feel a great desire to jump on a plane and rekindle the intimacy we once shared. After we sign off, more internal discussions fill my skull. I still feel highly attracted to Marlene. How could it work? Would she move here?

I hear back from Sophie.

"I love the book Adam. I would like to tidy up the language in a few places and I have some suggestions on editing it to help keep the reader turning the pages."

I arrange to meet up with Josephine in London after seeing Sophie. We meet at her home early afternoon. I step in carrying my manuscript with Sophie's recommendations.

"I would love a massage if you are not too tired."

I am too tired but acquiesce. I walk into her bathroom to wash my hands. When I return she is lying naked face down on a large red bath towel spread out over her bed. She has placed a bottle of almond oil on the table. I am shocked given her previous nervousness of being even partially undressed around me. I warm the oil in my hands before spreading it over her back. She feels a little fuller than before but still slim and delicate. I work carefully down her back softening the long muscles either side of her spine. I carry on over her small firm buttocks and down her legs. All the time I am wondering how to react. Why did she undress? She could have kept her underwear on, covered herself with a towel.

Was this a play to have sex with me, to start a relationship? What if we have sex and then I do not want to have a relationship. I spend a long time on her calf muscles and soles of her feet before suggesting she turns over. I can feel myself become aroused as Josephine lies on her back. I start with her feet and work up her legs being careful not to touch her in an overtly sexual manner. I feel the warmth of her inner thigh and abdomen. I massage her arms and shoulders and without thinking let my palms slide across her breasts. They feel firm and her nipples are erect. Then feeling self conscious I concentrate on Josephine's stomach.,

"Adam, I'm feeling cold can you snuggle under the duvet with me."

I pause, looking for the right words.

"Jo I am enjoying massaging you and I'm sure you realise I find you highly attractive and arousing lying here naked but are sure this is right?"

Josephine raises her head and looks quizzically at me.

"What do you mean?"

"I mean if I get into bed with you I will want to have sex but I am not sure that I am ready for that kind of relationship yet."

"I have thought about this for a long time, Adam. You're not in a relationship with anyone right now are you?"

"Well, no."

"So if you are currently free and I am too, what worries you?"

"I just don't want to feel close to you and then find that I am letting you down in the future. I don't want a repeat of what happened before, where you felt hurt and stopped talking to me. You are too important to me for that."

Josephine sits up, I notice her breasts take on a new shape, she tilts her head and puts her hands around my neck. We kiss, tentatively at first.

"Please don't make this complicated, Adam, it's not easy for me. I want the first time to be with you."

I undress whilst Josephine slides under the duvet. I climb in, still feeling apprehensive. I put my hand around Josephine and we kiss again, more passionately this time. I feel her breasts against my chest, I feel her slide her leg over mine, I enjoy the feel of the oil on her skin. Josephine pulls my buttocks towards her, as she rolls onto her back, she is pushing her leg out, encouraging me to lie between her thighs.

For a moment I am back under the willow tree with Anne. Josephine is looking into my eyes with the same intensity, I feel myself falling into her pupils. The orange candlelight gives Jo a warmer hue. We kiss, deeper and deeper, I let my hand slide up to her breast and arch my neck to kiss her nipple. We kiss again and Josephine reaches down to guide me. I feel a resistance. My eyes lock into hers.

"Yes, now Adam, do it."

Pushing harder, Josephine flinches, I feel her finger nails in the flesh of my bottom as I slide in. I pause to let her get used to me. Slowly we find our rhythm letting our emotions gain momentum. Squeezing my buttocks with her hands, she encourages me to be more forceful. Inevitably she tips me over the edge, I try to withdraw but Josephine grips me too strongly as she opens her mouth and cries out. It has been so long I have little self-control. My orgasm is almost too intense, shivers run up body as I convulse. She lies next to me and we caress each other. A few residual spasms of pleasure ripple inside my abdomen. As she runs her hand over my body, I sense her curiosity as her fingers explore my skin. I bite her shoulders playfully. It feels good just resting next to her, soaking up her energy.

The last time I made love to a virgin was nearly twenty years ago with Sandy. I feel a mixture of being honoured and proud of myself. I know this is irrational as there is nothing to be proud of but somehow it feels manly, conquering, I feel like an alpha male, my primal urges feel completely satisfied.

Josephine is lying across my chest, her hair trailing across my shoulder. Thinking back to first meeting her at the shiatsu class I am amazed at the transformation. Has she changed or have I? I would never have imagined Josephine would be someone I would be cocooned with in the warmth of this afternoon's passion.

I've missed my train. The saintly Mrs Llewellyn obliges and will stay in the cottage.

We stay in bed. It feels very comfortable, very cosy, very natural. I notice a sense of contentment I have not experienced since Christine was alive. Reminded of Christine I think of what she would think of Josephine and Marlene. They are so different, one gentle, deep, careful, considerate, supportive, slowly drawing the best out of me. The other fun, outgoing, exciting, someone who makes me laugh, ambitious and experienced in the way the world functions. Christine gravitated to people who were more extrovert so I expect Marlene would be her immediate choice. But would she change her mind if she knew Josephine as I do now? It takes a long time to know Josephine. I wonder how much more there is.

After dinner Josephine starts to read my manuscript. Suddenly she kicks me hard on the shin.

"Is that what you thought of me?"

I feel embarrassed and try to take the manuscript away from her but she fights back continuing to read my initial impression of her.

"You have to remember I was very different then. And anyway Josephine, you've changed a lot, you're certainly very attractive now. You look much stronger, more feminine and yes beautiful. I can change anything, I have the power to turn you into a queen in my book."

"No don't worry, I don't mind, you must write what you felt at the time," and then turning to me with a frown. "I hope my character improves later on."

She giggles when she reads further.

"Most amusing Adam, I love your description of Jane, but I

can't believe you were so judgemental then."

Later Josephine expresses a desire to meet my spiritual motivator Aaron again. I imagine she will revise her opinion when she reads his views on relationships.

I am tempted to declare my love for Josephine and ask her to come back to Borth-y-guest with me but I manage to restrain myself. I want my next relationship to last, ideally a lifetime, and part of me is telling me not to be impulsive. I need to consider Matthew and Eleanor. Aaron's test is to take a girl on a long holiday, the trials of travelling through Asia will surely test any relationship, presumably why none have survived.

Josephine becomes more talkative and open than I have ever known her when we cuddle on a bean bag.

"So why did you strip off and lie on my bed like that? You were always so uptight when I used to give you those ginger compresses."

"Yes, I have always felt uncomfortable being undressed. I was very thin and gangly as a child. I remember feeling horrified at the reflection of my white, bony body. I told you my upbringing was quite strict. Nudity was not encouraged and sex only in wedlock. I had a crush on you Adam, and I didn't want to put you off. I felt I looked better in clothes."

I kiss her on the lips.

"I promised myself that I would bring it all to some kind of conclusion. If I just carried on as my normal self I would never know. Never find out if you could want me, you know, be attracted to me."

I lean forward and hold her hands.

"Well I am glad, because now you know I am very attracted to you."

I look into Jo's eyes losing myself.

"I can't rush this because I want it to be right. It is possible that you could find me irritating, selfish, unreliable or whatever. It takes time. Can you be patient?"

Josephine purses her lips and nods turning her hands so I can lay my hands in her palms. As I lie in bed with Josephine sleeping across me I experience a slight pang of anxiety. I wonder whether Jo could now be pregnant.

In the morning I leave for Wales. It was a warm farewell and I do not feel any emptiness on the way home. That feeling of contentment is still present in my abdomen. It feels warm, satisfying.

A few days later Marlene phones me and suggests I get a web cam so we can see each other. For the first time we talk about our night together in the motel and the newspaper scandal.

"I have to admit I had very strong feelings towards you after. I still catch myself fantasising about being closer to you. Any room for a fun loving girl in your cottage?"

For a moment I am paralysed. I am frozen by the fear that I could say yes and she would be here in my arms or no and put her off forever.

"I need a little time. You must know I am highly attracted to you. Each time we talk I feel close to you. This is very difficult Marlene but I have to tell you that I slept with an old friend and I'm a little confused emotionally."

I am aware I am sounding like one of those men I read about with commitment phobia. There was a pause.

"No problem. I understand."

"No, it's not like that, I really feel highly attracted to you, please let's keep in touch and let our relationship grow organically."

My head is full of images of Marlene in my cottage, in my bed. I did not want this all to become a choice between Josephine and Marlene and retreat to get greater clarity.

I try not to think of Marlene, Josephine or relationships. Just let my mind open and relax whilst I engage in my normal activities. I keep in regular contact with both. After a few weeks Josephine calls me.

"Adam, I notice in your book you visited your parents graves, Anne and George's graves. I want to visit my parents but it is a part of my life I have shut away, fearing it would be an area that is too painful to enter."

I offer to take her. The following weekend I hire a car to take her out to the cemetery her parents were buried in. We kneel on the grass and I remain silent as she tries to connect. I breathe in feelings of loss, rejection and anger that drift out to the surface and lay my hands on her shoulders and remain passive. I feel her shoulders tremble as she begins to sob. Convulsions erupt, shaking her body. Perhaps this physical motion makes it easier to release the deeper emotional energy, a natural form of chi kung. I let the waves subside naturally before holding her close.

We drive back to Josephine's little flat and I tell her about the shrine I made for Christine. I help her collect the few reminders she has of her parents and we arrange the photographs, her mother's broach, a pair of binoculars and an envelope containing letters, candles, flowers and water on a shelf near the window along with stones from her parent's graves. The atmosphere feels very fragile, delicate and brittle.

I take her out to Myama for diner. I feel calm enough to just sit with Josephine without saying much. I drop her off and I am pleased with myself for being able to drive straight back to Wales, through the night, keeping my promise to Marlene.

CHAPTER TWENTY-EIGHT

This morning I notice it no longer bothers me to see parents feeding their children junk food. I no longer feel angry when I see an overweight child given a bag of crisps, chocolate or cola.

Last night I realised that nature has set humans boundaries to live in. Now that humans have crossed the boundaries, now that we are a threat to the existence of our planet, other forces have taken over. I suspect we will see a great reduction of the human population. The cosmic energy running through us appears to have made us eat or at least give our children the very foods that would make us prone to degenerative diseases and make it harder to breed. I feel in awe of the power and magnitude of the universe. I smile to myself as I think how all the great religions warned of the consequences of straying from the boundaries.

I no longer feel the need to intervene, to preach or lecture.

I slide into bed and turn my light off when I hear the sound of a car, loud knocking on the door follows. I run downstairs in my dressing gown and open the door.

"Hello! Pauline? Pauline what are you doing here?"

Pauline gestures to the taxi driver and he drives off. I stand back to let her in.

"Adam it was me."

"What? What was you?"

"Adam, I am so sorry it was me..."

Pauline starts crying. I am too stunned to react for a moment and then step forward taking her into my arms.

"Pauline, please what do you mean? What was you?"

Pauline is sobbing too strongly to talk so I sit her down on the sofa. I bring tissues and tea.

"Adam it was me that told the papers. I told them about you and Marlene."

More crying. I must be tired because it takes me a while to

work it out.

"I've been living with this terrible guilt all this time, it's been eating me up, although I'm sure not as bad as all you've gone through. Lucia convinced me to just do it. Get on a plane and see you in person. So here I am."

We both fall silent. I cannot collect myself, it is all too bizarre. Slowly it all makes sense, Pauline disappearing, not talking to me.

"Why?"

"I've asked myself so many times, I've even gone to therapy to try and find out. At the funeral you made your relationship with Christine sound so special but back in Philadelphia Cheryl told me you and Marlene had been having an affair all the time."

I want to explain it was only once, but what was the point? The word that had been planted in everybody's mind was affair and I did not want to appear to trivialise my actions by splitting hairs over the definition. She went on.

"You let me think you were virtuous, trustworthy and yet you were cheating on your wife just like the other gurus. It was a snap reaction. I made a phone call to an old school friend at a news agency and regretted it straight after. But once it's out you can't take it back. Neither of you denied it so the story ran. I am so sorry. Perhaps I was jealous, maybe I set too high standards for you. I wanted you to be different, to be faithful, just like I wanted my mother and I to be the only people in my father's life."

More silence.

"Can you ever forgive me? I'll leave if you like."

"No, please stay. I am still trying to catch up with you being here. Having my faults published in every paper was very painful at the time but perhaps I deserved it. As you say, it does all sound terribly hypocritical. But I did mean every word I said in the church. If I look on the positive side the newspapers forced me to move here. They put me in a situation where I could write my book. At least I was already in hiding when people said I had not helped anyone."

"That wasn't me."

We reverted to small talk, partly I suspect to move away from the gravity and drama of Pauline selling me out to the press.

"You know Marilyn is still very active. I think she really got it. She took off from where you left us. I listened to one of her talks. Very inspiring. And she does some healing now too. You should go and visit her. I'm sure she would welcome the support. Like you she doesn't charge fees, just donations."

"I'm not sure if I'm ready for America yet."

Pauline carried on distractedly making conversation.

"Cheryl's busy with her cooking school. Brad still hangs around with her. No romance, Brad is without a boyfriend. Mike promotes the classes and gives them foods to sample and they send folk to his shop. The last time I heard, Steve and Marlene wanted to run a long course, training people to do what you did. Sounded quite expensive. Hiring hotel conference centres, assessments, in fact all the stuff that you condemned in LA. And Stoosh is Stoosh. He came out to LA for a while because he felt he was next on the hit list. Dark forces hunting him down. I think he hangs out with Seriously now. Seriously was the big surprise. Really opened up. He still believes in you. Just waiting for you to bounce back. The last I heard he was recording with Marilyn."

"We've kept in touch. He did an amazing job on the gig."

Pauline is on east coast time and happy to talk but after a long yawn I give in.

"I have to sleep. You can have my bed and I will sleep here."

"No way. You go to your bed. I'll be fine, I'm too wired to sleep."

I help her make up the sofa bed and retire. Sleep came quickly.

When I wake Pauline is lying next to me. I turn onto my side to see her. She opens an eye. I smile.

"Did you have a good sleep?"

"Yes but not enough. Sorry I felt a bit insecure downstairs, I hope you don't mind," Pauline opens her eyes wider.

I can't stop myself, I feel like Don Giovanni. Instead of me persuading Aaron to settle and start a family I'm absorbing his free love philosophy.

I move closer and kiss Pauline on the forehead. My curiosity leads me to slide my hand up the outside of her leg. She is wearing knickers and a pink T-shirt. I pull her top up pretending to massage her back. I feel a strong desire to see her breasts, my hand reaches up to them. She responds by letting her hand slide across my back.

Pauline expresses herself verbally during sex. She whispers in my ear, tells me how stimulated she feels, how much she wants me. Pauline turns me onto my back, straddles me and pins my arms down. She tickles my side making me squirm and wriggle, she laughs. Sex with Pauline is a playful experience. Very different from my musings after the slightly intense massage she gave me at Ringing Rocks.

When she rolls off me and we disconnect I turn to look at the clock.

"I have to take Matthew and Eleanor to school. You relax, I'll be back in an hour."

When I return I fry some mochi and simmer a pot of kukicha and take them up to Pauline.

"Pauline there is something I must tell you. I should have told you a little earlier." I was not sure how to compose the next sentence. I remember our conversation on the plane, I remember how she does not want to compete with other women. "I had very similar experiences recently with Josephine and I am in close contact with Marlene."

Pauline raises her eyebrows.

"Perhaps Marilyn and Cheryl will be next." I experience an unwelcomed flash of excitement at the thought. Pauline moves closer to me. "Listen I only came here to apologise. I am not angling to ensnare you. I'm happy for now. I might not feel the same tomorrow, next week or next month but," she shrugged her shoulders and left the rest unsaid.

"I do not want to hurt anyone."

"So basically you want me to keep quiet."

"Yes."

Pauline laughs.

"I have just become complicit in the very thing I sold you out for. So what do you do on a sunny day in Wales?"

As I have no car I borrow a bicycle for Pauline and we cycle around the interesting sites. Later we pick Matthew and Eleanor up from school and go down to the beaches. Pauline insists on taking us out for dinner so I phone for a taxi to take us to the Castle restaurant. For the first time for many months I laugh a lot. This is a happy period in my life. I know it cannot go on but each surprise, each gift lifts my spirits to a new high. Is this the lifestyle the Aaron has maintained all these years? When we go to bed Pauline starts a pillow fight. In the end I wrestle her onto the bed resulting in the inevitable.

In the quieter moments Pauline and I discuss philosophy, healing and ecology. She catches me off guard with her impatient switching of subjects. In the Borth-y-guest tea room she snaps from giving me a new recipe for miso soup with garlic, ginger and olive oil to asking me what it felt like making love to a vegan woman.

"Was I the first? How did I taste Adam? You're sensitive to human energy. How did I feel?"

I see old Mr Evans shuffle to hear better.

"Amazing, we'll talk more later."

We agree on most topics but when we find a difference we argue passionately. I enjoy my discussions with Pauline, she challenges me, sees the weakness of my argument, forces me to think deeper, question more.

In the afternoon Pauline gives me a regenerative healing session. Highly energising, similar to my massage in LA but without the aid of a dream. We then swap over and Pauline shows me how to place my fingertips lightly at the top of her pubic bone and feed energy into her reproductive chakra. I can feel her fill with a hot primal energy and I become highly aroused again. She then encourages me to feed my energy into her abdominal chakra with my free hand. As my hand warms I move on up to her stomach and then on to her heart. Pauline's breathing speeds up noticeably and she pulls me towards her.

Initially our love making is frenzied and almost violent before subsiding into a slow sensual swim towards orgasm. As Pauline starts to come she wriggles her finger inside me stimulating my prostrate, producing an immediate, intense climax. This had never happened to me before and I feel slightly naive and innocent. Pauline was clearly experienced in the art of tantric love making.

I am happy to play the host. I am now an expert, taking in a range of morning activities, picking up Matthew and Eleanor from school, carrying on with the itinerary and still able to cook dinner. I notice them become more open to Pauline. Eleanor sits on her lap and when we walk up the Roman steps Matthew takes her hand. Is he just feeling more comfortable having women around or is it Pauline? She makes them laugh and spends a lot of time enthusing, building up their strengths. She reminds me of what amazing children they are. Listening to Pauline I feel so proud of them, I see her boost their self esteem.

On Sunday morning the clouds lift, losing their darkness. Beginning to feel claustrophobic I try to motivate everyone to go for a walk. Persevering in the face of resistance from Eleanor we set off in boots and long coats. The tide is out so we drag the dingy down to the water and row across to the sand banks. From here we walk towards Portmerion. It feels surreal on the open sand with the damp wind blowing into our faces; exposed, open, small compared to the vast flat terrain.

Pauline takes lots of pictures with a wide-angle lens stretching out the scenery, making it more infinite. I keep checking my clock, aware of the need to head back before the tide turns and reaches the long anchor.

Matthew falls over in one of the pools and my initial irritation is swamped by the others' laughter. He insists the water is warmer than the air.

Out in the open, with the wind blowing our superficial energy Matthew and Eleanor respond by running and shouting. Pauline and I find excuses to stop and put our arms around each other. On the way back the clouds open up releasing a fine rain with such density that I soon feel my wet clothes clinging to me and the squelch of watery socks.

Once home I put Matthew and Eleanor into a bath. Pauline shivers trying to revive the fire. Clouds the colours of slate merge into the cottage roofs, Pauline curls up on the sofa reading my manuscript.

"I sense you love Josephine deeply. Something special happened in that shiatsu class."

"Yes, I only realised recently. I do love her."

The weather seems to want to contain us in our little cottage, pressing close to the windows, softly massaging the walls with light rain.

On the last evening I take Pauline out to the Portmerion Hotel for dinner. The hotel has one of the most interesting atmospheres for dining I have experienced. Nestling in a wooded bay the mock Italian village is made up of colourful houses set in a tiered semi circle with the hotel near the sea at the bottom. The entrance has an old, established feel with a large open fire. We walk through to the lounge and order drinks. Wooden elephants give this space a colonial feel. The dining room looks over the estuary, currently swollen with dark green seawater. The food is a little too rich for my taste but imaginative and creative enough to make the event feel special. We have to make a special request to get vegan dishes for Pauline.

At the end of her stay I feel the same awkwardness, what can I do? I am very happy around Pauline but if I think of Josephine or Marlene I feel anxious. I am too much of a coward to mention Pauline to Marlene or Josephine.

I recognise I like being close to three different women. Is this the life Aaron loves so much? I try to explain it to Justin.

"Is it all a trick? Regardless of how elevated our society becomes, despite all the culture and civilisation, we never escape those base instincts to copulate. For two years now I have immersed myself in all the trappings of living on a higher plane and yet each time a woman comes into my life I am all too ready to strip off any pretensions of having evolved into a superior being and return to my primal desires."

I see him snigger but continue. "Derek has the willpower to commit to Sophie and never waver. At the other end of the spectrum Aaron has no self imposed restrictions. None of this would cause him any concern."

"What you did all three of them? Wow, you lucky bastard."

After a pause I reorient myself to Justin's world. "You know what Justin, you and I are going out and I am going find you a woman."

An image of me organising everything and having to be in bed with them helping Justin through the whole process flashed through my mind. There are no singles bars I know of nearby but I did manage to introduce him to Rhonda, a similarly aged single woman at the local health food shop.

CHAPTER TWENTY-NINE

Emily arrives for a long weekend with Pete. This is our first meeting and we both try a little too hard to hit it off immediately. Aware of Emily's scrutiny I sense we both get too excited when it appears we both enjoy listening to Radiohead.

I really want to talk to Emily about my love life and as soon as the initial catching up subsides I tell her about Marlene, Josephine and Pauline. I sense Emily being a little uptight about Marlene. I assume she still has negative feelings about our affair.

"Which do you feel closest to energetically?"

"As in?"

"Remember how Sigeyo explained the idea of how eating, drinking and smoking together allow your energy to harmonise?"

"Yes."

"Well, would you say that one of these women will eat with you in a way that will allow you to develop a long-lasting biological bond?"

"I think Pauline has been macrobiotic the longest and seems to like similar food to us. Marlene likes to eat out a lot and Jo is still playing on the fringe."

I could see Pete looking on suspiciously.

"What do you think Pete?"

"Oh, I think if one really turns you on then start there."

Emily glares at him.

"Is that why you're with me?"

I could see where this was going. "No, he is with you because of macrobiotics, your dress sense, intelligence, humour and personality, right Pete."

"Exactly."

"Come on let's get out and show Pete around."

Too soon I was kissing Emily goodbye.

I have started healing again. It feels very different after a period absence and after a time when I have been through so much. I have torn up the maps I used to follow and my work is much more intuitive. No more meridians, tsubos, five elements, yin and yang just what is inside me. I like to think I am working from my soul and connecting with my patients' soul for guidance on what they what from me. There is less of me imprinting my ideas into someone else's being. It feels like I am being in service whilst also being myself and living my own truth when I lay my hands on someone. I feel closer to connecting with love and as an experience I love it.

Aaron comes to stay next. He does not need the tours so we spend most of the time walking, sailing, sitting in cafés and relaxing on the beach. I am obsessed with his opinions about Marlene, Josephine and Pauline. I want him to help me through my dilemma to be someone I can bounce ideas off.

"Oh Ads, you sleep with three women and now you want to marry them all. You are so hopeless, I despair. You're the sort of man who would spend a couple of hours with a prostitute, have amazing sex and then propose to her. It's romance gone mad. Where's the reality?"

"It's just the way I feel. And it's not like I don't know them. I've already had a minor relationship with Marlene and spent a lot of time with her. I felt very close to Pauline in America and Josephine's been a special friend for longer. I could understand your point if this was the first time I'd met them but it's not. I know each of them and they know me, they've seen me for better and worse."

"But why do you have to settle down with one of them. Why make it so final? If it was me, I would just hang out with whoever I could and see where it leads. Be practical Adam, if you do not move to America you're taking a big risk on Pauline or Marlene coming here and liking it. You don't even know if Pauline wants to be with you. Maybe she's gone back to Greg or Dick back home.

Josephine's already here, she's not tied down. She would be able to move in with you, if that is so important. Then wait and see."

"I've thought of that. I know what you mean but I do want to find someone to spend the rest of my life with, living here has taught me I'm not a loner. It's different when you have children, I can't just try someone out and see what happens, I don't want to be in a new relationship every six months."

"If it is for life you must really want her, its not just a question of picking up the phone and saying I've chosen you, it needs to be someone so special you would make huge sacrifices for, someone you who will add to the rest of your life. Not just the sex but who will still keep adding even after you have gone through the honeymoon period, after you have gone through all the mutual discovery. I can't believe you have these feelings for all these women. Do you honestly love any of them? If not, walk away before you lose three good friends. I've been with hundreds of women but I haven't found anyone yet. Is it possible that three women would turn up in your life at same time? Is it simply that after being celibate for so long the sex has gone to your head? Tell me honestly Ads, if Marilyn came here and was in and out of your bed for a couple of weeks, wouldn't you suddenly feel she was the one?"

"Oh please, don't confuse me further. Who would I sacrifice the most for?" I space out, lying back against a rock and looking at the sky. "Josephine's delicacy would make me want to do a lot for her, maybe because she's much younger, more vulnerable than the others. Pauline has a deep soft side, I think I would look after her and I think she would genuinely appreciate it." I told Adam about our conversation on the plane back from LA. "Marlene is the most self sufficient, so maybe I would not feel so emotionally drawn in. But then maybe we would make a better team. I don't know Aaron, I've been chasing my tail for nearly a month now. The real point is that I crave the bliss I shared with Christine after I got my life back. That's not just sex and fun for a few months. It touched me so deeply, it became such a source of happiness that not having it has become a real void in my life."

"Perhaps you should become a Mormon and marry all three," Aaron moves closer. "Or is it that you cannot bear the thought of losing one of them. How would you feel if I started a relationship with Josephine?"

"No I promise you it is not that. If I genuinely thought you would be happy together I would be more than happy. I'd only be upset if you saw her as a few months of sex. I am being driven mad by too much choice. It would be so much easier if only one was available."

"But which one? Have you tried using nine ki?"

"Yes but that just tells me what I already know. Josephine is mainly earth and with her I might have a secure home life, greater stability and a stronger foundation to take on more myself. It would be back to being with the energy of my mother and Christine. I think she would be the most supportive. With Pauline I share more similar ki, I suppose making us soul mates, we would understand each other but we also share weaknesses. With Marlene it is more dynamic. She is more fiery, outgoing, fun and we would make a better team, each having the strengths that would compensate for the other's weaknesses."
"Well you've obviously done the maths, now it has to come from the heart. In the past you've gone up a mountain or fasted to reach a decision. Shall we climb Snowdon tomorrow?"

Snowdon is my least favourite mountain because being the highest peak it attracts the most visitors. That would not be so bad in itself but at its peak is the world's most depressing café. A concrete bunker serving the most unhealthy food imaginable, even the coffee is instant.

"OK, but let's climb Hebog."

I go round to the ever helpful Mrs Llewellyn and ask for a lift to Beddgelert. She offers to pick Matthew and Eleanor up from school to make our day more relaxing. That evening I start a simple fast by just eating whole grains and vegetables. Whole oat porridge in the morning and rice balls for the trip.

I enjoy climbing with Aaron. We match each others' pace well. We avoid any mention of the women. Mostly we discuss my book and Aaron's recent trip to Argentina. It gives me the chance to talk to him about using another name, whether he would feel exposed by my writing of our private conversations examining relationships. Initially he was surprised that I left them in.

"What possible relevance is it to your story?"

"You're the most important character and I wanted to show the difference in our situations, our approach to relationships, it emphasises your free spirited approach, I hope the contrast makes it more interesting."

"If I remember some of those conversations correctly, your book will sabotage any chance of another relationship."

"Perhaps women will see you as more of a challenge, try a little harder to be the one that finally captures you all for herself. Anyway I can't imagine too many of your potential girlfriends will ever read it. And would you ever want to settle down anyway?"

"I sometimes have this horrible fear that your absurd attitude to women is leaking into my soul. The other day I found myself day dreaming of having children. The one bit you have got right is the idea that we hang onto those happy periods beyond their expiry date. I was so happy during my late teens and twenties but lately it has all been a bit empty. Trying to relive the things that gave me such a buzz ten years ago is hollow now. I do need a new phase in my life. Would children complete the circle as you claim? I'm too nervous to let go Adam. Perhaps it is too late to make compromises."

At the peak we sit in silence. I open myself up to the mountain, to try to feel the energy surging up through the rocks, feel the concentration of energy between the earth and heaven at the peak. Sitting there I look up to the sky, letting myself be an aerial, the first point of contact as the energy from the cosmos contacts this part of the globe.

My ability to focus on simple things like my breathing is strong and I can avoid distractions for a long period of time. After an hour or so we eat our rice balls. I chew each mouthful one hundred times. This becomes a meditation in itself.

Time to descend. I feel open, light, fresh. I am also aware that I do not feel any clearer in my heart. When we return we take Matthew and Eleanor down to the harbour. Aaron plays with them whilst I scramble across the rocks at the end of the headland. I continue my meditation looking out at the sea. I watch the waves slap up against the rocks, follow the eddies and currents, watch a piece of driftwood float out towards the sea on the falling tide. Walking back to cottage I reason that if no inspiration comes today there will always be other times. The main thing is not to continue to devote so much energy into finding an answer, that is just confusing me more.

In the evening I cook a miso soup, pressure cooked rice, spelt and black soya beans along with a variety of steamed vegetables. After a long session of chewing we relax by playing cards.

The mountain climb made me tired so I go to bed early and fall asleep quickly. I dream of Anne. I am chasing her, she is laughing, I cannot catch her even though she is dancing and skipping across a poppy field. The harder I try the more she laughs. I run out of breath when I fall into the long grass she flops down on top of me. She pushes her nose to my ear. When she talks she reminds me of another woman.

I wake in a sweat. The house is quiet, Aaron must have gone to sleep. I wash myself. It takes me a long time to fall asleep again. This time Christine comes to me. I have not dreamt of her for a long time. She walks into the bedroom and sits on the bed next to me. Smiling sweetly she takes my hand, massaging it distractedly, before leading me out of the bedroom. I follow her down a soft sandy path. When we arrive at the clearing I see Matthew and

Eleanor running, circling two adults sitting on a rug with their backs to me. One turns round, it is me. Then I hear the voice again, she turns slightly to kiss my cheek and I know who it is.

CHAPTER THIRTY

Fifteen months later.

We are sitting in Luscious Organic in Kensington High Street eating our macrobiotic lunches. Josephine is sitting opposite me. Her pregnant tummy presses against the table. She looks radiant.

"You must try some of my sea vegetable salad Jo. See if you like it. You know how it is meant to increase the baby's intelligence."

Josephine smiles serenely.

"You don't think he or she would be happier being a few cards short of the full deck? Why do we all assume intelligence is good, from my experience simple people are the happiest," Aaron replies smiling.

She turns and put her hand in Aaron's and kisses him on the neck. I look hard at Aaron, searching for any sign that he might be losing interest, as I have for nearly a year. He turns and pats her bulge. I am still coming to terms with the transformation. Could my book have influenced him that much? Aaron has finally found someone he wants to settle with and it's Josephine of all people. Somehow I always imagined it would be someone more overtly sexual, expressive, passionate. Am I jealous after all? Maybe a little, seeing them together does produce the odd flash feeling of what might have been.

"Ow, you've made our baby kick me."

Marlene raises her glass. "Here's to a healthy baby and happy parents."

We all touch our glasses.

Marlene turns to me. "Hey and thank you for the tour yesterday. I loved the Tate Modern. It was so cool to walk across the river from St Paul's."

"You're welcome my dear."

"Can I have a juice dad?"

"Certainly Matthew, you too darling." Eleanor nods.

I watch Pauline as she tells a story about Lucia. She is animated, waving her hands, tossing her long hair back. My mind returns to the period after my dream. Initially I just felt relieved that my soul had made a decision for me. I didn't act for some time. I enjoyed feeling my energy free up as the pressure of making a decision lifted. Was it that I was still not sure? No, but I was apprehensive of starting a new relationship. I was not even sure that she would want to be in the kind of relationship I was looking for.

As I remained becalmed Aaron told me he was meeting up with Josephine. I did feel uncomfortable. Aaron explained how reading my manuscript had tipped him over the edge he had been teetering on for some time. Starting a family was the next adventure. If my book only influences one person I am glad it is Aaron.

It was Josephine's eyes that drew him in and I knew how he felt. It has occurred to me that just as I have a piece of George Wadkins' spirit floating around me that perhaps Josephine has some of Anne's energy in her eyes. Was it all meant to be some kind of cosmic reunion? The relationship that was cheated by war reignited sixty years later in London.

To find my love I went back to Philadelphia. She wasn't at home but I managed to track her down at Mike's shop. She was having a miso soup in the corner. I was standing right next to her when she looked up. I couldn't speak, my heart raced and I felt myself perspire. A shot of nervous tension flew up from my stomach to my heart.

She stood and put her arms around me. We found each other's mouths and I felt her envelope me. My legs began to shake and I had to sit down.

"Pauline, I want to spend my life with you."

The fear spread as Pauline started crying. Had she found someone else? She must have sensed my anxiety.

"Sorry Adam," she took a paper napkin and wiped her eyes. "I'm crying because that is what I never dared hope to hear you say."

I can feel Pauline's hand on my leg, I am close enough to smell her hair. We have been living in London together for nearly a year and are now planning another trip to America, back to spend some time with Seriously and Marilyn. It's not the same as with Christine, I know that, but I am in love and I feel loved. It doesn't get any better than that for me.

It's early morning and I still cannot sleep. Sitting on the floor by the sofa I write another list:

I'm in a loving relationship with someone who has a different energy from my mother.

I am accepting of other healers' desire to earn money.

I enjoy the financial security the royalties have brought me.

I am less judgemental of others.

Have started an internet macrobiotic discussion group with Emily.

I ate a purely vegan macrobiotic diet last spring to cleanse myself.

I may have played a small part in Aaron becoming a father, Justin forming a relationship with Rhonda and perhaps most gratifying, dear Josephine feeling closer to people.

I still feel Christine……

ACKNOWLEDGEMENTS

I would like to offer my huge appreciation to my sister Melanie who helped give this novel its style and to my lover Dragana who initially edited the book and helped me define the characters.

Big influences in my writing of this book were my dearest friend Jeremy Parkin as well as Patrick Bennet, who indirectly initiated my macrobiotic adventure by falling in love with my sister. My teachers Shizuko Yamamoto, Michio Kushi and Takashi Yoshikawa provided great inspiration.

Some of the ideas have been partially borrowed from others and mixed up into the philosophies of the characters. These include, George Ohsawa, Greg Johnson, Bill Tara, Phiya Kushi, Serge Benhayon and Byron Katy. Thanks.

Many insights came from my children Christopher, Alexander, Nicholas and Michael where my involvement in their growth and development has completely changed my own philosophy on life and allowed me to see myself differently.

I am hugely grateful to Amy Carroll for commissioning me to write *Practical Wabi Sabi* which turned out to be a life changing process for me. Much of the wabi sabi thinking found its way into *The Healer.*

Most of my gratitude goes to all my friends, students, clients, authors of books I have read (including *A Prayer For Owen Meany* by John Irvine and published by Transworld / William Morrow from which I used a short excerpt), members of my macrobiotic discussion group and colleagues who have been part of my life and stimulated me to look at life in a way I felt I had something to write about.

ABOUT THE AUTHOR

I started macrobiotics in 1980 when challenged by my sister, Melanie to try it for three months. Within weeks I was feeling so much better I knew I could not go back to my old foods.

This led to me taking macrobiotic cooking classes, learning shiatsu and immersing myself, with some skepticism, in macrobiotic philosophy. In 1984 I gave up my job as an engineer and moved from London to Philadelphia to help Denny Waxman run the Macrobiotic Association of Pennsylvania. Denny was a huge influence on my life at that time and helped me experience the macrobiotic life. During this time I was able to study and work with Michio Kushi, Aveline Kushi, Herman Aihara, Shizuko Yamamoto and a huge range of prominent macrobiotic teachers.

In 1986 I was invited to run the East West Centre / Community Health Foundation. This was housed in a large Victorian school building in London and ran a huge range of courses. This includes everything from tai chi to acupuncture, shiatsu to martial arts and a full range of macrobiotic classes.

During this time Michio and Aveline Kushi along with Shizuko Yamamoto were regular visitors to run workshops. Later we ran the first big feng shui courses in the UK with William Spear and Takashi Yoshikawa.

After seven years as director of the Community Health Foundation I left to work as a freelance consultant and teacher and to write books. My first books were on feng shui and these went on to become best sellers. Many books later I was able to go back to my roots and write *Modern Day Macrobiotics*.

During this time I wanted to spend more time with my four sons and was able to enjoy a more balanced family life working from home. My feng shui work took off and I travelled the world teaching and helping people create more healing homes. During this time I took on large projects with The Body Shop, British

Airways and International Airports.

I am currently the chairperson of the Macrobiotic Association of Great Britain and Feng Shui Society of Great Britain. I run an internet discussion group with Melanie and my partner Dragana. Dragana and I also share an interest in a macrobiotic food store and café in London, run by Dragana. I am still busy helping people start macrobiotics and teaching students to become macrobiotic practitioners, giving shiatus and providing feng shui consultations.

The Healer is my first novel and has given me the freedom to express my ideas on healing through the characters in the story that would not be appropriate in my other books. I hope *The Healer* provides an interesting format to learn ideas and try on a life changing philosophy.

OTHER BOOKS BY SIMON BROWN

Macrobiotics For Life – North Atlantic
The Feng Shui Life Coach – Godsfield Press
The Secrets of Face Reading – Godfield Press / Face Reading
Secrets of Chinese Masters - Sterling
Practical Wabi Sabi – Carroll & Brown
Modern Day Macrobiotics – Carroll & Brown / North Atlantic
The Feng Shui Bible – Godsfield Press / Sterling
Feng Shui in a Weekend – Hamlyn / Sterling
Chi Energy Workbook – Carroll & Brown / Sterling
Astrology by Numbers – Carroll & Brown
Practical Feng Shui – Cassell Illustrated / Sterling
The Principles of Feng Shui – Thorsons

SIMON BROWN'S SERVICES

I am happy to provide healing sessions, help in starting macrobiotics, feng shui consultations and help in becoming a practitioner yourself.

SIMON BROWN'S CONTACT DETAILS:

Tel: +44 (0) 20 7431 9897
Email: simon@chienergy.co.uk
http://www.chienergy.co.uk/

Please visit http://www.chienergy.co.uk/newsletter.htm and join my newsletter for updates and news. You will need to look out for an email from Bravenet and click on the link to confirm your subscription.

To join my macrobiotic group please go to http://www.chienergy.co.uk/ and look for a link to my macrobiotic